With very best ~

to Maureen and Peter.

I hope you enjoy reading this as
much as I did writing it.

Ian Cousins — 7th April 2022.

Together
Through Eternity

Ian Robinson

Grosvenor House
Publishing Limited

This book is published by
Grosvenor House Publishing Ltd
Link House
140 The Broadway, Tolworth, Surrey, KT6 7HT.
www.grosvenorhousepublishing.co.uk

This book is a work of fiction. Any resemblance to
people or events, past or present, is purely coincidental.

A CIP record for this book
is available from the British Library

Paperback ISBN 978-1-83975-915-4
Hardback ISBN 978-1-83975-880-5
Ebook ISBN 978-1-80381-035-5

For Christine, with much love.

Preface

Thank you for even contemplating reading this book. If you do decide to read it, I offer you my heartfelt thanks, and hope it gives you as much pleasure in the reading as I obtained from the writing.

I did not embark on this whole exercise as a money-making project, indeed I would be deeply flattered if I covered my costs, but please be assured that any profits, if there were to be any, I am pledged to give away to St. Luke's Church Holbeck in Leeds, who endeavour to help and support people living in one of the most deprived areas of Leeds.

I am privileged to worship God there, together with my lovely wife, Christine and close friends Cathy and Mike, in the fellowship of the whole church family comprising people from at least fifteen nations, under the loving and practical guidance of the Vicar, Revd. Alistair Kaye.

I wrote this book at the age of seventy four; it is my first venture into the world of writing, and I enjoyed it so much, I have already started on my second book.

Despite rumours to the contrary, Ralph is not me, although I have to confess that there are small elements of my life included in the story of an otherwise fictional character.

The funny thing is, that as I grew to like Ralph more and more as his character developed, I found that I had to alter the ending of the book, as I didn't want him to suffer the conclusion I had previously planned for him.

This is a story of love.

It is never too late....

'Dante looks around and sees two sinners clamped tightly together, breast-to-breast, and asks them who they are, to which they do not reply but butt their heads together like goats.'

Dante's Inferno

'They will be tormented day and night for ever and ever.'

Revelation Ch. 20 v 10

Acknowledgements

Firstly, I'd like to say a huge thank you to my good friend, Cathy Wrigglesworth, who has 'oohed and aahed' in all the right places, as she has read the chapters as I have written them; giving me much encouragement as the book developed.

Then, there's my friend Tim Loker, already a published author, who read through the first rough manuscript, and offered me much advice, which I am pleased to say I took on board and put into practice, to good effect.

I mention in the book a song by Janis Ian, Seventeen; a beautiful song which so captures that strange and crazy age, at least, looking back it was for me.

I also refer in chapter two, to men being from Mars and women being from Venus. This, of course is a reference to *Men Are from Mars, Women Are from Venus*, a 1992 book by John Gray PhD. His book sold more than 15 million copies and embedded the concept into modern folklore. That part of my story is based in the 1960's, way before John Gray's book, but I am however, claiming 'Author's licence' to make the gag work.

Thank you to the friends who have encouraged me, especially Sandra, Christine's sister, and Ken and Fran.

Sometimes in life you just know when something is meant to be; and that happened when Grosvenor House Publishing appointed Melanie Bartle to look after me and take me through the whole publishing process. It turns out that, although she now lives and works in the South, she was actually born and brought up about a mile away from where I live, in Pudsey. Thank you so much, Melanie, for your kindness, enthusiasm and encouragement, as you guided me through the whole process of having this book published.

Most of all though, my main thanks go to the love of my life; my constant companion, my best friend; the lady who has supported me through thick and thin, and to whom this book is dedicated - my wife Christine.

Chapter 1

Ralph Ernest Diggerby looked up from reading his newspaper and smiled inwardly; he leaned forward and took a sip from his now cooling cup of coffee, which he'd temporarily forgotten about as he'd become increasingly immersed in the article in the morning paper.

A shadow loomed across him, as a pleasant, friendly voice said, 'shall I get you a fresh cup, Mr. Ralph?'

'That's very kind of you, Everton; yes please,' answered Ralph as he carefully folded the newspaper, with the scrutinised story on the inside. 'I think I'll take my coffee up to my room and finish reading my paper up there.'

Everton, who was the on-duty care assistant poured Ralph a fresh coffee and handed him the cup, which Ralph carried carefully to the lift, with his newspaper tucked safely under his arm.

Ralph's room was on the first floor of the Retirement Home, almost hidden away at the end of the short corridor, once you had turned left out of the lift. Ralph nearly always rode up in the lift as the stairs, although the healthier option, were just an unnecessary chore, as he saw it. He paused by his door and glanced out of the window which overlooked the well-tended, large gardens to the western side of the building. He inserted the key into its lock and gave it the required customary push as it always seemed to need, making a mental note to remind the lovely Jessica again, to apply some WD40. The home was really quite well run and catered for most of his routine requirements, but it was always the attention to detail that served to irritate Ralph.

'Why couldn't Jessica just for once remember to complete a simple task, like applying some WD40 or whatever to the lock on his door? Anyway whatever, she's a lovely young lady,' he muttered out loud to no one in particular, and pushed gently at the door. At least the door itself opened and closed effortlessly. The room still had that newly painted smell, and the aroma of new wool carpet, seemed to catch in the back of his throat; it was as if you could actually just feel the microscopic threads of wool tickling gently in your nostrils.

What pleased Ralph was that, although he had already lived in Downwood, as the home was named, for just over three months, his room still had that new feel and smell. The light, airy atmosphere to the interior space was provided by the two windows that it had; indeed, that was what had attracted Ralph to this particular room when he had first looked at the accommodation. The room was at the western end of the new wing and because of this it had two outward facing walls, allowing for the two windows, whereas most of the other rooms in the home had space for only the one.

The interior walls were decorated in a light cream emulsion and the carpet and curtains added to the plainness. There were no photographs adorning the walls, no reminders of family anywhere in the room; indeed, the only interruption to the smoothness, being the single painting hanging in the middle of the main wall; an original oil landscape, reminiscent of the style of Bob Ross and depicting an imaginary mountain range with a few trees and a small river along the bottom of the valley, which seemed to run off the canvass beneath the gilded frame. The water always seemed to be so real to Ralph that he could almost imagine the need for a container on the floor, to catch the overflow.

The ample room was made smaller by the furniture, which comprised a comfortable three-quarter bed; a plainly but expensively upholstered easy chair; a walnut writing desk, complete with drawers; and a small walnut dining table, with one matching dining chair, neatly drawn up tight against the table. The accommodation was served by a well-appointed shower room; with a wc, and wash basin and an accessible walk-in shower; the room being tastefully tiled in light grey from ceiling to floor, with matching floor tiles.

A shelf, attached to the corner wall between the two windows, supported a red, somehow inappropriate, electric kettle sitting next to a small tea pot and a bone China cup and saucer, with a bowl containing lumped-sugar and a small jug half filled with fresh milk; whilst a rosewood tea-caddy and a single teaspoon completed the collection of items thereupon.

Home, thought Ralph as he quickly glanced around, and then he dropped his folded newspaper onto the table next to the coffee cup, which he had placed on the coaster which was left permanently in place on the table top; then he moved the single chair from beneath the table and placed it adjacent to the writing desk, and sat down.

Ralph took the key to the top drawer of the desk from his trouser pocket; unlocked the drawer and extracted the file that lay alone inside it. Reaching up, he pulled down the angled sloping top of the desk which, when opened, provided Ralph with the space he needed to rest the file on. Ralph moved his hand slowly across the surface of the, as yet, unopened file, in an almost caressing gesture.

He sat for a long moment just staring at the file and wondered why it always smelt so ....er... I suppose musty is the word I'm searching for, he thought. The file, which was in faded orangey brown card, smelt as if it had been stored in a damp attic for years, whereas in fact it had always been locked away in his safe up until the time he had moved into Downwood; and thereafter it had remained locked in his writing desk top drawer.

Ralph searched in one of the small drawers inside the writing desk for the pair of scissors, that had lain there for years. *Brackleys Bank Ltd* could still be seen faintly etched into the discoloured metal work. He moved the scissors from side-to-side metronome-like using his middle finger and thumb, whilst the desk at Brackleys Bank came onto his mind's video screen.

He could smell again, even after the passing of more than 50 years, the furniture polish; burnt sealing wax and dust that the old drawer had been impregnated with. He visualised the golden age-created richness of the wood of that old desk, with the black, scarred burns from the spilt molten wax, and the deep scars created by the Luftwaffe when the Brackleys Bank Thornston branch had had a direct hit from a Junkers 52 in 1941, when a young disillusioned German pilot had got fed up with looking for his nominated target, through the fog that wasn't supposed to have been below him, at least according to the German weather forecasters, so he had released his load. That, of course had been well before Ralph's time at the Bank, but the desk had been carefully stored and replaced into the rebuilt branch, shortly after the war. Typical bank, thought Ralph, always look after the pennies and the pounds will look after themselves.

Returning to the present, Ralph reached across for the newspaper, and opened it at the page he had been reading downstairs, checked the article again and proceeded to cut around its edges.

Once it was removed from the newspaper, he lay the article on top of the folder, and dropped the remaining paper into the small wicker-woven basket at the side of the desk. He re-read the article, smiling again inwardly, and untied the stained string holding the folder together. From the bottom of the folder, he pulled out one of those transparent plastic sleeves, A4 sized and slipped the newspaper cutting into it, and placed it after the last existing entry, untying the Treasury tag that held the collection together and then refastening the tag to include the new addition.

Sliding the collection of items back into the folder, he closed it, carefully re-tying it with the string. The folder was then placed back where it had come from, in the drawer; the drawer locked and the key replaced in Ralph's trouser pocket. Ralph patted the key through the trouser material, reassuring himself that it was safely tucked away.

Ralph picked up the coffee cup and took a sip; even before the first drop reached his lips, realising the coffee had gone cold again, and he put the cup back down. It's no wonder I don't drink much coffee, thought Ralph, I never seem to get to the cup whilst the liquid is still warm. He looked up as a light knock sounded at his door.

'Come in,' called Ralph, clearing his throat as he tried to speak the words clearly.

The door opened halfway and Everton appeared in the opening, 'you alright, Mr Ralph?' he asked, in his warm voice which, although he had lived in the UK since the age of six, still had undertones of the beaches and the palms of his origins, in Barbados.

Everton's voice resonated from his deep chest and seemed to come down to Ralph from on high, as Everton was solidly built, as a result of the amount of time he spent in the gym, and his height, just over six feet three, as he delighted in reminding anyone who asked.

'Oh, you let your coffee get cold again, Mr Ralph. I'll go and get you another one, but mind you drink this next one; we're blocking the drains with your undrunk coffee,' Everton laughed as he spoke the words.

'You're a very kind man, Everton,' smiled Ralph, 'but I may as well wait until lunch time. I mean, that's only an hour or so away, and I share your concern for the drains' Ralph laughed as he uttered the last words and surprised even himself with the touch of humour. Truth to tell, he'd not had that much to smile about down the years, come to think of it.

'You sure you're alright, Mr Ralph?' Everton repeated his question of a moment ago.

'Oh, I'm fine thank you Everton,' smiled Ralph; 'I'm quite content with my own company, most of the time. There's no need for you to concern yourself about me.'

'Don't you have any family or friends to visit with you?' asked Everton in a slightly concerned voice. 'I can't recall anybody coming to see you since you moved in here.'

'I've no living relatives, and only my once long-time-ago best friend Allan Briggs, who has only recently gone into care himself.' answered Ralph, glancing out of the window as he spoke. 'You can just about make out the Weighbridge Nursing Home, where he is, from here.'

Turning back to look at Everton's kindly face, Ralph continued, 'they recently sold his house, to help pay for the cost of his care. Damned disgrace if you ask me. I mean, if we lived in Scotland, that's all taken care of. Not that that concerns me personally, as I've no one to leave anything to, not on a personal basis, anyway; I've left my remaining estate to various charities. Most of them are local ones, as I don't trust the big organisations; they have far too many overheads. I don't agree with keeping the chief executive's posh car on the forecourt, with my donations. Keep it local, I say. You've a better idea of where your money's going, that way.'

'That's something that's never given me much concern, Mr Ralph,' smiled Everton, 'as I ain't got that much, to be givin' any away. But I do tithe to my church. Maybe we could fix up a visit for you to see this Allan, sometime soon? I mean, if he's local, we could organise a taxi for you?'

'Well, that's very thoughtful of you, Everton,' said Ralph, smiling thinly at the man, 'but I don't think that'll be something I'll be needing to do for yet a while.' Abruptly changing the subject, Ralph asked, 'what's for lunch today?'

'Well, it was gonna be shepherd's pie, but,' laughed Everton, 'we's fresh out of shepherds, so ham salad it is. See you in an hour or so, Mr Ralph.' Turning, Everton left the room, closing Ralph's door quietly behind him.

Take a taxi to go visit Allan; I don't bloody think so, Ralph thought. He sat a while with his eyes shut, and then he swung the desk top back into place, stood up and returned the chair from whence it came, tight against the walnut table.

Glancing at his watch, he realised it was still fifty minutes short of lunch-time, so he sank into the familiar comfort of his easy chair, and closed his eyes again.

Allan Briggs. I wonder what your retirement home is like in comparison to this one? Do you have comfort, and your own choice of new carpet? Or is the carpet one that the previous occupant has soiled and dirtied? Or is the food like school dinners? Once all these thoughts had flitted through his mind, Ralph opened his eyes and glanced around his room and smiled. Home, he thought for the second time in the last twenty minutes or so. Feeling somewhat satisfied with his situation, his eyes became heavy once more.

Chapter 2

'What'll it be, love?' Asked the rather attractive young lady behind the glass counter, 'do you want tea or coffee with your sandwich?'

Ralph felt himself going red and he muttered embarrassedly, 'tea please, with two sugars.'

'Just help yourself to sugar from the table at the end, please love. That'll be three shillings and eleven pence please,' said the attractive young lady behind the glass counter. She took the two florins that Ralph offered and smiled sweetly at him whilst registering the sale in her till. The till stood on the shelf at the end of the worktops behind the counter. Turning back to face him she said, 'penny change. Who's next, please?'

Ralph had never been to Coopers Café for his lunch before as his mother had always made him a sandwich, placed neatly wrapped in greaseproof paper, together with his favourite daily Kit-Kat biscuit in his metal snap-tin. That morning Mrs Diggerby had slept in slightly later than usual and hadn't had time to send him off to work properly as she liked to think.

'Oh, don't worry mum,' Ralph had said to her, 'I can try a new experience and buy myself a sandwich in Coopers Café. I haven't yet been out for my lunch like some of the other fellows do, so it'll make a pleasant change.'

Ralph found a seat at an empty table in the corner of the café, which was well out of the centre of the room. The atmosphere in the café was lively and it bustled with the chatter of the lunch-time office workers, and the clinking of cutlery on plates and cups. From his table Ralph could just make out the attractive young lady behind the glass counter, and he sighed as he watched her.

Ralph had never had a proper girlfriend; oh, there'd been a couple of girls at school who he'd been to the pictures with a couple of times but neither had lasted long and he'd been too shy to even hold hands. Maybe that was why neither had lasted long, he mused, as he bit into his cheese sandwich.

Glancing back again in the direction of the attractive young lady behind the glass counter, he swallowed his mouthful and thought, I wonder what her name is? She's rather nice, but I'd have no chance there. He absent-mindedly took another bite of his sandwich.

He looked around at his surroundings and noted the rather austere wooden panelling; the smoke-stained, what had once been cream painted, ceiling; and this wonderful oak block flooring with a patina brought about by thousands and thousands of feet over time.

I wonder how many people have come in here over the years he wondered? Let's see, if there's sixty people in now, and that turns over, say four times a lunch-time; and they're open six days per week; that's one thousand four hundred and forty people per week; times fifty-two weeks, no, times fifty-one weeks, because they are closed for the week following Christmas; so that's seventy-three thousand four hundred and forty people per year....

'Shall I take your plate love, if you've finished with it?' Ralph was startled back into the here and now by the attractive young lady who was no longer behind the glass counter but was now the attractive young lady standing next to his shoulder.

He could feel the warmth from her body and detected the delicate musk of deodorant and starch from her pristine blouse, she was that close.

'Oh, er, yes please,' Ralph muttered, slightly overcome by embarrassment at the proximity of the attractive young lady who was now leaning across him to collect his plate. It didn't of course, occur to Ralph that she had absolutely no need to lean that close to him just to pick up his plate, but he found he enjoyed the experience nevertheless.

Having stood up, Ralph carefully replaced his chair under the table, as he had been taught to do, and started to make his way to the doorway. 'Sorry,' he said to the man who pushed his way past Ralph, coming into the café.

Ralph stepped out onto Market Street, out into the warm sun of an early summer day; suddenly feeling that life had a little extra meaning, that for some reason his brain didn't quite fathom. He realised that he had started to walk along Market Street in the opposite direction from the Bank, where he worked as a counter clerk. He also found, much to his surprise that he was whistling as he walked.

Normally, Ralph would go back to the office if he had eaten his lunch outside; if it was a sunny day he would eat his sandwich seated on one of the benches surrounding the grassy area in the centre of town nearby to the Town Hall. Then he would return to sit quietly in the staff room until his hour was up and it was time to return to his place behind the counter. Today though, he was walking in the opposite direction and was enjoying the feel of the sun on his face and shoulders.

The Town hall clock suddenly chimed the three-quarter hour and Ralph realised that he needed to hurry back to the office, as he was due back on the counter to relieve Allan, on the hour. It wouldn't do to be late, in fact he had *never* been late either arriving at work first thing in the morning or getting back after lunch.

Late getting back after lunch? Ralph thought, I've never been anywhere after lunch other than straight back to the office. What am I doing? He had wandered further from the Bank than he had at first realised, but now he walked with a determined spring in his step and arrived on station behind the bank counter, via the cloakroom just as the Town Hall clock boomed the hour.

'You're looking a tad flushed old man,' said Allan as he passed Ralph on his way out to lunch, 'you look like you've just come back from a good, strong walk; or have you just had a glimpse of Mary's stocking tops in secretarial?' Mary was the manager's secretary and was famous for her shorter than average skirts.

Ralph often pondered why Mary was always pulling her skirt down a bit, whilst wearing such short skirts.

What's the point of that, he would ask himself, why not just wear a longer skirt, then she wouldn't have to keep pulling at it?

He had once mentioned this to Allan, who seemed to know more about these sorts of things, what with having three sisters, and he had said it was all to do with Mars and Venus. As hard as he tried Ralph couldn't see the connection between deep space and the length of Mary's skirts.

Ralph absent-mindedly unlocked his till drawer and set the till up for business. Standing there, his mind returned to the subject of the footfall in the café over the years. Seventy-three thousand four hundred and forty people per year walking on the floor in that lunch-time café; spending say, an average of four shillings and six pence per person....

'Is this till open, young man?' A rather stout customer, wearing a natty dog-tooth suit, and standing clutching his cloth money bag in his hand, brought Ralph back once again to the here and now; 'only you haven't got a till closed sign up.'

'Yes sir, it is open; I do apologise sir, I was just trying to calculate whether I had enough coin to last the rest of the day,' Ralph lied. 'Let's see what you have for us today.'

The remainder of the early afternoon shift passed with no real incident or anything to store into the memory, and soon enough Allan appeared back on the scene, his return being his customary seven minutes late.

I wonder why the Chief Clerk never seems to notice Allan's tardiness? There's a wonderful word, Ralph mused; tardiness.

Tardiness comes from the Latin word tardus, meaning slow, sluggish, dull or stupid; although it's used to mean the quality of lateness; but Allan could hardly be described as dull or stupid.

Allan was Ralph's best friend, or closest acquaintance, would have been a more apt description of their relationship; and had been since they had both joined the bank on the same day, over two years ago now. It was true however that opposites attract because really strictly speaking neither Ralph nor Allan had very much at all in common.

Ralph was quiet and shy and rather lacking in confidence, diffident; and he had a tendency to day-dream whilst Allan was confident and somewhat brash, and full of personality.

Ralph felt that Allan was good for him, indeed they were a good counter-balance for each other, but maybe Allan would influence Ralph more than the other way around.

Anyway, seventy-three thousand four hundred and forty people per year walking on the floor in that lunch-time café; spending say, an average of four shillings and six pence per person....

'Sixteen thousand five hundred and twenty-four pounds per year,' Ralph suddenly said aloud.

'No, just twenty pounds in one-pound notes please,' said Mrs Dunstan, who laughed as she pushed her personal cheque, made out to cash for £20 across the counter towards Ralph.

'Where were you just then,' – she glanced down at his name plate on the counter in front of him – 'Ralph? On some desert island, with a bikini-clad young woman in a grass skirt, perhaps, dear?'

'So sorry Mrs Dunstan, I was trying to remember the first line of the Bills of Exchange Act 1882, and the amount of the Governor of the Bank of England's annual salary,' Ralph lied, 'I've got part one of my banking exams next week and I'm trying to revise in my head.'

As Mrs Dunstan walked away towards the door Ralph found himself thinking about that stupid expression, desert island. How could you have a desert on an island? Or an island in the desert? How would the coconuts grow on trees in a desert? Besides, if *he* was ever marooned on a desert island, he'd probably find out he was allergic to coconuts. Ralph laughed quietly, inwardly at his own joke.

Mercifully the clock finally ticked around to 3.30pm, the magic hour as far as Ralph was concerned; for at 3.30pm the Bank could close its doors to customers for the day and that signalled the time for Ralph to balance his till; to reconcile all the credits and debits with the cash in his till.

There was just one customer left in the Banking Hall as the space in front of the counter was grandly titled; and that was Mrs Sykes, a fairly wealthy woman, according to her bank statement and the cut of the clothes she wore. She was waiting as usual to be served by Allan.

A thought occurred to Ralph that Mrs Sykes frequently came into the Bank just as it was closing time and waited, as was her custom to be served by Allan, or Mr Briggs, as she referred to him. It seemed to take for ever for Allan to serve Mrs Sykes; Ralph could hear them whispering and laughing as they dealt with whatever transactions there were, and yet, as often as not it seemed to be only a matter of cashing a personal cheque in the sum of £20, 'for some pin money,' as Mrs Sykes had clearly said on more than one occasion.

Ralph glanced up from his till ledger and could just see Mrs Sykes as she stood leaning slightly towards Allan, across the counter; I wonder what she does with all these pins she buys, he thought, and what do they find to talk about at such length?

Allan finally emerged from behind the counter to show Mrs Sykes out through the front door. Ralph wandered down to Allan's till to see if he had any spare note bands; the paper bands that wrapped each £100 of one-pound notes. He noticed that there was a single one-pound note on the counter top, so Ralph, for safety's sake, and in the interests of tidiness, popped this into the collection of £1 notes in Allan's till drawer.

Allan, his ushering duties completed, came round to the rear of the counter again and sat on his stool.

'I've pinched a couple of £100 note wrappers off your till Allan,' said Ralph without looking up from his note counting.

'Was there a single £1 note on the counter top, old man?' replied Allan.

'Yes', said Ralph, still without looking up, 'I popped it into your drawer.'

'Where abouts, old man?'

'Well, just in with the other £1 notes, in the drawer,' answered Ralph.

Suddenly Allan was standing next to him, looking slightly flushed. 'Where exactly did you put it, old man?' he whispered loudly.

Ralph wrapped the one hundred one-pound notes inside the wrapper and stamped it with the Bank's date stamp.

'Well, I don't know where exactly, but it's in the drawer with the others. What's the problem anyway?' Ralph asked, as Allan looked at him in a somewhat agitated manner.

'I need that £1 note, old man,' Allan said.

'Well just take the first one at the front', Ralph replied.

'No, no, you don't understand, you fool, I need *that* particular note.' Allan seemed to be getting rather more agitated.

'Well, they're all the same; what's the matter with you, Allan?' asked Ralph trying to concentrate on balancing his till.

'That one had her address, and telephone number on and the time her husband goes to the Golf Club tonight.' Allan reddened.

'Ooops,' Ralph didn't look up, but kept his eyes focused on the ledger on his counter. Ralph reddened too. 'Give me a minute, Allan and I'll help you sort through all your £1 notes; sorry.' Ralph replied rather nervously.

Less than two hours later Ralph was standing waiting at the number 37 bus stop, on Prospect Parade which was situated just around the corner from Market Street. That was one of the advantages of working where he did, the bus stop was just around the corner from the Bank, and at the other end of his journey, he would alight from the bus at the end of the road, or street where he lived with his mother in the house which she rented from the Council.

Although it was owned by the Council, it wasn't the stereotypical council house, as it was a pleasant three bedroomed stone-built terraced house; the end one in a block of four, in a quiet private residential area.

The builder of the houses had gone bankrupt many years before, just on completion of the block where Ralph's mother's house was, and the Council had bought three of the four in the block, at a much knocked-down price; the opposite end one having already been purchased privately. To all intents and purposes, to the outside world, it appeared as though Ralph and his mother lived in a privately owned house, which somewhat pleased Ralph.

They had been allowed to rent the house from the Council because Ralph's father Eric, sadly deceased now, had been a clerk in the Town Hall Housing Department at the time. Fortuitously, Eric had been asked to prepare the letting arrangements for the three houses, and had asked the Senior Clerk of the Housing Department whether he, Eric would qualify as a prospective tenant.

He and his wife of some 3 years were now expecting their first baby and would need to be re-housed from their one-bedroomed Council flat, as soon after the baby was born as possible. Permission had been granted, partly because of Eric's favourable employment position, and partly because the Council had an unwritten policy of selection for certain properties. This was denied, of course if ever this was suspected to be the case and questions were asked.

So, the couple, later to be a small family, moved into the house where Ralph was literally born within one month of Eric's request.

The bus arrived, the brakes squealing, as it came to a halt just past the stop. The bus terminus was only two stops back in Town Hall square, so by the time it reached Prospect Parade it usually still had empty seats.

Ralph preferred to ride upstairs on the bus, as somehow, he felt safer and more isolated from his fellow passengers up there; the only problem being that smokers went upstairs and he neither smoked, nor did he like the smoky atmosphere; but Ralph felt that this was a small price to pay for the seclusion; besides there was a better view from upstairs.

The bus lurched forwards as it set off, and Ralph had to make a quick grab for the handle on the nearest seat; and feeling acutely embarrassed, he quickly sat down in the available place, just in front of where he had stood swaying. Ralph neither looked left or right, but kept his head down and studied his shoes intently.

'Note to self,' Ralph muttered under his breath; (he had heard the Chief Clerk, of the Bank, Mr Mawson, say that on a couple of occasions, and he liked the expression; and had decided that that was one he was going to adopt) 'must clean shoes on arrival home, and replace broken shoe-lace on right-hand shoe.'

Funny that, he mused silently; right-hand shoe. It can't really be a right-hand shoe, can it? I mean you can have a right-hand glove, but a right-foot shoe sounds odd.......

'Hello, did you enjoy your lunch-time sandwich?' asked a vaguely familiar voice.

Ralph returned once again to the here and now, and immediately became aware of the musky deodorant and starch combination in his nostrils. It was then that he realised he was seated next to the attractive young lady from behind the glass in the café, who was now the attractive young lady *sitting next to him*, on the bus.

Ralph felt his face and neck going redder and redder, and his mouth suddenly filling with water from somewhere and his eyes having similar water, and his mouth then seemed to develop lock-jaw.

Somehow, he didn't know how, he managed to squeak, 'very much, thank you. I, er, don't think I've noticed you on this bus before now.'

'I'm having tea at me mate's house in Kensington street; her name's Laura, Laura Hetherington. Do you know her? This is only the second time I've been to her house, during the working week so it's only the second time I've been on this bus, at this time. Where do you get off?'

Ralph pondered a moment all the information fired at him, temporarily his mind froze; 'I get off at Wellington Street, that's where I live – with my mum,' he managed to say. His voice sounded very strained in his own ears, and he snatched a quick glance at the attractive young lady who was *sitting next to him*. She was smiling…. at *him*.

'I don't know where Wellington Street is,' she said, 'I think it might be after my stop'

'Yes, it's …' Ralph was interrupted in full flow by the conductress, coming upstairs and asking; 'any more fares, please?'

Ralph put his hand out with four coppers resting on his sweating palm. 'Four pence to Wellington Street, please', he said, much more confidently than he felt.

'You were saying where Wellington Street is before the conductress came upstairs, and interrupted what you were saying,' said the attractive young lady who was *sitting next to him*.

Ralph's tension had eased a little by now and he was able to say without too much strain, 'oh, yes it's about six stops further on than Kensington Street, and no, I don't believe I am familiar with your friends name. I'm not too good with names, anyway. I've already forgotten what you said Lena's second name was.'

'Laura, it's Laura, not Lena; and it's Hetherington,' smiled the attractive young lady. 'Do you want to know what my name is, or would you forget my name too if I told you what it is?' asked the attractive young lady.

'Oh, yes please. I'd love to know what your name is, and I'd make sure I didn't forget *that*.' Ralph found himself saying.

'Well, my name is Sheila Cooper,' said the attractive young lady.

Ralph repeated, 'Sheila Cooper,' and thought that now that he knew her name she would no longer need to be referred to or thought of as the attractive young lady. Well no, that is, she still is an attractive young lady, a *very* attractive young lady, but she has a name, and now I know what that is. Sheila Cooper.

'I'll write my name on a piece of paper for you, and let you have it, next time you have your lunch in the café, if you like. My friends all call me Sheil.'

There was a few seconds of silence between them as the bus continued to roar in second gear up the incline out of the town centre. Eventually Sheila said, 'well, aren't you gonna tell me your name?' and she smiled encouragingly at Ralph.

'Er, oh, yes, of course; it's Ralph, Ralph Diggerby, and I've only got one friend and he calls me Ralph, or old man. We work together at the Bank, that's Brackleys Bank, just on Market Street. I work on the counter; I'm a cashier.'

Ralph was feeling much more confident as the moments passed, and as his confidence improved so did his conversation.

Suddenly Sheila jumped up out of her seat saying, 'this is where I get off. No, there's no need to move, I'll squeeze past you.'

Ralph sat mesmerised as the familiar musk and starch aroma wafted within inches of his nose. He had been going to spring out of his seat, but Sheila was up, past him, and gone before he was able to react.

Ralph moved across into the seat that had been occupied by Sheila, feeling the comforting, pleasant warmth permeating into his clothing from where her body had been just a few seconds previously. He looked out of the bus window down at the street, just in time to catch a glimpse of her as she ran from the bus towards Kensington Street, turning quickly she waved and threw him a delicious smile.

Ralph gawped and managed to wave back, then she disappeared into Kensington Street, and he turned to face the front of the bus, but now, for some reason that he didn't quite fathom he found he was able to sit up straight, and look around him.

It seemed no time at all until the familiar bus stop came into view and the vehicle started to slow down; Ralph bounced out of the seat and floated down the stairs onto the platform just as the bus came to a halt. He stepped off and walking briskly he turned up Wellington Street and found that he was whistling to himself, as he seemed to glide along the pavement to number 17. He pushed open the gate.

'Someone sounds cheerful,' said his mother, turning from the rose bush that she was fussing with.

'Hello mum,' Ralph answered, and smiled at his mother. 'No more cheerful, or uncheerful than usual,' he said, not sure if he even felt as casual as he hoped he sounded.

'What kind of day have you had, Ralph dear?' his mother asked, starting to precede him through the front door, into the house. Over her shoulder she also asked, 'did you manage to get yourself a decent something for lunch?'

'My day has been pretty much the same as usual; not much different from the routine it normally follows, and my lunch was really quite nice,' he answered. 'I even went for a walk, which was really pleasant in the sunshine; that was after I had been to the café.'

Ralph followed his mother into the hallway, removing his coat, and he hung it in its usual place on the hall coat stand. 'What sort of day have you had, mum?' Ralph looked at his mother with affection, 'did you get to work on time?'

'Yes, I was on time, dear, thank you,' she answered, and walked through into the kitchen. Then, whilst lighting the gas under the potato pan, she continued, 'and my day was pretty much the same as usual, like yours. Although I've got a busy day ahead of me tomorrow, that I do know; Mr Mercer has asked me to go in to work a few minutes earlier to type up some notes from the meeting tonight, so he can get them in the post by tomorrow lunchtime.'

Ralph had followed his mother into the kitchen, and a thought suddenly struck him, and he said as casually as he could manage, 'would it help you if I went for my lunch to Coopers Café again tomorrow? It would maybe help you if you didn't have to make a sandwich for my lunch, before you go to work. Save you a few minutes, at least, wouldn't it?'

'Well, how kind and thoughtful you are, Ralph,' his mother smiled lovingly at him. 'That would be very helpful, dear. If you're sure you don't mind?'

Ralph became aware that he was sighing a sigh of relief inwardly, and he wasn't really sure why, but his pulse slightly quickened. 'Don't worry about me, mum; I'll be fine,' he breathed.

'Thank you dear. How much did your lunch cost you today?' His mother had just felt a pang of remorse, as if somehow, she wasn't looking after her boy as she should, by not providing him with his lunch.

'Actually, it was three shillings and eleven pence, and that included the cup of tea. I had a cheese sandwich this lunchtime, but there was also a choice of ham or potted beef with sliced tomato. I wouldn't mind doing that again, particularly if it helps you.' Ralph found that he couldn't look his mother in the eye, and *he* felt slightly guilty too.

So here they both were, with a feeling of culpability towards each other, but neither fully realising why, and neither actually aware of the other's feelings.

Ralph's mother busied herself preparing the evening meal, and then turning to her son she said, 'I feel responsible for making sure you are getting an adequate lunch, but it would help me in a morning if I didn't have that extra little chore of packing up your lunch. Why don't I give you four shillings each morning, and you can eat at the café every day, just like your colleagues do? I can take it out of your board money, and that way I would feel responsible for providing your midday meal.'

Ralph, had a sensation flow through him that was a mixture of relief, pleasure, excitement and for some reason that he couldn't fully understand, let alone explain, there was that feeling of guilt again.

'Whatever is best for you mum,' he said.

Once the evening meal was finished and the dishes were all washed up and sided, or put away, the two of them retired to the front room, as was their evening custom.

Evelyn, as Ralph's mother was called, sat down in her armchair which was placed just to the left side of the fireplace, leaned down and took her knitting out of the canvass bag which lived permanently on the floor next to her chair and began click-clacking on the needles.

Ralph had brought his copy of The Institute of Bankers Exam Revision Questions into the front room with the avowed intention of revising for next week's exams.

Once the book was opened at where he had left off the previous time, and he had tried to commence reading, his mind started to wander again, which really wasn't unusual for Ralph at all.

He found it so difficult to concentrate on the task in hand, but concentrate he must, in order to have the remotest chance of passing next week's Part One papers; the central point of which seemed to be The Bills of Exchange Act 1882. He had even bought his own copy of the flippin' Act in the hope that it would help.

He glanced across at his mother, and smiled in her direction, thinking what a kind loving person she was. He wondered if he would ever find a lady in his life, like his mum?

He asked her, 'Mum, where did you and Dad meet, that is; how did you and Dad meet?'

Chapter 3

'Mister Ralph? Mister Ralph?' Ralph slowly opened his eyes as Everton stood in the doorway to the room. Everton's kindly smiling face came into focus round the door opening, 'you're going to be late for your lunch, Mr Ralph, and your ham salad is going to be getting cold,' Everton laughed at his own joke. 'Were you trying to have a short doze? So would I, given half the chance,' he added. 'Come on now, your lunch is ready and waiting on the table for you.'

Everton, a gentle and kindly look on his face, waited by the open door whilst Ralph gathered his wits about him, as his mother used to urge him, eventually rising out of the comfort of his arm chair, straightening his sweater with a downward brushing motion of his hand; he did this out of force of habit, whether or not it was wrinkled and creased.

'Lead on, kind Sir. Let us attack, or should that be lettuce attack?' Ralph was rather pleased with his own joke and laughed out loud, but Everton, who hadn't quite got the joke, just smiled and let go of the open door after Ralph had passed through the opening, into the corridor.

The two men travelled downstairs in the lift together in silence, and entered the dining room side by side.

Suddenly, Ralph became fully awake as the dining room was a hubbub of noise; conversations, and the clatter of cutlery on plates, and spoons being driven around the inside of tea cups. Ralph politely nodded acknowledgements to several people as he found the way to his table.

He still hadn't managed to get around to making any particular friendships or even acquaintances but he was on nodding terms with several of the people seated in the room. This did not overconcern Ralph as he had a life-time habit of being insular. He ate his lunch and drank his cup of tea; declined the pudding of apple pie and custard; gently wiped his mouth using the napkin, which he carefully refolded and replaced on the table; rose from his chair and left the dining room, making for the lift to return to his room from whence he had come some thirty minutes or so earlier.

Actually, no I won't go back to my room, immediately, he thought, and turning to his left he made his way through the side door from the entrance lobby, as the lift and stairs area was known, and went outside into the garden. That's another of life's language quirks, Ralph thought, I'm going outside, into the garden.

The sun was warm and the sky was a Simpsons one; as he had always referred to one that was, mainly blue but had lines of distant clouds, and Ralph sauntered along the gravel path that dipped down to the seating area about seventy yards away, where he seated himself and enjoyed the sensation of the warm sun on his face.

Two memorial wooden benches were placed opposite one another under a structure that had once been a pergola, but which was now quite clearly supported only by the climbing roses and clematis stems than intertwined the rotting framework, which had long since ceased supporting the planting, he noticed; the roles now being reversed.

Still, it was pleasant, here in the warm sunshine; and secluded too. Ralph was aware that he had mentioned the warmth of the sun, and how pleasant it was, to himself several times now, but he was used to talking to himself, sometimes out loud, as he had been pursuing that course of action for many years past. The seating area was just out of sight of the main building because of the dip in the landscape, and Ralph felt comfortable there.

A dunnock, often mistaken for a sparrow by those who didn't know better, swooped into view and alighted on the top point of the pergola and started to sing the most beautiful set of bird-song notes; the sound was clear and sharp and gave a lift to Ralph's inner being.

'Beautiful little creatures' he murmured out loud, to no one in particular.

Downwood had once been the family home of John Poppleton a wealthy paper mill owner and his wife, Edwina, who between them had owned much of the town itself. The property had originally got its name from the large wooded area, stretching down through the hollow in the landscape and ending up surrounding and running alongside the beck which still marked the boundary of the property.

The original family home had been constructed just on the summit of the rise in the land that stood above the wooded valley, indeed the attic windows were the apex of the whole surrounding area and commanded a view stretching for several miles to the far horizon. Today's view to the horizon was a markedly different one to the original when the house had been built, as there had been a vista of nothing but green fields and meadows, at the outset; but now there were groups of houses and other low-rise buildings as far as the eye could see; but Downwood's boundaries had remained untouched for some six generations.

The use of the imposing and sturdy Victorian structure had changed somewhat, as indeed, had the construction of the west side of the property, which boasted a brand-new wing; although much of the original structure remained intact, including most of the fine interior decorative art-work.

The main dining room for example, where Ralph had just eaten his lunch, was based on the design work of the three Scottish Adams brothers; Robert; James and William; who had originally introduced the neo-classical interior design based mainly on Roman styling, after the 1750's. Downwood had though, not been constructed until the 1890's but still benefitted from the influence of the Adam boys' ideas when a revival in their styles of interior design, came about in the

Victorian and Edwardian eras, as a result of the influential *Paris Exposition* of 1867. Ralph had read all about this in the brochure, advertising the new rooms, one of which he now happily occupied.

'Sorry to disturb you, Mr Diggerby,' a softly spoken voice whispered near his ear, 'it's me, Jessica and I'm just going up to tidy your room, and guess what? I've got some of that WD40 stuff to squirt in your door lock. I'm just letting you know, so that you don't go getting it all over your hands from when you put your key in the lock. We don't want all that oily stuff or whatever it is, all over your nice clothes and furniture now, do we?'

Ralph had to shield his eyes from the sunlight as he opened them, in order to make out Jessica's face, even though she was only two feet away from his.

'Wonderful, my dear Jessica,' Ralph smiled at her pleasant young face, and Jessica returned the smile. 'Thank you very much. Hopefully I can give up on the body-building classes now, so I can just push the key in without all that much effort.'

Jessica giggled, and turning to go she said, 'Ooh, Mr Diggerby, you are funny. Tarra for now'

Ralph, still shielding his eyes from the sun, watched her retreat towards the side door of the building, and just as she was going out of sight from where he was sitting, she turned and waved.

What a pleasant young lady she is, thought Ralph, I suppose she'll break some poor bloke's heart before she's done. Ah, deary me. He sighed and closed his eyes again.

The words of Janis Ian's song Seventeen drifted into Ralph's mind as he sat there, and he hummed the tune to himself as he saw the words come up on his mind's video....

....'I learned the truth at seventeen

That love was meant for beauty queens'.....

Released in 1975, but not heard for the first time by Ralph until he was in his late-thirties, probably around 1978 or 79, he mused, the song stirred in him a distant memory, a sensation he could *feel* in his bones.

There was still an emptiness; a shyness, that was so acute it occasionally caused him physical pain. He felt again the longing to be 'like all the others'; but quickly swallowed the feeling as if it was bile that had risen up from his stomach.

It seemed to Ralph that Jessica was a little like that, too; pleasant and hard-working but somewhat shy. The girl wasn't exactly a physical beauty, but nevertheless she was attractive in her own way; and possessed a cheeky, impish side to her nature. She always seemed to be happy, and was a young lady that you couldn't help but like. To his mind, she appeared to be one of those young people who had not yet found her own confidence, and had not yet recognised her own positives, and potential; but hopefully she would; and when she did, she'd break some poor bloke's heart before she's done; he repeated his earlier thought.

A breeze gently rustled the leaves and flowers of the clematis supporting the pergola, and brought with it a very sweet scent from the summer jasmine which was also winding its way up and across the structure surrounding Ralph.

The little dunnock returned to his favourite post at the highest point of the pergola and sang another couple of bars of his Intro.

Intro, Ralph recalled, is the first stanza of the song; it is called the Intro. (Introduction) as it is found at the beginning of the song and it sets up the song. The intro establishes the song's important elements, like the key, rhythmic feel, tempo, and other aspects such as energy and attitude.

No need to Google that, he concluded; and glancing up at the Dunnock he thought, this little guy certainly fits that definition; energy and attitude, he's calling his territory markers, and there's no doubt that it's *his* territory.

Ralph had always had a fondness for birds, and wildlife in general, but especially so for birds. He remembered the robin that had been resident in his garden over a period of three or so years, so many years ago now.

Percy, they had called him; and he had been so tame that he had eaten out of Ralph's hand. He had loved grated cheese and would always come when called.

Come on, cheeses, Ralph remembered calling, and Percy would fly to a branch nearby wherever Ralph would be standing in the garden, at the time. It had taken some time to encourage him to be that tame but what an exhilarating feeling it had been when Ralph had first felt Percy's little feet on his thumb, coupled with the gentle peck of his beak as he gathered up the individual cheese morsels, that had been resting on his palm.

'Sorry to disturb you again, Mr Diggerby,' the same softly spoken voice whispered near his ear, in exactly the same fashion as she had done a few moments earlier, 'it's me, Jessica. Carlo, the chef says to tell you it's roast lamb for dinner tonight, but Everton told him you won't eat lamb. Can he do you some poached salmon instead he says?'

Ralph shielded his eyes again and looked round at Jessica, 'salmon would be just fine for dinner tonight, if you would kindly pass that reply on to Carlo,' answered Ralph.

'What's up with lamb then?' asked Jessica, 'don't you like it?'

Ralph's body stiffened, not so much that Jessica would have noticed, but enough for Ralph's breathing to be ever so slightly laboured.

'I never eat lamb in any form, and haven't done for many years,' he stated with a flat tone to his voice. It was a tone that said to Jessica, that that was the end of that piece of conversation. Mr Diggerby did not eat lamb; however, it was presented. End of.

'I'll tell Carlo that salmon is alright for tonight's dinner, and lamb is _never_ alright, whether it's chops or stew or roast or however it's served,' she smiled at him, but a tighter smile than before; not the cheery open, relaxed smile of their previous conversation.

'Thank you, my dear Jessica,' replied Ralph. 'I didn't mean to be snappy, it's just that I am rather averse to lamb.'

'Oh, no offence, Mr Diggerby,' Jessica had regained her relaxed smile, and turned and walked back up the path towards the house. Just as before, Ralph watched her go, and just as before she turned prior to disappearing from sight and waved.

'Oh, deary me,' Ralph said aloud, as if confiding in the Dunnock, 'I hope I haven't gone and spoilt our friendship. But then, why would a young girl like Jessica want to be friends with someone like me anyway?'

Ralph turned his head to face forwards again, and allowed his eyes to close. He recalled again, the question he had asked his mother, all those years ago.... Mum, where did you and Dad meet, that is; how did you and Dad meet?

Chapter 4

⁓⁓⁓

The noise emanating from Room 4 was just a cacophony, like a crowd coming away from a Football League match at full-time after a five-nil victory.

Evelyn Fuller was just standing, motionless, in the doorway of Room five, shyly waiting to leave, but was prevented from doing so by the temporary flow of young masculine bodies, all seemingly releasing the pent-up tension of having sat through one and a half hours of Mr J K Thompson's lessons on Council Housing Law and Legalities.

Although not the most enthralling of topics, it was nevertheless a necessary requirement in Eric Diggerby's relentless march to qualifications, and as such, had therefore, to be endured and tolerated.

Eric rather enjoyed his job as a junior clerk, in the Council's Housing Department; but he found the evening classes after a long day at work rather tedious; however he accepted that it was something that he just had to put up with.

He stood back from the crowd of boisterous young men who were excitedly pushing their way out of the classroom, to allow them to get clean away, which made him more or less the last person to leave. He was looking down at his text book as he sauntered unimpeded from the room and didn't see the young lady who happened to set off from her room just at the same moment that he was passing.

The collision was delicious; Evelyn, smelling of fresh lily of the valley, from the soap she used walked right into Eric's side and knocked all his books from out of his grasp; the books cascading down to the floor.

Evelyn's hands went to her mouth, her long slender, young fingers overlapping, her face rapidly reddening, 'Oh,' she gasped, 'I'm so dreadfully sorry, how clumsy am I?'

She immediately stooped down in an attempt to assist in the recovery of the situation, as well as of the books.

Eric was already collecting up the scattering of books, and when he stood, having gathered them together, he looked at his assailant, and gave her a reassuring smile.

'It's really not a problem, think nothing of it; I was slow in leaving the room after the other boys, as I don't really enjoy being in the melee,' he said.

Having gathered both himself and the books back together, Eric had the opportunity to appraise the young lady who was now standing in front of him holding in her hands the one book that she had recovered from the floor. She looked into his face and smiled as she handed him the book.

What Eric saw was a delight to his eyes; here before him was a slender girl, for she had not quite, it seemed to him, to have become a young woman as yet. She was petite, with her lack of height seemingly emphasised by the flat white ballet pumps she wore on her feet. Her light-coloured hair had a wispy appearance, and her slim shoulders, encased in a cotton dress and thin knitted woollen jacket, came only just above Eric's elbow. Her fresh smile was set off by deep blue eyes, which although they were now gazing shyly towards the floor, he had managed to catch a glimpse of the mischief hiding therein.

'C, could I see you home?' Eric managed to half stammer, whilst feeling himself reddening.

'Oh, that won't be necessary, thank you,' Evelyn answered, 'my mother will be waiting for me at the gates and we always walk home together.'

Slightly crestfallen, Eric managed to utter a tumbling cascade of words, as they were now walking along the corridor towards the too fast approaching door.

'Will you be here next Tuesday evening? If so, do you think I could walk you home next week? I'd see you safely home;

your mother wouldn't need to worry. By the way my name's Eric, Eric Diggerby; I'm a clerk with the Council and I'm doing Housing. What are you doing?'

'My name is Evelyn Fuller, I work as a junior clerk at Page's Solicitors, but I'm doing a Pitman's course on office administration and short-hand and typing, as I want to be a legal secretary, because that sounds exciting. I'm learning to type on an Underwood Number 5, it's what they use in the office; and I don't know whether my mum would let me walk home with you next week or not, but I'll ask her if it would be alright, as I would like that. Oh, and thank you for asking me,' Evelyn added shyly.

By now they had reached the door, and Eric held it open for her and stood back just inside in the shadow, in an attempt to keep out of sight, until she had walked a few yards towards the gate where a lady, who was obviously Evelyn's mother was standing. She was clearly Evelyn's mother as she was a slightly older looking carbon copy of the girl, he had just met.

Despite standing back behind the door, and waiting a few seconds before exiting, and trying desperately to maintain an innocent detached air, which Eric thought he had managed successfully; Evelyn's mother's first words to her daughter upon them meeting outside the gates were.

'And just who was that young man, that you were talking to?' Evelyn's mother turned her head slightly to the side in order that Evelyn wouldn't see the warm smile on her face.

'He says his name's Eric, and he works for the Council and he's studying something to do with Housing Laws and he's asked if he can walk me home next week after class, and he seems a very polite young man,' Evelyn managed to get out all in one breath, whilst carefully avoiding catching her mother's eye. 'And I would like it very much if he did walk me home next week; please,' she added as a hopeful afterthought.

Mrs Fuller smiled inwardly as she replied, 'I'm going to have to ask your father, and discuss it with him first.'

'But mum, would *you* mind?' Evelyn asked, knowing full well that her mother hardly ever consulted with Mr Fuller on such matters; nor on most other things in their joint lives that required a decision, come to think of it. Evelyn knew within herself that any decision regarding the matter in question would be made solely by her mother.

They walked on in silence for a few minutes before Mrs Fuller turned to her beloved daughter, and said, 'maybe that young man, Eric, did you say his name was, could walk us *both* home next week.'

The matter was settled then; no further discussion with Mr Fuller or anyone else would be necessary, but this way mother would get to assess this young man for herself.

A warm glow of maternal affection spread throughout Mrs Fuller's being, for she loved her only daughter with a love that could hardly be expressed in words; and all she wanted for her offspring was for her to be happy, and have contentment and fulfilment in her life.

Her feelings and emotions for her daughter were echoed by Evelyn back towards her mother; they had a happy, warm and open relationship. Mrs Fuller was acutely aware of her daughter's shy quiet nature, but at the same time knew that there was a happy little soul hidden inside her daughter, just waiting to be set free.

Mother and daughter spoke not another word between them and the remainder of their walk home was completed in silence, although each one knew of the other's satisfaction at the outcome of the short discussion, and decision that mother had made.

Eric had spent the entire week that followed, in a state of perpetual worry, wondering whether Evelyn had managed to ask her mother about him walking her home and whether her mother would have given her permission.

As a result, he found it so very difficult to concentrate during Mr J K Thompson's current lesson on Council Housing Law and Legalities.

He had spent a goodly length of time, staring blankly at the blackboard.

Let's face it, he thought, I don't even know for sure whether she's attending her class this week. What if she is attending her class this week and her mother has said I can't walk her home? What if she's attending her class this week and she hasn't dared to ask her mother? Oh dear, what if she's attending her class this week and she doesn't want me to walk her home, because she's changed her mind?

Eric glanced at the old, round, wood-framed clock on the wall behind Mr J K Thompson; the big hand was just moving up to the X; meaning there was still another agonising ten minutes to go; it seemed to have taken an eon to move from the IX.

Finally, after a time that seemed long enough to have melted both polar icecaps, the bell rang to announce the end of this week's lesson, and now Eric's heart was pounding and his mouth had gone strangely dry; because now he had to wait for the end of the stampede as he described his colleagues exit as they left the room, before he could leave also. Hanging back as he usually did, he eventually emerged from Room four's doorway, and – joy upon joy, Evelyn was standing quietly in the doorway to Room five apparently waiting for him.

'Hello, Evelyn,' he managed, 'have you had a good week?'

'I've had a lovely week, thank you,' she replied with a shy smile, 'what about your week, how has your week been?'

'Oh, I've had a lovely week too,' Eric lied.

Although, he thought, it's actually turned out alright, just because Evelyn is here waiting. Of course the thing that would top the week off completely would be the right answer to the next question. Dare he ask the question?

Eric paused, and having taken a deep breath, he asked, 'did you ask your mother about me being allowed to walk you home?'

The two seconds that elapsed between the question leaving his lips and her answer reaching his ears, seemed like endless minutes.

'Yes, I did ask her.' She was teasing him now, and she stood and looked at his face for a moment before adding, 'and she said yes.'

Suddenly this was Christmas morning! Eric felt as if he had just unwrapped that most special present, the one that he had been hoping for, for ever.

'But,' Evelyn interrupted his internal celebrations, 'she did suggest however, that it would be nice if you walked both her and me home this week.'

Evelyn's addition to the answer did not dampen Eric's spirits one iota, he was just *so* happy. They walked together along the corridor, to the door; neither feeling the need to actually speak. Eric held the door open for Evelyn to go through before he did, and then he let it go, so it closed behind them as they made their way to the gate, where Mrs Fuller was standing watching them. Her heart warmed towards Eric before he had got within 10 yards of where she was standing.

'Hello, I'm Mrs Fuller, Evelyn's mother,' she said proffering her hand towards Eric, which he tentatively accepted and noticed the warmth in her fingers.

'Hello, Mrs Fuller. I'm Eric Diggerby, pleased to meet you. May I say how grateful I am to you for letting me walk home with you both.'

Mrs Fuller simply smiled in reply, but knew instantly in her heart that when the question arose as to whether she would allow Eric to walk Evelyn home alone next week, the answer would be a yes.

Here in front of her was the ideal young man she had long dreamed that her daughter would one day bring home to tea. He appeared smartly dressed, although only in his working clothes; he was quiet and seemed very polite and well mannered, and he sounded as if he had prospects; and she could tell from the expression on his open, honest face that he was very attracted to her daughter, Evelyn. Glancing at Evelyn's face she observed that the feeling was obviously mutual.

It took the shortest ten minutes of Eric's life to walk to Mrs Fuller's house and the conversation was light and friendly. When they reached the gate, Eric turned to go back the way he had come, but before he could say good evening, Mrs Fuller asked him whether he had his meal before evening class on a Tuesday.

'No, I usually have something to eat afterwards. Mother keeps my dinner warm over a saucepan for me until I get home,' he replied.

'Perhaps,' Mrs Fuller said, smiling warmly, and directly at Eric, 'you'd like to come and have tea with us next Tuesday after you've safely delivered Evelyn back home, without my help?'

'Do you mean I will be allowed to walk Evelyn home, next week, just the two of us?' Eric beamed at Mrs Fuller. 'oh, and yes please, I would love to have tea with you next week, and thank you so much for inviting me. I'm afraid I'll be wearing the suit I dress in for work, and not my Sunday best, if that's alright with you?' Eric gushed.

Mrs Fuller laughed gently, and replied, 'it's you I'm inviting to tea Eric, and you look perfectly presentable, just as you are, bless you my dear.'

The following months passed like a dream for both Eric and Evelyn, in fact they hardly paid any attention to anything else going on around them; even the 3rd of September 1939 pretty much passed them by. The fact that England had declared war on Germany that day seemed of little consequence to either of them.

Their lives moved along in a dream, both continuing with their respective occupations until reality struck on the morning of Eric's 18th birthday; the fifteenth of November 1940.

Under the terms of The National Service (Armed Forces) Act, which had come into force, unnoticed by neither Eric nor

Evelyn, on the day of the declaration of war, Eric had now become eligible for call up to the war effort.

For on the aforesaid morning, the arrival of the postman brought a small bundle of birthday wishes in addition to which he also brought the brown envelope that floated down onto the mat behind the door, the brown envelope that contained Eric's call-up papers.

Eric, it read, was required to register his name, and make himself available for possible military service.

Chapter 5

'It's Mr Diggerby, isn't it? Are you alright, Mr Diggerby? Were you asleep; did we wake you? This is a beautiful part of the garden especially when the sun begins to turn down to the horizon, we both think.'

Ralph struggled back to consciousness, and half opened one eye, but carefully, in order to see who it was that had alighted on the bench opposite to his. He groaned inwardly as his half-opened eye revealed the identity of the person, or perhaps people behind the words. It was the Misses Cotton.

Audrey and Brenda Cotton; the unmarried twin ladies who shared a double room in Downwood; they shared a double room as it kept the cost down. They went by the names of Audrey and Brenda; as their father had said that would make them A, B and C. Ralph had overheard them telling these tedious stories more times than he had spent days actually living in Downwood.

'Yes, it's Diggerby; and yes, I'm fine thank you, thank you for asking; and yes, I <u>was</u> asleep; and yes, you <u>did</u> wake me, for which I thank you as I have been sitting in the sun a mite too long.'

Ralph said the last few words as he was already planning his escape, and he was just about managing to contain his irritation, but the Misses Cotton were oblivious to most of the negative reactions they engendered in their fellow humans as they lived in this "pink world" where reality was but a blur.

One of the ladies leaned slightly forward in a conspiratorial fashion, as if wishing to share a secret, 'We're the Cotton sisters, I'm Audrey, and this is my twin, Brenda. Our father....'

'.... who art in Heaven, (where he's thankfully, safe)' Ralph interrupted under his breath.

'Our father named me Audrey, because I was the first-born and then my sister was named Brenda as she was the second born; and our surname is Cotton, so our father referred to us as the ABC twins. Don't you think that's funny, Mr Diggerby?' The two ladies looked at each other and giggled.

Ralph immediately had a flash-back to a scene from the film, Four Weddings and a Funeral, that he remembered having seen many years before, where one of the characters played by Simon Callow was cringing at the rear of the church whilst a young couple sang "Can't Live Without You" whilst accompanying themselves on the guitar.

'Not really,' Ralph answered, as he stood up. 'It strikes me it was just a matter of alphabetical identification. Now, if you'll excuse me ladies, I have something which requires my immediate attention inside.' And with that Ralph marched swiftly, if somewhat stiffly away up the path.

'Can't live without you....' he sang quietly to himself, as he walked. He did turn around just the once to look back, but the Misses Cotton appeared to be completely engaged in whatever it was that they were now discussing.

'Say goodnight to the folks, Gracie' Ralph muttered aloud to himself as he went through the door.

'Isn't he a pleasant man dear?' asked Audrey. 'Who is, dear?' her sister, Brenda replied.

It took a few moments for Ralph's eyes to adjust to the light as he walked into the lobby area, as he headed towards the lift, but he could just make out Everton pushing a tea trolley towards him.

'Hey, Mr Ralph, would you be wantin' a cup of tea?' Everton had this wonderful natural way of making the word 'wanting' sound rounded, somehow.

Ralph pondered a moment, 'yes please Everton,' he answered, looking straight at the man standing in front of him; the two of them being separated from one another by the tea trolley. Everton was one very good reason why Ralph felt that this place, Downwood where he now lived, was so pleasant. Him and Jessica, both.

'Couldn't help but notice that you came back inside, just as soon as them there two cotton buds walked down to where you were sitting.' Everton opened his big eyes wide and rolled his eyeballs, and laughed aloud. 'No disrespect meant to them, Mr Ralph, they're sweet old ladies, but they sure do make a man laugh, sometimes. Gonna jump down, turn around, pick a bale o' cotton,' Everton sang quietly under his breath whilst pouring Ralph's cup of tea and handing it to him.

'See you later then, Mr Ralph,' said Everton turning the tea trolley around and walking away swaying whilst continuing to hum his song.

Ralph gratefully took his cup of tea into the lift as he was on his way up to his room, and once inside there, he gently placed the cup and saucer onto the table. He found that his thoughts were once more drawing him to look inside the orangey brown folder in the top drawer of the writing desk. Finding the key in his trouser pocket, he removed it from its resting place and unlocked the drawer; extracting the folder from out of the drawer and placing it on the writing desk top which he had opened.

It's so strange, he thought, how all my life can be summed up in the contents of this one tatty, slim, orangey brown folder.

After opening the folder, Ralph took out the top item which was his Birth Certificate; Date of Birth, it read, 16th May 1947; Father Eric Diggerby, occupation Town Hall Clerk; Mother's name, Evelyn Diggerby, nee Fuller, occupation Solicitors' Secretary.

In the next file compartment down, there was the only photograph that the whole file contained; it was a photograph of a young man, dressed in a World War Two styled military uniform standing stiffly to attention next to a young woman in a very smart woollen material suit. The woman was holding a small posey of what looked like short-stemmed roses; and both young people were smiling rather nervously into the camera lens.

There were no other people in that photograph, and both the posers could be identified by turning the photograph over to where someone had written, in pencil, "Eric and Evelyn, wedding day 5th March 1941."

'Eric and Evelyn; mum and dad,' murmured Ralph out loud, gazing at the photograph.

Ralph sadly, couldn't remember much about his father, as he had died in 1958, just after Ralph had reached the age of 11 years old.

What he did remember though, was that his father had come home one Wednesday afternoon, earlier than expected, as he had been sent home from work complaining of a very severe headache. Ralph remembered that the headache had seemed no better the following morning and that his mother had walked with her husband to the Doctor's surgery, to ensure that they obtained an appointment for him.

The doctor's consultation had resulted in a referral to the local infirmary; and also the Doctor had written a letter to his employer, explaining that he would be unfit for work for a short while. Together with that, the doctor had proceeded to write a letter to a Mr Fenton, Consultant Surgeon, Thornston Royal Infirmary; the letter was to be taken and handed to the surgeon's secretary when the appointment was being made; a task which was duly completed that same afternoon and an appointment secured to consult with Mr Fenton, early on the following Monday morning.

When Ralph had returned home from school that following Monday afternoon, he had been aware of the sombre mood in the house as soon as he had walked in; and his parents were sitting in the front room, which in itself was unusual, as that room was generally reserved for weekends, particularly Sundays. The couple had been sitting side by side on the settee, each with a cup of tea in their hands and they were not conversing; just sitting quietly.

'Hello, son,' his father had said, 'come and sit down lad, your mother has something to tell you.'

His mother had flashed a quick questioning look at her husband, but he had nodded his head at her, so she coughed and started to speak to Ralph.

'As you know, Ralph, your father and I had to go to the Infirmary this morning for your father to be examined by a consultant about the headaches he has been having. He has had a series of tests and x-rays and the Consultant, Mr Fenton has unfortunately informed us that your father, has developed something called a brain tumour; that is a growth of some kind in his brain.' Evelyn was bravely fighting back the tears, determined not to let her son see just how upset she was, and trying desperately thereby to reassure Ralph that there was no need for him to worry as everything would work out alright in the end.

She continued, 'your father will be having an operation as soon as possible; the tumour will be removed and then there will be an amount of time needed to convalesce, to help him to recover and after that he will be able to return to work, and normal life, will be resumed.'

Ralph glanced up from his writing desk, and had a mouthful of his tea. He remembered that day, some sixty-odd years ago, with great clarity. The following days and even weeks passed by in a blur; his father had had the operation and recovered; then he had come home and gone to bed, where he had stayed for a week or two.

There had, Ralph remembered, been several visits from the Doctor, always followed by hushed conversations between the doctor and his mother.

He remembered too that one day when he had come home from school and started to climb the stairs, in order to tell his father about his day, which had always seemed to please father; mother had called him into the front room before he had had the chance to start the ascent.

'Your father is not upstairs, Ralph dear, he has been taken back to the hospital, as he has become rather unwell again,' she had said quietly.

Ralph remembered, that for some reason he had realised that at that moment he was not required to ask any questions; just to accept his mother's statement.

In the stillness of his room, all these years afterwards, Ralph sat at his writing desk and recalled again, the scene two days after his mother had spoken to him in the front room. He would never, ever forget that day.

The class was halfway through the afternoon story when a girl had knocked at the door of his classroom and whispered to Ralph's teacher, Mr Callaghan, that the Headmistress wanted to see Ralph immediately in her room, and he was to go straight there.

He had been excused from class by Mr Callaghan and had gone with the nameless girl to Miss Beswick's room. The girl had knocked at the door and the sound of 'come in' had been called from the inside.

The girl had opened the door and gently pushed Ralph, encouraging him to go inside the room. Ralph had never set foot inside Miss Beswick's room before and it seemed to him to be an enormous cavern, with a large wooden desk right in the centre.

Ralph had looked at the Headmistress, and suddenly became aware that his mother was sitting in a chair on the opposite side of the desk, to Miss Beswick, clasping a cup of tea in her hands, her eyes full of big, fat, round tears; a couple of which were finding their way down the front of her face.

'Come in, Ralph dear,' said Miss Beswick kindly, 'please sit on the chair next to your mother; she has something to tell you, dear'

Ralph had never seen his mother so upset, and he wondered what ever could be the matter with her.

'What's the matter mum?' he had asked gently, sensing even in his young eleven-year-old mind that something in his life was about to change for ever.

Mother had suddenly leaned towards him, wrapped her arms tightly about his thin body, let out a huge sob, and managed to say, 'Ralphie, your father has died.'

Evelyn sobbed again; deep wracking sobs, that seemed to cut right into Ralph through his insides. 'He died at the Infirmary this afternoon,' she said.

Ralph didn't fully comprehend exactly what this all meant, but he suddenly had felt the need to follow his mother into sobs, and the tears started to stream down his young face. He blinked repeatedly, and he was just vaguely aware of Miss Beswick saying something to his mother.

'Best take him home now, go home together; I've had Ralph's coat sent to my room. Here it is. Don't worry about his not attending school for a while; we understand. Just recover as best you can and send him back when he's ready.' She added, I'll inform his class teacher Mr Callaghan, and the other children, just so they'll be aware of the situation.'

Ralph looked back down at his writing desk; the next item down in the file, his father's death certificate had slipped out, and it lay face up as if looking at him.

Ralph could vaguely recall having returned to school within a few days, and how kind the other children and in particular Mr Callaghan had been.

The only other thing that Ralph remembered about that time was an occasion a few weeks later; when he had been sitting with his mother after the evening meal and had asked her, 'Mum, what's going to happen to us, are we going to be alright?'

His mother had put her arms around him and reassured him that everything would be fine. They would be able to continue to live in the house; and she had now applied to work full-time at the Solicitor's and permission had been granted. There would not be quite as much money now of course, but if they were careful, they would manage just fine.

Ralph remembered having been suitably reassured, mainly by his mother's quiet calm and confidence.

Ralph returned his father's death certificate to the place where it had fallen from in the file, and in so doing dislodged the pristine £1 note that was the next item down.

Its unmistakable corner was now in view, and Ralph hesitated to touch it. The tension in his body became so palpable, and he felt distinctly uncomfortable, and a sheen of sweat appeared on his hands; his breathing altered, and he told himself to calm down; to remember that it's only a bank note; an out of date, no longer legal tender, £1 bank note.

With his middle finger and his thumb he pinched the corner of it that was protruding from the file, and gently eased the bank note out; and now there it was on the writing desk in front of him, seemingly staring at him, or at least the monarch's eyes in the note's royal image seemed to be.

He carefully turned it over to read again what was written on the reverse, and his breath momentarily caught in his throat.

Chapter 6

'What'll it be, Ralph?' asked the rather attractive young lady behind the glass counter, who was now identified as Sheila, Sheila Cooper; 'do you want tea or coffee with your sandwich?' Sheila lowered her eyelids as she asked the question of Ralph.

'Oh, tea please, er, Sheila. I'll help myself to sugar at the end table. Thank you, Sheila,' he said as he took the cup from Sheila and placed it onto his tray next to the ham and tomato sandwich that he had decided was going to be today's lunch.

'That'll be exactly four shillings, please. The extra penny is because it's ham; the cheese like you had yesterday, is one penny cheaper, er I mean less.' Sheila smiled sweetly at Ralph and took his proffered two florin coins.

As he went to turn away from her counter to find a table, Sheila slipped a small piece of paper onto his tray, with her name, address and mother's telephone number written in blue biro.

'That's for you, as promised,' Sheila beamed at him. 'Who's next please?'

Ralph returned her smile but in a somewhat more nervous fashion; and now, actually completing the move of turning away from the counter, his eyes searched the crowded room for a vacant table. There, as luck would have it, he spotted the same table that he had occupied the previous day, and like yesterday at this time, it was currently unused. Ralph made his way across the room, placed his tray on the table and sat down.

Then he stood up again and, feeling awkward, removed his overcoat, draping it over the chair that was opposite the one that he had chosen to sit on. He sat down again, and immediately realised he had not helped himself to sugar from the end table.

'I think I'd like to try my tea without sugar today,' he said out loud, in an attempt to convince himself that this was what he wanted to do, rather than risk the embarrassment of rising from his table again to obtain some sugar.

Instead he unbuttoned his suit jacket and carefully picked up the half of the ham and tomato sandwich nearest to him on the plate.

He took a deep bite and glanced up at the counter as he did so, only to be thrown into embarrassed confusion by finding that Sheila was staring intently, straight at him. She threw him a delicious smile, both with her mouth and her eyes; Ralph tried to return the smile but found himself reddening by the second.

He did glance over his left shoulder, just to make sure that there was no one behind him that she could be smiling at, but there was no one, as Ralph's table was against the wood-panelled wall. Pleasantly reassured, Ralph resumed the eating of his lunch, just sneaking another glance at the counter as he finished the first half of his ham and tomato sandwich.

Disappointed, by the fact that Sheila was now not where she had been a couple of moments ago, he looked back down at his plate. At that same moment, he became aware of that aroma again, the musk smell from the deodorant and starch from the crisp white blouse that Sheila wore. As yesterday, she leaned unnecessarily close to him as she placed something onto his plate from inside her cupped hand; Ralph looked up into her face, and straight back down to his plate, to find a coconut macaroon nestling next to the remains of his sandwich.

'Oh, th-thank you,' he stammered.

Ralph immediately thought back to when he had arrived at work earlier that morning and had busied himself with opening the days mail, which had been stacked high on the mail-room table, as usual. It was his first task of each day, to take a Bank paper-knife and slit open all the envelopes and pile them neatly, ready for a more senior clerk from the Securities Department to actually open each envelope to reveal the contents and then to apportion them to whichever department of the Bank that they needed to go to be dealt with.

Having accomplished the day's first task, Ralph had gone onto the counter to tidy it and ready it for the day's business.

In the meantime, his till drawer, along with the others that were to be operational that day had come up in the lift from the strongroom. The first thing that Ralph had done upon unlocking and opening his till drawer had been to take a cheque from the inside pocket of his suit jacket, one that he had made out to "cash" for £2, and entered it into his ledger, putting the cheque in the entries wire basket behind the counter, and had then placed one carefully selected brand new £1 note into his wallet; the other pound he had taken from his till in change, mainly florins, as two-shilling pieces were referred to in the Bank.

Ralph also recalled to mind the incident between himself and Allan of the previous day, where Allan had had the 'special' £1 note, with Mrs Sykes' personal details written on it.

The romance of that had appealed to Ralph's senses and he had determined over night to draw a new £1 note, it had to be a new one, and he would ask Sheila to write her name, address and telephone number on it, so that he could put it into his wallet, and thereby have something similar to what Allan had.

The idea of doing that and the planning of that exercise had been easy enough but, suddenly returning to the here and now, Ralph tensed as he realised that *now* it was the time for action.

'I wonder if I could ask you to do something, er, Sheila?' he blurted out. 'If you have a moment or two to spare, do you think that you could, er, possibly....?'

'.... write my name and details on that new £1 note you are clutching in your left hand?' said Sheila, finishing Ralph's sentence for him.

'Oh, er, yes, that's right,' Ralph managed to say. 'How did you know that that was what I was going to ask?'

Ralph sat motionless as Sheila smiled knowingly at him, removed a black biro pen from her apron, bent low over the table and carefully copied her name, address and mother's telephone number onto the back of the £1 note, before sliding it across the table to him, until her fingers just touched his. Sheila delayed letting go of the £1 note, so her fingers rested against Ralph's for just half a second, but it was more than enough time to send an electric shock, all the way up Ralph's left arm, straight into his pounding heart. Sheila smiled at him and returned to her position behind the counter.

When he had recovered and his breathing had returned to near normal, he picked up the £1 note and carefully folded it into a very precise half and put it into his wallet; but not in the section where notes were normally kept, but into a separate section with a small zip.

Several moments later after Ralph had cleared his plate and cup of their contents, Sheila appeared as if by magic at his side again; and again as yesterday she leaned in deliciously closer than she needed to, just in order to clear his plate and cup and saucer.

'Was everything alright for you today, sir?' Sheila had asked in her waitress' voice, 'and shall we have the pleasure of seeing you in here again tomorrow, sir?' She smiled at him with her eyes.

'Everything was fine, today, thank you,' replied Ralph, 'and I'm certain I shall be back tomorrow.' Sheila was already starting to wipe his table even as Ralph was putting on his overcoat, ready to leave.

'Do you particularly like this table; only you sat here yesterday, as I recall?' Sheila asked, 'I only mention it as I can reserve this table for you if you will be coming in at the same time, tomorrow.'

Ralph particularly liked this table as it was against the wall just at the point where the stairs rose to whatever was on the upper floor, but it afforded him a certain level of anonymity, tucked away as it was, in the corner. He felt sheltered there and certainly not in full view of the remainder of the people occupying tables in the café.

'I would certainly appreciate it, if you could do that for me,' Ralph replied with genuine enthusiasm. 'Thank you very much, Sheila. I shall look forward to seeing you again tomorrow.'

With that said, Ralph, carefully replaced his chair under the table and made his way to the door of the café and stepped out into Market Street.

The sun wasn't shining as it had been yesterday and there was a stiff breeze blowing, hence Ralph's need to wear his overcoat, but nevertheless, Ralph felt a warm glow within, which of course he put down to the cup of tea he had just drunk.

Despite the breeze, his steps were light as he found himself walking away from the Bank; as he had indeed done the previous day. He didn't walk quite as far as he had done the previous day, remembering the need to hurry back, when he'd gone further than he had realised. Today, he walked briskly towards the Town hall again, but this time he turned back upon himself, at a point that he knew would give him sufficient time to comfortably walk back to the office in time to restart work punctually at 1.00pm.

Indeed he arrived back, ready to recommence serving the Bank's customers, spruced up and feeling on top of the world, with a few moments to spare.

'You're back in good time old man,' said Allan. 'Did you have a good lunch?'

'I most certainly did,' enthused Ralph, 'followed by a brisk walk. Why don't you slip off the counter now Allan, whilst it's quiet? I'll take over.'

'That's awfully decent of you, old man,' gushed Allan, already moving towards the exit. 'See you later,' he called over his shoulder.

'By heck! Where was he rushing off to?'

Ralph looked up to find Allan's father Arthur, standing adjacent to his till.

'He nearly knocked his own father over in his haste to leave the building,' Mr Briggs senior, laughed.

Taking his chequebook out of his pocket, Arthur Briggs said, 'I need to withdraw a couple of hundred pounds from the business account, Ralph, please. Do I make the cheque out to myself? I can never remember what to do. All in tenners, if you will, please?'

Ralph smiled at Mr Briggs, whom he liked; he was a strongly built man and although he appeared to have a gruff exterior, he was extremely pleasant when you took the trouble to get to know him a little. He had obviously come straight to the Bank from the building site where he was currently working.

Mr Briggs had his own small building firm, through which he employed two other men, one of whom was the labourer; and he had been extremely disappointed when his son, Allan had shown no inclination whatsoever of joining the firm and following him into the building trade.

'Allan couldn't throw two bricks into a straight line to save his life,' Mr Briggs had moaned once before when he had talked to Ralph at the counter, whilst Ralph was busy counting out some notes for him.

The same was happening again now, and Mr Briggs was bemoaning the same tale to Ralph, but this time he added, 'how proud I am that a son of mine is bright enough to hold down a job in a Bank. I've never had the brains for figures and a lot of reading and writing; I've allus worked with me hands. Just think, he might even bring some status to the Briggs family,' he laughed again.

'There you are Mr Briggs, two hundred pounds in crisp ten pound notes,' Ralph handed the money to Allan's father with a smile; a smile that wasn't just "Bank politeness" but a smile of genuine warmth, as Arthur Briggs was one of the few men that Ralph felt genuinely comfortable with.

'Thank you, Mr Briggs, hope to see you again soon.'

'Aye lad, but I know that you bank men only really like to see a customer when he's payin' money in, not drawing it out.' Mr Briggs laughed his deep throated laugh, whilst turning and heading for the door. 'Tarra lad, thank you,' he called over his broad shoulder.

Without warning, a cloth money bag containing different denomination notes and a paying in book, were thrust towards Ralph by Mr West, the proprietor of "Go West For Fish & Chips".

Ralph could tell without looking up that it was Mr West because of the smell of stale cooking fat and fish batter, mingling with the tang of day old vinegar. Still, he always paid in a regular, goodly amount of money from the takings from his gold mine known as the afore mentioned "Go West For Fish & Chips".

The only problem being the amount of grease that was left clinging to the bank notes and the smell it left on Ralph's fingers after he had counted and bundled all of them. Mr West didn't say very much when he came to the bank and always seemed to look dark eyed and tired, but I suppose thought Ralph that'll be because he has to get up so early in the morning to deal with all those potatoes he has to peel and chip.

'Good afternoon Mr West,' Ralph greeted his customer in as pleasant a manner as he could. He didn't expect a reply, and wasn't disappointed in his expectation, as Mr West just leaned against the counter, silently watching Ralph count the money and tick the amounts off on the paying in slip. 'That all seems in order, thank you Mr West,' said Ralph, whilst stamping the Bank's date stamp on both copies of the paying in book.

'Is there anything else we can help you with today?'

Mr West simply pushed himself upright from the leaning position, flicked a £10 note from his hand across the counter towards Ralph, and quietly said, 'two mixed bags of silver, lad.'

'Thank you, Mr West, hope to see you again soon,' was Ralph's closing remark as Mr West made for the door, without reply.

'Hello, Mrs Perryman,' smiled Ralph at the next customer who appeared at his till, 'would you mind awfully if I just pop off the counter for just a moment, I just have a need to wash my hands?'

'Of course not, young man. I can smell that fish and chip money from here. It's disgusting. It's a pity you can't wear rubber gloves when you're having to handle that; but then it wouldn't look right, I don't suppose, a young man like you behind a bank counter wearing Marigolds.'

Mrs Perryman suddenly laughed. 'Off you go then.'

The chief cashier, a certain Mr Melrose, came from his position at the far end of the counter and asked Mrs Perryman whether Ralph was attending to her, to which she replied that she was 'being very well looked after, thank you.'

Despite that reassurance, Ralph did get a stern look from the aforementioned Mr Melrose upon his return to the counter, a few moments later.

'So sorry about that Mrs Perryman, so sorry to have kept you waiting,' Ralph said with an apologetic smile, 'now, what can I do for you today?'

'I just want to pay in my Grattan account today, please,' she answered.

After a short pause she added conspiratorially, following a quick glance down the counter to where Mr Melrose was now engaged with a customer, 'you want to watch him, yonder; he can be a nasty piece of work; not my place, I know, but you'd be best advised to keep your eye on him.'

Ralph smiled at her, as he replied, 'thanks for the advice Mrs Perryman, I'll keep that in mind. Bye for now.'

Ralph knew that Mr Melrose was irritated by people who only came to pay in their catalogue money; they were mostly people who didn't even have an account of their own with the Bank. 'Treat the Bank like a bloody post office, some people,' he had said to Ralph one lunch-time when the subject had raised itself.

Personally, Ralph couldn't see the problem with it, but he had learnt to keep his opinions on such matters very much to himself, especially when Mr Melrose was "on a rant".

Mr Melrose was the youngest of three brothers, born to wealthy parents; the eldest son of whom had become a surgeon at a London Hospital; the second son, was a solicitor in Dorset, and then there was Duncan.

Duncan Melrose; if you like, the "runt of the litter" who had originally gone into the army, but had been "asked to leave" Sandhurst for some unspoken about misdemeanour, and had been "persuaded" to accept a position with Brackleys Bank after his father had pulled a few strings.

Ralph allowed the thought that Duncan had gone from being cashiered out of the army to being a cashier in the bank to run through his mind. Ralph also often laughed inwardly whenever he thought that there must have been a lot of strings needed pulling, which was why Mr Melrose always seemed to be so wound up with life.

Duncan Melrose, now in his middle fifties, had inherited well from his parents' estate, and really only continued with his position at the Bank as "something to keep himself occupied".

'Hey? Are you serving customers or what, lad?' Ralph looked up from his thoughts and there was Mr Walter Metcalfe standing in front of him with his paying in book to the farm account and also, as usual two or three fivers in his deposit account pass book.

Mr Metcalfe was the archetypal dales farmer; weather beaten face, stockily built, but strong, and a bit on t' dour side.

Walter Metcalfe had been paying £5 notes into his deposit account for over thirty years, and the account showed a total of an astonishing (to Ralph anyway) amount of over £38,000. Considering, Ralph thought, that someone could buy a house for around £2500, that £38,000 was an awful lot of money; and Mr Metcalfe, Ralph had often noted had never, ever drawn any money out of his account.

'Sorry, Mr Metcalfe, just doing some calculations in my head,' Ralph lied.

'Aye well, you want to stop all that calculatin' and gerron wi' some work, and get folk served. Us proper workin' folk haven't got time to be calculating.'

Mr Metcalfe thrust both his farm account paying in book and his deposit account passbook at Ralph with a scowl on his weathered face. Ralph checked that the entries balanced with the cheques from the Milk Marketing Board, stamped both copies of the paying in book, tore out the bank copy and handed the book back to Mr Metcalfe, followed by the deposit account passbook, suitably updated and signed.

'Thank you, Mr Metcalfe, looking forward to seeing you again soon,' said Ralph, fighting hard inwardly, to hold back the laughter he felt brimming to the surface. He liked Mr Metcalfe, he really did, but why wouldn't the man ever smile?

A small hand clutching tightly to a ten shilling note waved just above the counter top, and a voice came from somewhere in that general direction, 'can me mam have ten shillings in silver for our meter please mister?'

Ralph leaned forward taking the proffered note from the small hand and counted out ten silver shillings, pushing them as far towards the other side of the counter top as he could reach.

'Thanks mister,' said the faceless voice and a hand came up and took the coins and disappeared.

A second or two later, a small thin girl in a cotton dress came into view as she reached the bank doorway, turned and gave the sweetest, cheekiest smile, then she waved and stepped out of the stygian gloom of the Banking Hall into the daylight outside.

The remainder of that afternoon drifted on and the Bank clock dragged its seemingly weary hands around to finally arrive at the magical three-thirty position on its face; time for the Bank's doors to be closed, and the task of writing up the till ledger and checking the accuracy of the final totals and then, counting all the cash in the till to ensure that the two balanced.

The till ledger showed how much cash there *should* be in the till and the counting then would show the actuality. There was always a sigh of relief when the two figures turned out to be the same.

'Sight balance.' Allan called from his till. A sight balance was where the two figures agreed on the first time of checking.

Ralph was however, ten shillings "short"; that is, he had ten shillings less in his till than the ledger said he should have had.

Ralph checked again; it was still ten shillings short.

Allan was now passing with his till balance entries ready for the machine room to "post" the figures into the day's work, when he happened to notice a ten shilling note lying on the floor under Ralph's till. It was just visible, sticking out from under a large cloth bag of uncounted silver coin.

'There's a ten-bob note there, old man; there, on the floor.'

Ralph followed the direction of Allan's pointing finger, and sure enough, there was the offending ten shilling note. Thinking back to the little girl who had come in wanting change "for her mam's gas meter" he realised that it was the one she had brought in for that loose change.

Ralph savoured the thought with a smile and recalled the memory of the cheeky grin on the girl's face as she had waved to him, on leaving the Bank, and now realised that he must have dropped the note off the counter top when the child had distracted him; and then, he remembered, Mr Melrose had also brought him the cloth bag containing £100 of loose silver, ready to be counted and to be bagged in any spare moment; although no such spare moment had arisen, on that busy afternoon.

'Thanks Allan,' said Ralph, and in the same breath called out, 'till four balanced.'

The final one and a half hours of the day's Bank routine passed and Ralph found himself once more standing, waiting at the number 37 bus stop for his transport home. He did just wonder whether the young lady from Cooper's Café would be on the bus again tonight, as she had been last night, but he concluded that she probably wouldn't be, as last night she had said she was only on that bus as she was going to tea at her friend, Lucy's – or whatever the friend's name was.

The bus arrived, the brakes squealing, as it came to a halt just past the stop; exactly the same sequence as last night, and every night.

'I wonder why the bus always comes to a halt about five paces beyond the stop?' Ralph pondered, and shrugging his shoulders, he stepped onto the bus platform and went straight upstairs in hope; but alas, no Shelia. He quickly found an empty seat and sat down on it, before the bus lurched forward.

Ralph alighted from the bus, at his usual stop, walked smartly up Wellington Street, as he normally did, and found his mother fussing with the rose in the front garden, as she usually was doing at this time of day.

'Hello, Ralph,' she greeted him, 'have you had a good day dear?'

'Hello mum,' Ralph answered, 'same sort of day as usual, thank you. What about you, have you had a good day?'

Evelyn had stopped fussing with the rose and was preceding Ralph into the house.

'What did you get yourself for your lunch today, dear? Did you go to the same café as you went to yesterday?'

Ralph was removing his overcoat and hanging it up by the front door, and answered, 'Yes, I went into Coopers Café, the same as I did yesterday, although today I had a ham and tomato sandwich. A very pleasant young lady brought me a coconut macaroon too, which I enjoyed.'

That's good, Ralph dear. I'm so glad that you had a good day. Now, wash your hands, your dinner is almost ready to go on the table.

And so, another working day ended in the same gentle way as had all the others preceding this one.

Chapter 7

There it was, in Sheila's own clear script, her name, address and her mother's telephone number; all written on the back of the still pristine £1 bank note, neatly folded and kept in the orangey-brown folder.

'Hmm', Ralph broke the silence of the room, and sitting on his chair at the writing desk, he couldn't help contemplating and wondering at all the trouble in his life that seemed to have been caused by that single, solitary £1 note.

He took a glance at his wrist watch, which showed that the time was just coming up to 5.15pm, which meant that there was still another three quarters of an hour to go before they served the evening meal in the Downwood dining room.

Ralph carefully returned all the items back into the folder, making sure they were all in the correct order. Each item in the folder was kept in its own plastic A4 sleeve, and all the sleeves were kept in place by the two oddly named Treasury tags.

Treasury tags were those pieces of cord with a metal strip fixed at either end; and were used to hold sheets of paper together, by slotting them through a hole in the papers. Ralph had wondered over the years about the origin of the name "Treasury tags"; what did these bits of string and cheap metal have to do with the Treasury?

Ralph had kept a small number of Treasury tags since his days with Brackleys Bank, and found them immeasurably useful from time to time.

The Treasury tags were kept in a small tin box, which he had kept as a memento of his father, together with the other random items that he had gathered as a collection over the years. There was an assortment of elastic bands, although most of those were just perished by the passage of time; some different coloured paperclips; a half-dozen or so drawing pins; an unused 3d postage stamp celebrating the Centenary of The Salvation Army, which had been folded down across one corner; a stub from a London bus ticket; a maroon coat button; and his cycling proficiency badge, which he had earned in 1959.

He couldn't really remember riding his bike much after that year, as he had started at Grammar School and the amount of homework he had been given, curtailed his hitherto evening freedom, which he had previously enjoyed at the end of each school day.

Just as he was about to return the folder to the writing desk drawer, one of the plastic sleeves slipped and jutted out; it was the one that contained the copy of the best man's speech at Ralph's wedding; the speech given by Allan. Allan Briggs. Best man. Best friend?

Ralph pushed the speech paper back into line in the folder, and then he returned the folder to its place of rest, inside the top drawer of the writing desk; slid the drawer shut; turned the key in the lock; extracted the key and returned it carefully to his trouser pocket, where force of habit commanded that he pat the key through the trouser material; just in order to confirm it was safe.

Standing up from the desk, Ralph took the three paces to the window, and leaning his hands on the windowsill he looked out at the view. He had realised that if he stood on tip-toes and craned his neck towards the right, he could just make out the heavy stone entrance to The Weighbridge.

The Weighbridge, had been, in its prime, just that; a working weighbridge, but around thirty years previously it had fallen into disuse and the building and grounds had suffered neglect, until fifteen years later, someone at the Council had had the bright idea of renovating the existing buildings, and extending them where appropriate, adding in some new buildings and converting the whole site into a Council owned and run retirement home and complex.

It was to The Weighbridge that Allan had eventually been confined; for he was now a resident in the Care Home section, as he was suffering from Alzheimer's. Ralph had been to visit him once, a couple of years previously, but Allan had not appeared to know who Ralph was. It was true to say that Ralph had not been 100% convinced that Allan, had truly not known him or recognised him, but actually Ralph, in all honesty preferred it that way.

Ralph stepped back from the window, and decided there was just time to re-enter the world of the book he was currently reading; Ken Follett's Whiteout. He had just managed to pick up the book, which was of course, the hardback edition; Ralph much preferred the hard back copies to the paperback versions; somehow a paperback didn't feel like a proper book to Ralph's way of thinking; when there was a light tapping at his room door.

'Come in' he called out to whoever this was, interrupting his afternoon.

'So sorry to bother you Mr Diggerby.' It was Jessica who stepped into the room; 'there's an envelope that's just been hand delivered for you downstairs; so I've brought it up for you, just in case.'

'That's very kind of you, Jessica,' Ralph answered, 'but, in case of what?'

'In case it contains something important that you need to read right away,' Jessica answered in wide eyed innocence. She had covered the distance between the door and his chair in a few dainty steps and handed the light blue envelope to Ralph.

"Ralph Diggerby, Downwood" was all that was written, in blue biro, on the front of the envelope.

'Thank you, so very much my dear Jessica,' he said, taking the envelope from her outstretched hand. Jessica remained standing next to Ralph for a few seconds, but Ralph made no move to open the envelope, merely remaining seated, staring at his name written on the front.

Eventually, Jessica said, 'right, I'll go back downstairs and leave you to it, Mr Diggerby.'

'Oh, er, yes alright, my dear,' said Ralph absent-mindedly.

He sat wondering who the envelope was from and what it contained, as he didn't know anyone really well enough to have them send him any personal correspondence.

Jessica had vacated the room whilst Ralph's mind had been lost in a twilight mist, and now coming back to the reality of the day, he said out loud, sternly to himself, 'there's little point just sitting staring at the envelope Ralph, wondering who it's from; the only way to find out is to open the thing.'

Ralph had always been of a suspicious mind when it came to situations like this, but eventually he slipped his little finger under the flap and opened the envelope. Pulling out the matching note paper from the eggshell blue envelope, he realised, once he'd glanced at the writing that the note was short; and was hand written, dated that day, and simply informed him that if he wanted to see his friend Mr Allan Briggs before he died, then they were expecting that to happen within the next forty eight hours or so. The short note was signed by the Manager of the Weighbridge Nursing Home; Ralph's first reaction was to wonder how anyone at the Weighbridge had known where to contact him.

Ralph refolded the letter and carefully replaced it back inside the envelope; and then watched it as it floated onto the carpet, by his chair, and he allowed his mind to drift for a moment or two.

He decided there and then that there would be very little point in visiting Allan as the real Allan had gone some years before; and because of Alzheimer's, that dreadful disease, the shell that was left was not the real Allan Briggs any more. Ralph thought it would be best to try to remember him as he had been, when they had first been friends.

Ralph leaned back in his chair and allowed his mind to drift back to a Monday morning in early July 1964; to a time when a very nervous, seventeen year old version of himself had arrived outside the front entrance of Brackleys Bank Thornston, ready to start his journey into the World of Work, as his mother had termed it; or into The Big Mister's World, as he had joked with his mother.

Whichever it was, it was his first day of paid employment. He had been just in the act of preparing himself to ring the bell, when a young man of similar age to Ralph stopped alongside him and spoke in a bright and cheery voice.

'Good morning, old man, my name's Allan Briggs and I'm starting work here today. This is my first proper job, but I did try working for my father in his building business, but obviously I wasn't cut out for that sort of work, as my father has made very plain.'

'Hello, Allan, my name is Ralph, er, Ralph Diggerby, and this is my first day here too.'

He pressed the front door bell, a large brass affair built into the wall, with the word "Press" written in black into the white surface of the bell's domed push mechanism. He noticed the stonework around the bell was stained green from the brass cleaner that was used to keep a shine on the bell's brass work, as indeed he noticed the shine on the big brass letterbox built into the stone wall just below the bell.

The two young men were standing just to the side of a pair of double doors constructed of solid oak, which were the main entrance to the Bank, and one half of which was opened a short way almost at once, by a middle-aged man, dressed in a smart navy blue uniform; although he kept the opening to a minimum and was looking out at them with a face that was just above a stout steel chain linking the two sides.

The man at the door had a stiff military appearance; he was smartly groomed and his face was adorned with a prominent grey moustache, and he said, somewhat brusquely, 'good morning gentlemen, how can I help you?'

'Er....' was as far as Ralph managed to get with his reply, as Allan cut across him with, 'good morning, I'm Allan and this is Ralph, and we are both here to start work with the Bank today.'

The door was still being held on the stiff metal chain by the blue-uniformed man who now asked if he could have sight of each of their letters of introduction, which were to be shown at the door upon arrival on their first morning. Each of the two young men reached into the inside pocket of his suit jacket, in Ralph's case, his brand new, first-time-on suit jacket, and produced the aforementioned letter.

The uniformed man took the letter offered by each individual and glanced down the page, noting the contents, seemingly satisfying himself that they were actually who they claimed to be, and then the oak door closed gently, only to be opened fully.

'Good morning Mr Diggerby and good morning Mr Briggs, welcome to Brackleys Bank. If you'd like to follow me, I'll show you where the staff cloakroom and restrooms are and then take you to introduce you to the Chief Clerk, Mr Mawson,' said uniformed man.

A young lady, in a very short skirt flounced past them both and smiled ever so sweetly saying gaily, 'good morning, boys.'

Uniformed man just turned to them both and raised his eyes heavenward, 'that's Mary, the Manager's secretary,' he said, by way of some explanation.

Ralph had felt himself blushing, whilst Allan had merely rubbed his hands together, as a big smile had spread across his face.

Uniformed man showed them both where the staff restroom, and the washrooms were situated, and both Ralph and Allan took the opportunity to freshen themselves up, before the introduction to Mr. Mawson.

Uniformed man had said he would leave them for a couple of moments to allow them to acclimatise themselves to their surroundings. Ralph checked his appearance in the full length mirror affixed to one of the white-tiled walls. He felt that he looked quite presentable in his new suit, which was in fact the first proper made to measure suit he had ever had.

True to form, his mother had accompanied him to the branch of O. S. Wain, in the High Street, to be measured for his first new suit. Ralph had felt acutely embarrassed standing in the shop, whilst his mother introduced them both to the eager tailors assistant.

She had gone to great length to explain that her son, Ralph of whom she inordinately proud had just been accepted for his first job at Brackleys Bank and she felt he ought to have a suit, properly measured for his new position in life.

Eventually the assistant had reached behind the counter and brought out several swatches of sample suiting material, and they had spent some twenty minutes debating; and travelling backwards and forwards to the window to "see it in a better light" before Ralph, or more accurately, his mother, decided on a medium grey cloth with a fine brown stripe running through it.

Then it had come to the measuring; which Ralph had found left him feeling extremely awkward; he felt stiff and tense and then caught sight of himself in the mirror, and wondered why he looked so pale.

He stifled an involuntary sound, as the assistant pushed the end of his tape measure uncomfortably up into Ralph's groin to get the trouser length measurement.

'Does Sir dress to the left or to the right?' the assistant asked.

Ralph stared blankly at the man; "dress to the left, or right?" he repeated in his mind.

Not having the faintest idea to which direction he "dressed", Ralph replied in all innocence, 'I normally get dressed in my bedroom, next to the wardrobe door.'

The assistant stared blankly at Ralph for a moment, realised that Ralph in his naivety had no idea what he was asking him, and said, 'shall we say that Sir dresses to the left?'

'Oh, yes, to the left,' repeated Ralph; still none the wiser.

Ralph, at age seventy four, still cringed with embarrassment over that memory.

'I think I'll go downstairs and treat myself to a small sherry, in the bar,' Ralph expressed this thought in a loud voice, to himself. 'Yes, I think I'll do just that,' he answered.

He stepped into his bathroom to check his appearance in the mirror, and once he was satisfied that he would be presentable to the public, as he always termed this inspection, he locked his room door behind himself and made his way to the lift.

The bar was a small private room just off the lobby, next to the dining room. It had three chrome-plated, tall bar stools, which were positioned adjacent to the bar, whilst the bar itself measured less than five feet in length and behind it, fixed to the wall, there were three glass shelves supporting a collection of various bottles.

The bar area was made complete by two small wooden tables with three wooden, padded chairs at each table. Hardly anyone in Downwood actually regularly frequented the bar, as it was only open for the half hour before dinner for aperitifs.

There didn't appear to be anyone in situ behind the bar when Ralph walked in and looked around the room, confirming to himself that it was not currently occupied.

All of a sudden, Everton appeared to unfold himself from behind the bar, as apparently, he had been crouching down replacing some clean glasses on the bottom shelf.

He spread his large hands on the bar top and greeted Ralph with, 'good evening, Mr Ralph; would you be seekin' an aperitif? If you are,' he added with a broad grin, which showed his wonderful white teeth in their best light, 'then you need to get yourself to a dentist, as that's where you can get a pair o' teeth. We only serve drinks.'

Everton's deep booming laugh filled the small room and Ralph joined with Everton in that laughter.

'Just a small cream sherry please, Everton,' Ralph requested when they had both stopped laughing.

Ralph really did like this man. 'Would you like to join me in a glass of sherry, Everton?'

'Thank you, no,' Everton responded, 'that's very kind of you to offer, but we'd never both fit in a glass of sherry.' Everton laughed that deep, booming laugh again and once again Ralph found himself laughing along with this gentle giant.

'Seriously, Mr Ralph, thank you, but I do not drink alcohol.'

Everton poured a generous measure of cream sherry into a glass and handed it to Ralph.

'By the way, I took the liberty of calling in at The Weighbridge this lunchtime on my way home, as I walk past it every day, just to enquire on your behalf about your friend Allan Briggs. It seems he's not very well. I hope that I didn't do wrong, but I was just trying to help you,' Everton added.

'Oh, thank you,' Ralph answered, 'at least that clears up the mystery of the written note, that I received this afternoon.'

Ralph did not like "loose ends" so, although he was slightly miffed at Everton's disclosure, it did at least gather up that particular loose end.

Bong! Bong! Bong! Bong! The six o'clock dinner gong sounded; and Ralph gathered up his sherry glass and found that he was one of the first into the dining room. He was seated at his table before most of the other residents entered the room.

'Good evening,' he muttered several times, as people, upon entering, acknowledged his presence.

The meal over, Ralph returned to his room, and crossing to the window that he had earlier looked out from, he stood once again on his toes and craned his neck to the right, and could just make out again, the large stone structure of the entry gates to the Weighbridge. He stood, looking in that direction until his feet, and the muscles in the backs of his legs would allow him to do so no longer; at which point he relaxed his muscles, allowing his feet to sink down flat to the carpet and crossed back to his easy chair, where he felt his body sink into the welcome, comfortable softness.

Ralph felt replete after the evening meal; the salmon had been cooked to perfection and the accompanying new potatoes and peas had rounded it off nicely. He had enjoyed the fresh fruit salad for afters, but he could have taken or left the soup first course, so he had left it after only a couple of spoonful's.

It was no surprise that before long his eyelids began to feel heavy, and he just managed to sip the last remaining drops of his sherry from the glass, before he put the empty glass on the carpet and he allowed his eyes to shut again.

Ralph's mind drifted back again to Coopers Café, and he could still clearly remember the fifth time he had gone in there for his lunchtime sandwich.

Chapter 8

'Hello Ralph, will you be wanting a tea to drink with your cheese sandwich?' asked Shelia.

She poured the cup of tea and placed the cup on Ralph's tray, together with what was becoming his regular "afters"', a coconut macaroon.

'That'll be just two shillings please, Ralph,' Sheila said taking just one of the two proffered coins.

'But –?' Ralph started to question why the cheese sandwich for which he had previously paid three shillings and eleven pence, had suddenly been reduced to two shillings; but the sweet smile on Sheila's face cut him short.

'Special price, just for you,' she whispered as she beamed at him. Then in her normal café voice, called out, 'who's next, please?'

'I'll have what he's having,' grinned the next man in the lunch-time queue, and nodded towards Ralph, who by now had made his way to his reserved table and seated himself.

'I don't think you will,' laughed Sheila, 'he's not getting it himself yet.' Both Sheila and the customer laughed at that.

Once again Ralph realised that he had forgotten to put two sugars into his tea, but embarrassment caused him to not bother to get up from the table, and he proceeded to drink it without.

As before, once he'd eaten most of his sandwich the now very familiar musk smell appeared at his shoulder, and Ralph could not help but feel the warmth from Sheila's body, as she leaned across him to tidy the table.

Ralph looked up at Sheila, although it was difficult to focus her clearly at this short distance, 'why was the cheese -?' he started to ask.

'Special rates for my favourite customers,' she answered the question before it had been fully asked.

Sheila looked into Ralph's face and smiled sweetly at him; he was such a nice young man, she thought, but he did appear to be so innocent. 'Er, Ralph, don't you like me?' she suddenly asked him quietly.

'I like you very much, actually,' Ralph reddened as he replied, 'why do you ask?'

'Well, wouldn't you like to be my *very* favourite customer; my *most* favourite customer?' she pouted gently.

'How do I become your most favourite customer?' Ralph asked, wondering, whatever could be the answer to that question?

Sheila looked at Ralph's face and the realisation dawned that he genuinely wasn't aware of the answer to that question.

'Oh Ralph,' she sighed loudly, 'don't you want to ask me out?'

'Of course I want to ask you out,' spluttered Ralph, 'I have wanted to ask you out, all along; ever since I first started coming in here'

'Well why haven't you, then?' Sheila, stood with each hand on its corresponding hip, doing a "double tea-pot".

'I didn't like to, in case you said no,' Ralph answered truthfully, suddenly feeling his shyness come bubbling to the surface.

He just lowered his eyes and stared at his plate for a moment. When he raised his eyes again to look at Sheila she was still standing in the "double tea-pot" pose, but she had a soft kindly smile on her face.

'Well, go on then,' she teased him with her eyes, and stabbed the fingers of her right hand gently into the top his left arm, 'ask me.'

'Er, would you like to go out with me somewhere, please,' Ralph duly asked.

'I'll have to think about it,' Sheila teased him, but then she quickly added, 'yes, of course I would,' when she had noticed the sudden crestfallen look which had passed across his face at the first part of her answer.

Inside his head, he was screaming, *wow*, but he managed to stay outwardly calm.

'Where would you like to go?' asked Ralph.

'Why don't *you* suggest somewhere?' Sheila replied. 'Why not think of something overnight and ask me tomorrow. In the meantime, I'll just clear your table.'

Sheila leaned *very* close in to Ralph as she collected his plate and cup and saucer together and placed them on the tray she had been carrying. Once again Ralph could feel the warmth of Sheila's body through the thin starched white blouse, and ooh, that delicious smell.

'See you tomorrow then,' Sheila laughed gently and turned away carrying the tray, in the direction of the door to the kitchens. She was gone before Ralph could reply.

He did, however manage a 'bye, see you tomorrow,' under his breath, almost as if talking to himself, which, in fact he realised he was doing, as she had gone.

Ralph turned left upon leaving the café, instead of his customary right turn, and found himself wandering around the ground floor shelves of WH Smith's book department. Without consciously aiming for them, he wandered in the direction of, and started browsing the "*Teach Yourself* ...." books, with their distinctive yellow and black dust jackets, although he did notice that one or two now had yellow and blue dust jackets.

Having dismissed the Teach Yourself Banking, as being totally unnecessary, he did however, for some unfathomable reason find himself scanning through the pages of, '*Teach Yourself Colloquial Arabic*' by Terence Frederick Mitchell, first published in 1962. Why on earth would I want to teach myself colloquial Arabic, Ralph wondered to himself?

'Hello, you're Mr Briggs' work colleague at the Bank, aren't you?' said a voice over Ralph's shoulder.

Upon turning Ralph recognised Mrs Sykes, Allan's "friend". 'Yes, it's Mrs Sykes, isn't it?' Ralph asked, in greeting her.

'Trying to improve yourself, are you Ralph?' she smiled at him, 'maybe I could do with looking through those titles too.'

Helpfully, Ralph held up a copy of "Teach Yourself Dress Making". 'Why not start with this?' he asked.

'Whatever makes you think I would want to take up dress-making as a hobby?' Mrs Sykes, smiled quizzically at him.

'Well you seem to spend a lot of money on pins,' said Ralph, innocently and in all seriousness, 'I can't help but hear you say to Allan that you want some pin money.'

Mrs Sykes threw her head back and laughed out loud, 'oh, you are a comic,' she said, turning to leave, 'bye, Ralph. Thank you for the really good laugh, you are funny.'

Ralph was really pleased that he had made someone laugh, and a glow came over him when he thought that Mrs Sykes, a sophisticated lady, thought that he was a comic, but it did puzzle Ralph as to why she should think that; he couldn't think of anything funny that he had said.

Replacing the Teach Yourself Colloquial Arabic, and the Teach Yourself Dressmaking back onto the shelf from whence they had come, Ralph left the store and returned at a saunter to the Bank.

The lunchtime session on the counter and the rest of the banking day passed without any incident of note; the only thing that Ralph remembered was Mr Metcalfe, the farmer, coming in with his customary three five pound notes in his deposit account pass book, and grunting his usual greeting at Ralph.

Three-thirty came and went; Ralph's till balanced first time. 'Sight balance' he had proudly and loudly called.

The clock had run round until, at last, the little hand had nestled at the five.

Ralph's bus journey home on the number 37 had drifted, hardly noticed; his mother was in the front garden as usual, fussing with that same rose, as he had reached the house.

'Hello, Ralph dear, have you had a good day?' she had asked in her customary fashion.

Once Ralph and his mother had sat down at the table for their evening meal, and commenced eating, Ralph asked his mother a question in what he thought was a very casual, if not an indifferent manner.

'Mum, just supposing, only supposing mind, but just supposing someone asked you to go out with them, when you were younger, Mum, where would you have liked to have been taken?'

Evelyn didn't look up from her plate, and in turn tried her best to answer Ralph's question casually.

'Oh, I think I would have liked to have been asked to go to the pictures. Actually, there's a very good film at the Regal this week, starring Julie Andrews; in fact it's been there for a couple of weeks now, The Sound of Music. Everyone seems to like it, it's definitely a film that a young lady would like to see, I should imagine. There is a new film on at the Palace, Born Free, which is about a lion cub and how it grows up; one of the young secretaries at work saw it last night and was saying how good the film was.'

There was a silence for a few moments as they both continued eating.

'Mr Metcalfe brought three more fivers in to pay into his deposit account,' said Ralph, breaking the silence, 'and I saw a customer whilst I was in WH Smiths, who thought I was very funny, in a comical sort of way.'

Ralph's mother just sat listening to what her son was saying as he tried to keep the conversation going. She smiled inwardly to herself knowingly, and merely responded with, 'that's nice Ralph, dear. Did that same young lady at the cafe provide you with a coconut macaroon again today, dear?'

Not another word was mentioned all evening about young ladies, films, or coconut macaroons, but Ralph did think it would be the right thing to do, to offer his mother the unspent two shillings from lunch-time.

'Well, the young lady at the café did say that there was a special offer on today for the café's best customers, and I suppose she must think that I'm one of them,' explained Ralph.

His mother declined the return of the two shillings but simply said, 'thank you for your honesty, Ralph dear, but you keep it.' She added as an afterthought, 'I'm sure that the young lady does think you are one of the café's best customers.'

Evelyn looked at her son from under her eyelids, smiled to herself and just for an instant wished that Eric could be there for these moments. She wondered how Eric would have reacted to Ralph's gradual emergence as a man. She accepted that Ralph was very naïve about many aspects of life, but experience she felt, was life's best educator. She couldn't help but feel that, now in June 1966, having just turned nineteen; his birthday having been only recently celebrated on the fifteenth of May, that Ralph should be experiencing more of the adult world, but she supposed that that would happen soon enough.

Evelyn felt quite proud though, that her son Ralph, was basically an honest young man as witnessed by the offer just now of the return of the unspent two shillings; and he seemed to be diligent at his work and with his studies for his Banking exams. The time was probably right for him to dip his toe into the pool of female company.

It did also cause her a little concern that Ralph seemed to be somewhat of a loner, as he didn't seem to have any particular friends, apart from the young man at work, Allan Briggs, who Ralph mentioned from time to time. This, she had to admit, didn't seem to trouble Ralph himself, so Evelyn tended to dismiss this worry from her mind, as "something Ralph would come to in his own good time."

She had mentioned this in passing to Margaret, her colleague at the solicitor's, and Margaret had reassured her that her son, David was pretty much the same, 'so I wouldn't let it worry you over much, Evelyn,' she had said.

Evelyn was aware that she did tend to worry a little over Ralph, and she was always relieved to see him walking up Wellington Street at the end of the working day. She always took herself out into the front garden to "fuss over her favourite rose" which, she conceded, was just an excuse to keep a watch out for the 37 bus, and Evelyn always breathed a silent sigh of relief when she caught sight of Ralph, alighting from it.

Thankfully, he hadn't seemed to notice the extraordinary amount of attention the rosebush in the front garden seemed to get from her, around coming home time.

I wonder how old will Ralph have to be, before I stop tending to the rose bush whilst waiting for his return? thought Evelyn, realising that that time was now probably closer than she had previously acknowledged.

Ralph spent most of the rest of the evening rehearsing how he was going to ask Sheila to go to the pictures on Saturday night with him.

'I wonder if you'd like to come with me to see Born Free, at the Palace on Saturday night?' asked Ralph as he guided his tray along the last twelve inches of the three chrome plated rails which ended adjacent to the till that Sheila was standing behind, as usual. Ralph waited with bated breath for her reply.

'There's your cup of tea, Ralph,' she answered, adding under her breath, 'no charge today, just take your tray to the table that's reserved for you, Sir. Who's next please?'

Ralph did as he was instructed, and had only taken two mouthfuls of his sardine paste sandwich, a new line that he was trying, before the musk-mingled with starch scent played with his nostrils again at close quarters.

'No charge for your lunch today, as you just became my very special favourite customer, when you asked me that question about going to the pictures on Saturday night. I'd love to go with you to the pictures, to see Born Free. It's got Virginia McKenna in. Laura saw it last week with her mum, and they both said it was really good, with lots of scenes of Africa in. I'd love to go to Africa, wouldn't you?'

Ralph pondered the question for a moment, 'I've never really thought about whether I would like to go to Africa. I should imagine it's very hot, and there are snakes. I don't like the idea of snakes. But if I got to go with you, I'm sure I'd enjoy it.'

Just as Sheila turned to go back to her till, Ralph asked, 'the film starts at seven thirty, shall we meet outside the pictures at seven fifteen?'

Sheila spun around and replied, 'why don't we meet at seven o'clock and go for a coffee in the Palace coffee bar first?'

Ralph was thrilled by that suggestion and readily agreed. Now, Sheila turned again and this time went back behind her till, but turned her head in Ralph's direction and gave him the sweetest smile. Ralph thought his chest would burst, until he realised, he had breathed in but not out. Ralph had finished eating his lunch and put his hand into his suit jacket pocket and removed his wallet; taking out the pristine, folded £1 note that was carefully secreted inside the zipped compartment, and sat looking at it.

'I told you that there was nothing to pay, for my very special customer,' said Sheila, who had come up alongside Ralph. The aroma of starch and musk deodorant was very strong in his nostrils as she leaned closer than ever across him to collect his lunch plate, cup and saucer from the table.

'No, this is not for use, not this £1 note, it's the one you wrote your name and address on for me.' Ralph just sat a moment and then replaced the £1 note back into its safe hiding place.

'Thank you for my lunch today.'

Saturday night at a quarter to seven, saw Ralph nervously, but excitedly waiting outside the Palace Picture House, wearing his best brown shoes, onto which he had managed to get a military shine to the leather on the toe-caps. Evelyn had put a smart, knife edged crease into his best grey trousers, and Ralph had decided to round it all off with his favourite casual checked shirt, and a light blue sweater. He did allow himself to feel somewhat chilly, or was it cool?

He hadn't been waiting long before he noticed Sheila walking towards him, but to his horror – she was accompanied by another girl. They were walking with their arms linked together and chatting in an animated fashion.

Oh, he hadn't bargained for that. Ralph suddenly felt acutely disappointed, and the evening that he had so eagerly looked forward to, was fast fading in the excitement stakes.

'Hello, Ralph,' Sheila greeted him, 'this is Laura Hetherington, my best friend, the one I was having tea with that night you and I were on the same bus.'

'Hello, pleased to meet you,' muttered Ralph, smiling thinly at Laura. He was doing his best not to let his disappointment show, but somehow, he didn't think he was succeeding.

'Don't look so worried, Ralph,' laughed Sheila whilst glancing at Laura, as she continued, 'told you he'd think we were both going to the pictures with him.'

Turning back to Ralph, she put a reassuring hand on his arm and said, 'I always have my tea at Laura's on a Saturday, and Laura is going to the skating rink to meet some friends, so we were just travelling into town together.

Laura suddenly smiled at Ralph and leaning forward, she gave him a peck on his cheek.

'Bye, you two, hope you have a wonderful time together, and enjoy the film.' With that she walked on past them both, in the direction of the skating rink.

Ralph thought he had detected the slightest hint of a wiggle, as she walked away from them.

Happily for him, Ralph now had a moment to look at Sheila, and oh, did he like what he saw? Sheila was dressed in a black and white shift mini dress with a cut away neck line, her brown hair which always had to be fastened up for work, was now being allowed to bob free just touching her shoulders. Ralph's eyes were drawn to her feet which were attractively adorned in a pair of black patent kitten heel shoes; and to Ralph's eyes she looked sensational.

'You look wonderful,' he said, enthusiastically. 'Just sensational.'

'Well, thank you, kind sir,' Sheila replied. 'Shall we go inside and have a coffee?'

The inside of the coffee bar was a revelation to Ralph; the subdued lighting; the shoosh of the espresso machine; the big juke box standing against the wall, with some music blaring out that sounded to Ralph to say, 'I see a rickshaw and I want it painted black'.

He vaguely recognised the Rolling Stones, but in all truthfulness, he couldn't make out the words clearly enough. The intimate space was not overcrowded, but busy enough with mainly people his own age.

Sheila spotted an empty table and went to sit down, 'just ask for two espressos,' she called over her shoulder.

By the time Ralph had obtained two coffees and brought them back to the table, "River Deep, Mountain High", by Ike and Tina Turner was giving forth from the juke box.

'What was the previous song, the one about a rickshaw?' asked Ralph.

There was brown sugar in a bowl on the table, something which Ralph had never tried before, and he loaded two heaped spoonsful into the froth at the top of the wide coffee cup and watched as it slowly sunk through the bubbles into the coffee that dwelt somewhere underneath.

Sheila had put just the single spoon of sugar into her coffee and was now slowly stirring the liquid.

'What was that about a rickshaw, Ralph?' she asked.

Ralph repeated his earlier question, and Sheila sat for a moment thinking; suddenly her face lit up into smiles.

'Did you mean, "I saw a red door and want it painted black?"' she laughed. 'It's Paint it Black, by the Rolling Stones; it's at number twelve this week. The record playing now is River Deep, Mountain High, by Ike and Tina Turner; and that's at number eight.'

'Well, it sounded like I want a rickshaw,' said Ralph, who blushed slightly, and was glad that that wouldn't be noticed in the semi-dark.

Fascinated by this new world that had suddenly opened up before him, Ralph asked, almost from a point of view of logic, 'so, what's at number one, this week?'

'The Beatles, Paperback Writer,' said Sheila, wondering how Ralph could not possibly know that fact.

As was typical of most young women of her age she spent most of Sunday every week listening to records on the radio or on her personal Dansette Record Player; and Alan "Fluff" Freeman was a must on a Sunday afternoon with his "Pick of the Pops" programme on the radio. "Hi, Pop Pickers."

'Time to go,' Sheila stood up and started for the door, closely followed by Ralph, who was now fumbling in his back pocket for the ten shilling note that he had put there specifically to pay for the pictures; hoping that the cost of the tickets was going to be no more than five shillings each. As it turned out the total cost of the two seats was seven shillings and six pence, leaving enough to buy an ice cream during the interval.

An usherette with a muted torch showed them to their seats, more towards the back of the stalls and they settled down to watch the Pathe News.

Ralph had just got settled when he became aware of the proximity of Sheila's warmth; giving him an instant reminder of how he felt on a lunch-time in the café, except there was just her and him, in the dark.

Sheila readjusted her position slightly and her arm was touching his.

What to do? Was this an accident? Should he move slightly away to allow her room for her arm, which she clearly wanted to position on the arm rest between the two seats? Had she accidentally leaned her arm on his? Should he move his arm?

Just at that moment, the young man sitting in the seat right in front of Ralph, and next to a young lady, suddenly raised his arm and put it across his companion's back, just above the ridge of the cinema seat and she, in turn appeared to snuggle into his shoulder.

Now Ralph *was* in a dilemma; clearly, Sheila had seen the activity in front of them, and what, Ralph wondered, had been her reaction? Should he do the same? Would Sheila think him too forward if he attempted the same manoeuvre? On the other hand, would she lean into his arm if he attempted to do the same thing? Oh, what to do?

Sheila leaned up to place her lips near to Ralph's ear.

'There's a bit of a draft on my neck; do you think you could do what the boy in front has done to keep his girlfriend warm?'

Ralph didn't require being asked twice, problem solved. He gingerly raised his arm, taking great care not to dislodge the hair on the back of Sheila's head and settled his arm gently across her shoulders. Sheila immediately snuggled into his arm and let out a small giggle.

'Didn't hurt too much, Ralph, did it? This is much nicer sitting like this, isn't it? Now we can really enjoy watching the film.'

For the next hour and a half, Ralph was only vaguely aware of some lions and a hot sunny film setting, as the heady aroma of Sheila's hair; perfume; and the smell of the new dress material, had Ralph on a film set of his own.

Much to Ralph's disappointment, the main feature ended, all too soon; the house lights went up and everyone started to file out of the cinema in great haste, in order to avoid the playing of the National Anthem.

It was still light when they emerged from the darkness of the cinema, and Ralph was very reluctant to let this wonderful evening come to an end. But end it must.

'Can I see you home?' he asked Sheila.

'That's very kind of you, Ralph, but my mother always meets me off the bus when I get home, but you can walk me to the bus stop, if you like.' Sheila took hold of Ralph's hand and set off walking in the direction of the Town Hall.

'I had a lovely evening, thank you,' said Sheila. 'Did you enjoy the film?'

'Yes, I did, thank *you*' ventured Ralph, and suddenly feeling emboldened, he added, 'but I enjoyed being with you, more.'

'Oh, thank you Ralph, that's sweet of you,' smiled Sheila

By now they had covered the distance from the Palace Cinema to the Town hall where Sheila's bus was waiting with its diesel engine gently ticking over.

'All aboard,' shouted the conductor.

Sheila suddenly let go of Ralph's hand, put her finger ends gently on his face and kissed his lips ever so quickly, then she turned and called out to him over her shoulder.

'Thank you for a lovely evening.'

She hurried the few yards to the bus and jumped on as the driver put the engine in first gear and set off with a roar, and a plume of diesel fumes.

Ralph stood alone on the pavement, his lips tingling and fizzing, and the light imprint of her fingers still lingering on his cheek.

Chapter 9

———⊸∞⊹∞⊸———

Ralph thought he felt the soft and gentle touch on his cheek, the fingers light and warm.

'Sorry to wake you up Mr Diggerby, do you want a cup of Ovaltine before bed-time?'

It was the lovely Jessica, who had come up to Ralph's room and having knocked a couple of times on his door, and getting no response had opened the door and tip-toed across to his easy chair, and still getting no response had touched his face to ensure he was actually alright.

Ralph opened his eyes and smiled warmly at Jessica.

'I'm so sorry to wake you, Mr Diggerby,' she repeated, 'but I was wondering whether you would want a cup of Ovaltine?'

'Thank you very much, my dear Jessica, I would love a cup of Ovaltine. Your touch reminded me of someone I used to know, many years ago now. Do you have a young man? I suppose you do.'

'No, Mr Diggerby, actually I'm not going out with anyone at the moment. I did have a boyfriend but he started at University in Manchester last October, and met someone else who's a lot cleverer than I am.'

'That young man might possibly be an academic, but he sounds like he's rather stupid, to me. Lovely young woman like you – what more could a man want? Anyway, sorry, that's nothing to do with me; I should keep quiet.'

Ralph looked at the eager young lady in front of him and risked a question.

'What would you like to be, given a chance? I mean would you like to go to college or university to study and if so what would you study?'

'Well mum couldn't afford for me to stay on at school for A-levels but I would love to go to college and do my A-levels and then maybe go to university to become a nurse. You have to go to university for that now, you can't just start in a hospital, but first I need my A-levels. I don't suppose there's much chance of that happening for me, but I don't mind too much; I'm quite happy as I am; but I do dream of being a nurse one day.'

'Anyway,' Ralph said, changing the subject, 'how come you're here at this time of night? It's been a long day for you, hasn't it?'

'I'm doing overtime, as I'm saving up for driving lessons; I'm going to learn with Jack Ellis School of Motoring, they cost £23 per lesson, but £200 if I book ten in advance.' Jessica smiled at the look of surprise on Ralph's face, 'that'll be just a tad more than it would have cost you, back in the day,' she continued, laughing.

'Cheeky monkey,' Ralph laughed with her. 'Now, get yourself down to that kitchen and fetch me a beaker, not a cup if you don't mind, of Ovaltine.'

Jessica giggled, and saluted, and turned smartly and left the room.

When she returned, about ten minutes later, with a beaker full of Ovaltine, and a small side-plate of rich tea biscuits, Ralph thanked her, smiling affectionately at her, and as she turned to leave the room, he held out his hand towards her.

'Here you are, my dear,' he said placing a twenty pound note and a five pound note into her hand, 'have the first lesson on me?'

Jessica looked at the two notes in her hand and seemed to be embarrassed by their being there. 'Oh, Mr Diggerby, that's ever so kind of you, but I wasn't hinting, honest.'

She extended her hand back towards him, with the notes between her fingers and said, 'I couldn't possibly accept this, I mean you're ever so kind, but you're retired, and I wasn't hinting,' she repeated.

Seeking to change the subject, somewhat, Ralph asked her, 'what does your mum do for a living?'

'My mum is a waitress at Coopers Café on Market Street, I don't know if you know it; it's been there for years. That's how my mum knows Jack Ellis, he has his lunch in the café every day, and my mum asked him if he would teach me to drive.'

Ralph's interest was suddenly sparked. 'Oh, I know of Coopers Café, my dear, Jessica. Do please tell me a little more about your mum.'

'She's the kindest loveliest person I know, and we have lived together, just the two of us in a Council flat on the third floor, ever since my dad left her for someone else.

We used to have our own little two bedroomed house when dad was still with us, but it had to be sold after the divorce. Its mum's dream to live in a house again and have a garden; but that dream's never likely to become reality, I'm afraid.'

Ralph looked at her earnest face, and smiled in her direction.

'If I had had children, which I wasn't fortunate enough to, because of circumstances, then happen I would by now have a granddaughter, just about your age, and I'd like to think that I'd be helping her out a little. But I haven't got a granddaughter, so you'll have to do.'

Ralph smiled warmly at her. 'Go on lass, take it. Please tell your mother, though, then there'll be no misunderstanding.'

'Oh, that is so kind of you, Mr Diggerby, thank you ever so much.' Taking Ralph completely by surprise, Jessica leaned forward and kissed him on the cheek, just lightly, and placed her hands just for a moment on each of his shoulders.

'Before you say anything, Gramps, that's only what a granddaughter would do in these circumstances,' Jessica giggled cheekily, turned and left the room.

A split second later the door re-opened, Jessica put her face round the door, and said, 'thank you, Mr Diggerby, and I will tell my mum, I promise. Goodnight, sleep tight, Granddad'.

The door closed behind her.

Ralph was left sitting in his easy chair, staring at the door for quite a few moments, his eyes just a little moist.

'What a lovely young lady; actually I wish she *was* my granddaughter. If she was *my* granddaughter, she wouldn't have to be working overtime just to save up to pay for some driving lessons; I'd have treated her to all the driving lessons that she needs.'

As he said these words aloud, breaking the stillness of his room, an idea began to form in Ralph's head, but he dismissed it for the present time as there was nothing he could do about anything, at this time of night.

Ralph roused himself out of the easy chair, took his dining chair from its place tight up against the dining table, and placed it adjacent to the writing desk. Feeling in his pocket for the writing desk drawer key, he took it out and inserted it into the lock. Out came the folder for the umpteenth time that day, and down came the writing desk top; once again he untied the string that held the folder together, and he started to leaf through the contents, stopping about seven items down, and carefully extracted the copy of his will that had lain there for some years, untouched.

Untouched, as Ralph had considered many years ago when he had made this will that that was how it was going to be; all his estate divided up between his favourite charities. After all there had been nobody in his life to leave his estate to.

The will had been drawn up by, and with the guidance of Mr Thomas Mercer, of Page, Mercer, and Forshaw Solicitors; the Mr Mercer for whom his mother Evelyn, had worked as secretary.

Ralph had gone to visit Mr Mercer after his mother's death, in order to get advice on making a will; and again, sometime later in life when Ralph's circumstances had altered, he had sought advice from the firm a second time; although Mr Mercer himself, had been deceased for a good few years by then, his son Thomas Mercer Junior, had succeeded his father in the firm's partnership, and he had been entrusted with the job.

Ralph placed the will onto the rear edge of the inside of the desk, retied the folder and replaced it back inside the drawer. He then proceeded to follow the usual ritual of locking the drawer, placing the key, well down into his trouser pocket, and feeling for it through the trouser material; lifting the writing desk top back into place, and replacing the dining chair again, tight up against the table.

Sometime later, when Ralph was lying in bed, realising that sleep's escape wasn't going to come yet awhile, he found his thoughts turning to young Jessica.

What a cheerful, pleasant and genuine young lady she seems to be, he mused. I've never heard her complain about her lot in life, she seems caring and respectful towards her mother. She obviously realises that her mother is not in a position to help her out very much financially, so seems determined to set to and work for what she wants. I wonder when her birthday is?

All these thoughts continued to drift through his mind, until eventually Ralph drifted off into a troubled sleep and dreamed dreams of such a complicated mixture; in the dream pot were cotton buds; a lamb bone; Jessica in a car, learning to drive; Everton, pouring a huge glass of sherry and then spilling it onto Allan's shirt; water dripping from the river in the oil painting on his wall, soaking the carpet and finally his mother, wearing gardening gloves and carrying a single orange rose, showing him into the Solicitor's office, to read his own will.

He woke up early, breathing hard and feeling quite warm, and it took a few moments to bring himself out of the dream state back to reality. He lay there staring up at the ceiling in the half light, which was being provided by the daylight squeezing into the room round the edges of his curtains. It felt like it was only six in the morning, and indeed, consulting his watch it confirmed he was just five minutes awry.

By nine o'clock, Ralph was shaved, showered, dressed, breakfasted, and ready to commence the tasks he had set himself for the day. This made him feel motivated, and he was pleased that he had some direction to his life, if only for the next couple of hours or so.

Picking up his phone he tapped with his index finger, the first number on his list, and waited for the call to be answered.

'Jack Ellis School of Motoring, good morning, how can I help you?'

'Hello, my name is Ralph Diggerby, and I'd like to pay for ten driving lessons, for my…. er, for a Miss Jessica, er, oh dear, I've just realised I don't know the young lady's surname, I just know her as Jessica.'

Ralph felt somewhat awkward, but he persevered.

'But I do know that you have your lunch in Coopers Café every day, and her mother works there, and that she has made enquiries about driving lessons for Jessica.'

'Oh that's Mrs Darley, Margaret Darley. Yes, she was enquiring about lessons for her daughter, Jessica, about four weeks ago. I think she's recently turned seventeen, in the last six or seven weeks or so. Apparently, she's currently saving up for some lessons.'

'Right, Jessica Darley,' said Ralph, writing the name down on the piece of paper in front of him. 'Well, I'd like to pay for her first ten lessons; I'm a friend of the family. How do I get the money to you?'

'Do you have a bank card, Mr Diggerby? If so, I can take your details over the phone now and the job's sorted,' said the person on the other end of the phone.

That job done, Ralph dialled the phone number of the estate agent dealing with the sale of his house at number seventeen Wellington Street; the house he had lived in all his life and in truth, had been very reluctant to sell. He tapped the end of his pen on the paper pad in front of him as the dialling tone sounded.

'Good morning, Carter and Stone, Estate Agents, Erica speaking, how can I help?'

'Good morning Erica, this is Ralph Diggerby here; you currently have my house at 17 Wellington Street on the market on my behalf. Can you tell me what the current position is with regard to the house?'

'Well, I'm sorry to tell you Mr Diggerby, that to date we have not had any offers for the house, in fact there sadly seems little interest in it at the moment.'

'That's good news, actually,' breathed Ralph. 'You see, there's been a change of plan, and I'd like you to remove the house from the market straight away. Please forward a bill for any costs you have incurred and I will settle that immediately upon receipt; and perhaps you would confirm in writing that the house is no longer on the market.'

That task completed, Ralph dialled the third number on his list, waited until the phone was answered, and spoke.

'Good morning, this is Ralph Diggerby, is it possible to speak to whoever has taken over the will department from Mr Thomas Mercer Junior?'

'Good morning Mr Diggerby, well, actually the person in charge of wills is Mr Thomas Mercer the third, who took over the department from his father, some ten years ago. I'll put you through, now.'

Ralph spent the following fifteen minutes or so, discussing the changes he wanted to make to his will, stressing the urgency of the matter to Thomas, as he insisted on being called, and an arrangement was made for Thomas to visit Downwood the following afternoon, for the completion of the actual paperwork.

Ralph switched off his phone, and sat back in his chair feeling greatly satisfied, with a warm glow surrounding him; rather reminiscent of an old *Ready Brek* television advert.

He stood up and stretched, and feeling like he had accomplished something really worthwhile from his morning's activities, left his room to go down in the lift to the lounge for a cup of mid-morning coffee.

As he entered the lounge, Jessica had just poured coffees for two of the other residents, who were carrying them to a table in the window.

Jessica smiled warmly at Ralph as she looked up and saw him walking towards her.

'Good morning Mr Diggerby,' she beamed at him. 'How are you this morning? Did you sleep well after your Ovaltine?'

Ralph could hardly contain himself, thinking about what he had accomplished with his morning's work.

'A very good morning to you, Miss Jessica Darley. I slept just like a baby, thank you; awake every hour crying my eyes out,' Ralph laughed at his own joke.

'Ooh, a bit formal aren't we, this morning, Mister Diggerby?' Jessica giggled.

'Ah, so Darley is correct then?' said Ralph, adding, 'could I possibly trouble you for a cup of coffee, please, with two sugars? Oh, and when you've got a minute or two, I'd like a quiet word?' Ralph further added.

As an additional four people were entering the lounge, Ralph decided that his room was probably the place that suited him best for drinking his coffee.

'I'll be upstairs in my room, when you are free, my dear,' he said, gathering up his cup and saucer and heading back to his room.

It was more than thirty minutes later that a light tapping announced the arrival of Jessica at Ralph's room door.

'Come in,' he called, looking up from his easy chair where he had been sitting waiting.

Ralph had placed the dining chair some short distance from his easy chair, facing it, and he invited Jessica to sit down.

Ralph took a deep breath, looked at Jessica's young, eager face, and started the conversation.

'I spoke with Mr Ellis this morning at the driving school, and I can now confirm that you are in a position where you can book your first driving lesson. I have paid for the first ten lessons.'

Ralph held up his hand to stifle anything that Jessica was about to say, and continued, 'we shall call that your belated seventeenth birthday present of a few weeks ago, shall we?'

Ralph took a clean handkerchief from his pocket and offered it to Jessica as a big fat tear rolled down each of her two pale cheeks.

'I - er, just don't know what to say. Th-thank you, Mr Diggerby. I don't know what to say,' Jessica repeated.

'Best say nothing at all then, you've said thank you, and that's good enough for me.'

Jessica launched herself from the chair and flung her arms around Ralph. 'Why?' she managed to ask.

Speaking in a muffled voice due to his face being hugged so tight, Ralph simply answered, 'because I am able to, and I want to.'

Jessica relaxed the vice-like grip on Ralph's neck and straightened up.

'Now,' Ralph said in a clearer voice after Jessica had straightened up and taken a step backwards, 'now, there is something else that I am able to do, and that I also want to do, but first I need to consult with your mother. Perhaps you would ask her if she would be kind enough to come and have a chat with me this afternoon after she has finished serving lunches at the café? I have a proposition I wish to put to her; and I would also be grateful if you would accompany your mother, when she comes to call. For now, I suggest that you run downstairs, and request a few minutes leave, and go to Coopers Cafe and tell your mum. Oh, and perhaps make some time to telephone to Mr Ellis.'

Suddenly Ralph felt an embarrassment creeping over him, which he tried to cover, by saying sternly, 'well, go on then jump to it.'

Jessica put her hand over her face and turning, half ran and half skipped to the door, and left the room.

Ralph remained seated, and went to wipe his eyes on his clean handkerchief, realising at that moment Jessica had taken it with her as she had left. So he just sat and allowed his face to get wet.

There was knock at the door.

'Come in,' called Ralph. Everton's big frame filled the doorway.

'Everything alright with you Mr Ralph?' Everton paused a moment before continuing with, 'has anything happened, I just passed Jessica coming from the Manager's office in floods of tears, saying 'it's Mr Diggerby, it's Mr Diggerby,' and then she ran out, heading into town. 'I wondered if you were alright?'

'Everton, I am fine thank you; I thank you too, for your concern. I confess that I might be the cause of Jessica's tears, as I have just been the bearer of what I think are glad tidings to Jessica and her mother, the details of which I am sure she will share with you once her mother and I have had a conversation.'

'Just so long as you are alright, Mr Ralph. I'll take your empty coffee cup downstairs. Makes a change for me to take your coffee cup downstairs empty,' Everton laughed, as he left the room. 'It'll be lunch in another hour and ten minutes,' he called as he closed the door.

With lunch over and done with, Ralph wandered down to the pergola area as he had done on the previous day. He sat with the warm sun on his face and he must have dozed off, for the next thing he was aware of happening, was that by now familiar soft touch to his cheek, and the recognisable soft voice saying.

'Mr Diggerby, so sorry to disturb you, but my mother's here to see you as you requested.'

Ralph opened his eyes, shielding them from the bright sunshine, so enabling him to make out Jessica and an older, similarly attractive woman, who Ralph knew to be Jessica's mother, as the likeness was unmistakable.

He stood slowly, proffered his hand saying, 'Mrs Darley, pleased to meet you, I'm Ralph Diggerby. Do please seat yourself on the bench next to me.'

He patted the empty space next to him on the bench, and waited until both women had sat themselves down. Jessica seated herself at the end of the bench, so that her mother would be nearest to Ralph.

Ralph waited until Mrs Darley had sat down and then seated himself, next to her and turned to face her.

After exchanging a few pleasantries, Ralph said, 'you must be wondering why I have asked to see you Mrs Darley. Jessica and I have had numerous conversations and in one of them she told me where you and she live, and about your dream to live again in a house with a garden. Well, I have made a decision.'

Ralph proceeded to explain, 'I own a house in Wellington Street, which I put on the market when I took up residence in Downwood. It is a stone built terraced house with a neat garden to the front and a larger lawned garden to the rear. It is the house that I was born in and indeed had lived in all my life until I came here; but I would love to offer it to you and your daughter to live in, at the same rent as you currently pay for the flat you are in. The house still contains all my furniture throughout, and you would be welcome to use that as you wish. You may keep any or all of the contents, and make use of them as you see fit. I have arranged over the phone with my solicitor that you, Mrs Darley may, if you so desire, live in the house for the rest of your life.'

Mrs Darley sat in stunned silence as Ralph turned towards Jessica, saying, 'I have made provision in my will that whoever takes over the house after my, er, demise, will be required to allow your mother to live there for as long as she chooses, continuing to pay the same rent, which will be fixed. There, Miss Darley, Mrs Darley, what do you think?'

There followed a few more moments of silence, as Jessica and her mother tried to take in what Ralph had just said to them.

'Oh, and by the way,' Ralph continued, you might like to ask the question; and when can we move in? The answer to which question being, as soon as you can; tomorrow, if that's not too soon,' Ralph laughed.

Mrs Darley sat for a moment looking intently into Ralph's eyes, which held her steady gaze, she reached out her hand and placed it gently on his, 'But, why?' she asked.

Whilst still maintaining eye contact, Ralph answered her question.

'I'll give you a similar answer to a similar question that Jessica asked some couple of hours ago, about driving lessons. I am making this offer because I am able to and I want to. The thought of someone I do not know living in that house, and maybe not tending the garden, that was my mother's pride and joy, is something I do not really want to contemplate. Also the thought that someone would tend the old rose bush in the front garden and treat it as my mother used to do, fills me with a great deal of comfort.'

After a continued momentary silence, Ralph added; 'I would be so grateful to you if you would accept my offer. You have a dream; I can fulfil it; please say you will accept? Your daughter, Jessica is kind and gentle and caring, and I can see at a glance that she inherits that from you. I would love it if my life-long home was in your care. Please say that will you accept my offer?'

Ralph took a set of keys from out of his jacket pocket, and placed them on the bench in the narrow gap that separated both Mrs Darley and himself.

'There,' he said, 'the other set are at the Estate Agents, but they will be returned within the next couple of days. What do you say, Mrs Darley?'

Margaret Darley turned to look at her daughter, who simply uttered, 'ooh, Mum,' and clasped her mother's hands gently between hers, and squeezed.

Jessica had such a gentle look on her face, and smiling at her mum, gave a barely perceptible nod of her head, whilst looking at Margaret through half closed eyes.

Turning back to look into Ralph's eyes again, Margaret Darley, whispered, 'thank you so very, very much, Mr Diggerby; I, that is, we accept.'

As the tears welled up in her eyes, she continued with, 'I can't say I understand, but I am so deeply grateful; we will not let you down, the rose will be loved beyond measure. Thank you, a million times over. With your permission we will go straight there to have a look at our, new home. Thank you, thank you.' She dabbed at her eyes with her small handkerchief, which she had just extracted from up her sleeve.

Both women stood, and without any warning both hugged the elderly man so tightly he found he could hardly breathe.

After they had both gone back up the path and disappeared out of his sight, Ralph sat awhile in the sunshine, and felt thoroughly content for the first time that he could remember in many, many years.

He was still sitting in the same position an hour later when Jessica had returned to finish her much interrupted shift.

He was brought back to the reality of the day as two young lips gently and briefly kissed his mouth. He opened one eye just enough to be able to see Jessica's face clearly in front of his.

'Thank you, Granddad Ralph,' she said and kissed him again.

He reclosed his eye, and remained still for a moment. That was so like the first kiss that I ever remember, Ralph thought; the sweetness, the delicate touch of the lips, the innocence.

Chapter 10

On their second date, Ralph had walked Sheila back to her bus stop, but unlike the first date they had arrived at the bus stop with a few moments to spare before the bus was due to set off. They had stood side by side, holding hands when Sheila had half-turned towards Ralph and looked up into his face.

'Thank you for a good time tonight, Ralph,' she had said, 'you can kiss me goodnight, if you would like to.'

Ralph remembered being rooted to the spot for what seemed like moments in time, until Sheila had leaned up to him, put her hand on his shoulder, pushed herself up onto her toes, and gently kissed him for just a second or two on the lips.

Suddenly, he was getting sugar, lemonade powder, rose water, and soft, soft skin, and warmth; for just a second or two he could feel her warm breath as it danced above his top lip; it was the most delicious sensation he had ever, ever, experienced. He wanted it to go on for ever, but it stopped. It stopped as Sheila pulled away from his face and allowing her feet to relax, she stood with her feet back, flat to the floor, and a knowing smile on her face.

Ralph asked her with his eyes, and she answered with hers, and this time it was Ralph's lips that made the first move. There was just something in his mind that half expected Sheila to move away as he approached, but she didn't, and their lips met in such a delicious, sensuous collision that Ralph felt he was going to pass out.

'All aboard,' shouted the bus conductor, and laughing in their direction, he added, 'come on you two, stop kissing in the clinches. Haven't you got any homes to go to?'

Ralph was surprised that he didn't feel very embarrassed, by this public finger pointing; indeed he was left feeling somewhat proud of himself.

They parted and Sheila tripped lightly to her bus, blowing him a kiss, calling over her shoulder, 'see you Monday?'

Ralph savoured every step of the way from Sheila's bus stop to his, which was about one hundred yards away; the bus was at the stop, engine silent, and he climbed on and went upstairs. It was as if he was alone on the bus.

The bus set off and he was hardly aware; the conductor collected his fare and he was hardly aware; and he only really came out of his dream state when he opened the front door to number seventeen Wellington Street, and Evelyn called out to him from the kitchen.

'Is that you Ralph? Did you have a nice time?'

By the time Ralph had hung his jacket up on the rounded newel post, ready to be taken upstairs later on his way to bed, his mother had come into the hallway, wiping her hands on the kitchen towel.

'I was just wondering to myself dear, if you are taking this young lady out again next Saturday, perhaps you'd like to invite her here for her tea before you go?'

'Oh, yes please mum, that would be lovely,' enthused Ralph, and continued, 'it would be a good opportunity for you to meet her. Her name is Sheila, I'm sure you'll like her,' he added

'Now you go and sit down in the front room and I'll make us both a nice mug of cocoa,' Evelyn suggested, as she returned to the kitchen, smiling to herself, after she had noticed the happy flush on Ralph's face.

The following Monday lunchtime saw Ralph in the queue at Coopers Café with his sandwich of choice for the day. Ham and tomato.

'Cup of tea, Ralph?'

'Yes please Sheila,' Ralph replied with a new confidence in his voice, that he didn't realise was there.

'Take your tray to your table and I'll be across in a while,' Sheila replied. 'Who's next please?'

The café was busier than normal today and Sheila was more occupied than usual, but she eventually managed to slip out from behind the counter and carry her tray to Ralph's table.

'I had a wonderful time on Saturday evening,' she said knowingly, whilst giving Ralph a huge wink, 'particularly the saying goodbye bit at the bus stop,' she added. 'You've got ever such nice lips,' she said, smiling, 'you should use them more often,' she now laughed.

Emboldened, Ralph replied, 'I will when I get another chance.'

Silent for a moment, Ralph then added, 'my mum has asked if you would like to come for your tea on Saturday, and then we can go out somewhere after?'

'Well as I've mentioned before, I always go to Laura's for tea on a Saturday, but I can put her off, I know she'll understand,' Sheila answered, as she, in her now customary fashion leaned very close to Ralph as she cleared away his lunch-time crockery. 'I'll look forward to that. I'd like to meet your mum too.'

Ralph breathed in deeply savouring the familiar aroma of musk and starched blouse. 'Mum wondered if there's anything you particularly like or don't like to eat?'

'You can tell your mum, that I'm sure that I'll enjoy eating whatever it is that she prepares. I'm pretty easy going,' she winked. 'See you tomorrow, I hope.'

Ralph took his time going back to the Bank, but was ready and willing to go back on the counter, five minutes early. 'Go when you're ready, Allan,' he said.

'He'll go at one pm precisely, said the stern voice of Mr Duncan Melrose, the First Cashier. Let me remind you, gentlemen, I am in charge of this Bank counter, and I say who goes where and at what time.'

'Yes, Mr Melrose.' The two young men chorused in unison, as each turned to his individual till.

'And I don't expect to see you back on this counter until your lunch-time is fully completed, in future, young Mr Diggerby. Your lunch hour is precisely that, one hour. You leave at twelve noon precisely and you return ready for action at one pm precisely; do I make myself clear?'

'Precisely,' answered Ralph.

The old hands on the Bank clock had just dragged themselves around past two in the afternoon, when the excitement really started. Ralph had served a couple of customers with routine matters, and looked up to find Mr Metcalfe, the farmer standing at his till.

Mr Metcalfe appeared different, somehow, and Ralph on closer inspection realised that Mr Metcalfe was wearing a tweed suit, which judging by its condition was a much worn, if not much loved, item of clothing. He certainly wasn't dressed in his normal farming garb which comprised of an old brown jacket over the top of his dungarees; in fact he looked quite smart, and he was clutching his Bank deposit account passbook, in his scrubbed-clean hands. The pass book was different too, in that there were no five pound notes protruding from it.

'Good afternoon, Mr Metcalfe, you look like you're having a day off today, what can I help you with?' asked Ralph, leaning across the counter, whilst holding out his hand ready to receive the passbook.

'I've decided to buy myself a new tractor, lad, so I'll be needing some of them there five pound notes I've been stashing into this deposit account, since I can't remember when. I'll be needing ten thousand pounds in cash please as I don't want to be messing about with cheques and what-not.'

Taking Mr Metcalfe's passbook from him Ralph started to write the withdrawal entry into the appropriate space.

Looking up as he started to write, Ralph asked, 'how would you like the money; in £20 notes?'

Mr Metcalfe looked at Ralph with a surprise on his weather beaten face. 'Nay, lad, I'll just have my own five pound notes from t' tin in t' safe, if you don't mind, please.'

'I beg your pardon,' said Ralph, stopping writing in mid date.

'The fivers, lad. In the tin box in t' safe. Just give us me own notes, please lad. There's no point 'em being in there all these years if I'm not going to use 'em now, when I'm buying summat, is there?'

'But, Mr Metcalfe, we don't keep the five pound notes in a box; there is no box, we just take the five pound notes, and write them up in....'

'Hey up,' Mr Metcalfe raised his voice as he cut across Ralph's sentence. 'What do you mean, there's no box? Where's all me money, then?' He was shouting now. 'I want me own money.'

Trying to bring some calm to the situation, Ralph said quietly, 'Mr Metcalfe, it doesn't work like that; you see, we take your money, and enter it into your passbook and then the notes go into general circulation, there is no tin box in our safe, not for you or for any other customer. We enter the sums into your passbook, and then when you need some money out, we enter it into the book as a withdrawal and give you the money from the till. That's how it is done.'

'You mean, all these years, since 1938 when I've been putting my money into my account and thinking it was safe with you, you've been handing me money out to STRANGERS?' Mr Metcalfe shouted the last word. 'I can't believe it lad. I need to have a word with the manager; in fact I need to have a word with the manager right now.'

Ralph, feeling somewhat flustered and irritated, left the counter and knocked on the large, polished, oak door with, Mr Arnold Lester Manager, emblazoned on a brass plate, which was affixed precisely in the centre of the door just at eye level.

'Come.' a voice boomed from inside the room, into which Ralph had rarely, if ever, entered.

'Excuse me Mr Lester, sir, would you mind having a word with Mr Metcalfe, the farmer, please? He seems to be having a bit of trouble understanding where his original five pound notes have gone; the ones that he's been paying into his passbook deposit account, since 1938. I've tried my best to explain, sir, but he's now insisting on talking to you. I'm sorry, Mr Lester.'

'Don't worry. Ralph, isn't it? I'll have a word and I'll soon sort him out. He's just a bit on the old fashioned side. Show him in.'

But Mr Metcalfe wasn't going to be "soon sorted out" by Mr Lester, or anyone else, and decided that he was going to close both his Farm Account and his Deposit Account and have them transferred to another Bank that "could be better trusted with his money." Nothing that anyone could do or say could persuade him to do differently.

Ralph felt guilty about the whole incident, as if he had somehow let the Bank down. He thought deeply about the whole matter and although he couldn't actually pin-point anything he had done wrong personally; he just couldn't rid himself of the feeling of guilt.

He asked to see Mr Lester in order to try and explain, and thereby clear the air, but Mr Lester was "too busy".

Mr Melrose the First Cashier, didn't seem to be remotely interested in the matter, when Ralph tentatively, broached the subject.

'Nothing to do with you or me lad, what goes on in that room,' he indicated with his head towards the door with Mr Lester's brass plate on it.

'My advice to you, Mr Diggerby is to just get on with your work, and have done with it.'

Allan, who had been listening in on this conversation, simply raised an eyebrow at Ralph as their gaze met, fleetingly.

Ralph settled back at his position on the counter, and just got on with his work, until the Bank clock showed itself at last, to be in what Ralph considered was its best position of the day; where the big hand was on twelve and the little hand had reached the five; namely five o'clock.

Ralph was walking towards the staff cloakroom, passing Mr Lester's door, when it opened and Mr Lester beckoned him to come inside.

'I don't want you to concern yourself overmuch about today's incident with Mr Metcalfe, Mr Diggerby. I don't believe that you did anything wrong, and there was not, in my opinion, anything you could have done personally to rectify the situation. I do hear good reports about your work in general, and particularly pleasing reports, from Mr Melrose about your attitude towards the Bank's customers in your dealings on the counter. May I suggest that you now go home; enjoy your evening meal and put the incident completely out of your mind.'

'Thank you sir, Mr Lester, sir,' Ralph managed to utter, before he was ushered from the room by Mr Lester, who Ralph noticed was actually smiling at him in a kindly way.

Feeling much reassured, Ralph set off for the number 37 bus, but because he had been delayed by the conversation with Mr Lester, his usual bus had already left and there was a wait of ten minutes for the next.

By the time he got home his mother had been fussing with the rose in the front garden until she couldn't think of anything else to attend to on it.

'Hello, Ralph dear. Have you had a good day?

'Hello mum, pretty much the same as usual thank you. I was, however told by Mr Lester, after he had called me into his room as I was about to leave the Bank, that he thought I was doing a good job on the counter. That's what made me miss my usual bus home.'

Evelyn looked at her son with some pride, 'oh, that's good Ralph, dear. I'm so pleased to hear that you are getting on well. I can't say that I noticed you were late,' she added.

Ralph followed his mother through the front door, into the house, where she continued on into the kitchen as Ralph removed his jacket, and hung it at the bottom of the stairs.

Going into the kitchen behind her, Ralph surprised Evelyn by kissing her on the cheek. Raising her fingers to the spot where his lips had brushed her face, Evelyn exclaimed with delight, 'oh, how lovely, Ralph. To what do I owe that show of affection? I can't recall you kissing me for some years.' She laughed, but her laughter was soft and warm, and her eyes spoke more than her mouth could say.

'Sheila says she would love to come to tea on Saturday, and she said that anything you prepare will be just lovely to eat.' Ralph was oblivious to the unspoken thoughts that were contained in his mother's eyes.

'Oh that'll be lovely then, dear,' was all Evelyn said in reply.

Saturday seemed to take for ever to finally arrive.

There was a gentle knocking on the front door, which was quickly answered by a nervous Ralph who had been hovering nearby.

For the previous fifteen minutes or so in truth, he had been waiting, and watching, from his viewpoint, just inside the front room, next to the window, behind the net curtain, so he had seen Sheila walking smartly up the road.

He had admired her pale green mid-thigh length, sleeveless dress, with the cut away neck line similar to the black and white shift dress she had worn on their first date. Ralph's eyes were drawn to her feet, just as they had been on their first date, and saw that they were in the same black patent kitten heel shoes.

He noticed for the first time though, just how attractive her legs looked. He also admired how her brown hair was again allowed the freedom to bounce gently on the tops of her shoulders, instead of being fastened up.

Evelyn had been keeping herself "busy" in the kitchen even though everything had been prepared beforehand and had been ready for at least the previous hour.

'Hello, Sheila, you look nice,' said Ralph shyly as she stepped into the hallway. 'My mother's in the kitchen, I'll just tell her you're here.'

'Why don't we both go into the kitchen and then you can introduce me to your mum? I'm dying to meet her,' smiled Sheila, standing with her hands together holding her black patent handbag in front of her.

Before either of them could move, Evelyn came into the hallway from the kitchen, wiping her hands on her apron, as she removed it carefully over her head, whilst making sure that her hair remained undisturbed.

Ralph saw immediately that his mother was wearing her "Sunday best", and that she was wearing her smartest outdoor shoes, her hair was nicely done and she had applied a touch of makeup.

'Hello my dear, I'm Evelyn, Ralph's mother, I'm so pleased to meet you, and to welcome you to our home.'

Sheila smiled very sweetly and replied, 'I'm pleased to meet you too, my name's Sheila.'

'Well, shall we go into the front room and sit down?' Evelyn suggested, whilst leaning in front of Ralph, who seemed temporarily stunned, to open the front room door, and motioning for them to go in.

Once Sheila was seated, Evelyn followed suit and turning to Ralph she said in a voice that was gently telling rather than asking, 'perhaps you'd like to make us all a cup of tea Ralph? The cups and saucers and everything you need are on the tray on the side in the kitchen; and the kettle has just boiled. You go and do that dear, whilst Sheila and I get to know each other a little.'

There was the slightest pause whilst Ralph seemed to be still rooted to the spot, but Evelyn, giving him one of those "mother's looks", almost hissed the words. 'Well, go on dear.'

Evelyn and Sheila exchanged pleasantries for a moment or two; which was just long enough for Ralph to brew the tea, or more precisely to pour the boiling water over the tea leaves that were already in the teapot.

By the time he was carrying the tray into the front room, he heard his mother ask Sheila, 'so, what does your mother do, dear?'

'My mum? Well she owns the café, and does most of the work in the kitchens.'

'Which café?' asked Ralph in surprise.

Sheila looked up at Ralph, as he was still busy arranging cups onto saucers on the table; gave him an amused frown and said, 'Coopers Café, of course.'

Sheila turned back towards Evelyn and continued with, 'my mum's name is Sandra Cooper, she took over the café when my dad died a few years back. Fortunately, my father had bought the café premises, and that was all left to my mum when he died. That's why I work there.'

Turning to smile at Ralph, she said, 'I thought you would have guessed, what with my name being Sheila Cooper,' she emphasised the name Cooper, and now giggled.

Ralph just stood with the tea pot in his hand and seemed mesmerised, and couldn't quite work out for himself how he had not realised the connection in the name. Cooper.

Evelyn broke the short silence by asking Sheila, 'do you have any brothers and sisters Sheila; or are you an only one?'

'No, Mrs Diggerby, my dad died shortly after I was born so there are no more children; I was the first but only one, as it turned out.'

Evelyn smiled her kindly smile, 'oh, that's so sad, my dear. Ralph's an only one too, as I didn't seem to be able to have any more children after he came along.'

Evelyn paused and looked at Ralph who had remained almost motionless with the teapot still clutched tightly in his hand. She stood up from her chair, raised her eyebrows heavenward whilst smiling at Sheila, and took the teapot from Ralph.

'How do you like your tea, Sheila dear? If we wait for Ralph to pour, we could all die of thirst.'

Evelyn motioned with her eyes for Ralph to sit down on the settee next to Sheila as she busied herself pouring the tea, and arranging the biscuits.

In answer to Evelyn's enquiry, Sheila, who was giggling at the situation between Ralph and his mum, answered, 'white, no sugar please, Mrs Diggerby.' As she said this she smiled at Evelyn, and gave an almost imperceptible shake of the head.

By now, Sheila had relaxed into the moment, and her eyes quickly took in the whole room. She rather liked what she saw; the highly polished Oak sideboard; the good quality but slightly worn carpet; the settee and two matching arm chairs, which again were of good quality, but were now bowing to the ravages of time. The room was she noted, spotlessly clean and tastefully decorated, though when the decorations had last been refreshed, it was difficult to tell. The room, indeed the whole house had a warmth and friendliness about it that she could feel, and that she liked.

Once the trio had progressed into the dining room, Ralph had sat and eaten his meal in relative silence as the two women chattered away, and indeed he found not only couldn't he get a word in edgeways, he was quite content not to try. Ralph was delighted that Sheila and his mother seemed to be getting along just fine and it amazed him just how much the two hitherto strangers suddenly found they had in common to talk about.

Evelyn had decided to bring the Sunday meal forward by one day, so they had dined on roast beef and all the vegetables, and finished off with homemade apple pie and custard. Evelyn's speciality was homemade apple pie and custard, and this particular offering was of her best.

After the meal was finished, Evelyn suggested that Sheila and Ralph retire to the front room, whilst she cleared the table, but Sheila adamantly insisted on helping, and on stepping into the kitchen she plunged her hands into the sink first, and commenced doing the washing up.

'It's what I do,' she gently insisted to Evelyn who instinctively felt awkward that a guest in her home was helping do the tidying *and* the washing up.

For a few minutes Ralph sat in the front room, totally oblivious to the activity going on in the kitchen, until it dawned on him that his mother and Sheila were laughing together and chatting away to the accompaniment of the scraping of plates and dishes.

'Shall I ...' Ralph started to say as he eventually braved an entry into the kitchen.

He was cut short by Sheila, who laughed and turning away from the sink, said to him, 'no, thank you; whatever it was you were offering, your mum and me are enjoying ourselves, you go and sit down.'

Evelyn in her turn looked at her son and laughed gently, and found she was joined in the laughter by her new found friend; this confident young lady with the cheeky smile, and infectious giggle.

When the two ladies re-joined Ralph in the front room, Evelyn suggested, 'that they had a small sherry each. I know this is probably the wrong way round as it is normally an aperitif, but I feel the occasion warrants a sherry.'

Before anyone had realised it, the evening had slipped away and the time was fast approaching twenty past nine. Evelyn suggested that Ralph should shortly consider accompanying Sheila home on the bus, to ensure she got there safely.

It didn't seem to matter to either Sheila or Ralph that they had not actually managed to go out on the Saturday evening, but nevertheless, they all agreed they had had a very pleasant evening together and Evelyn was particularly pleased to have had company in her home on a Saturday evening, although she did feel just a tad guilty that she had prevented the young couple from going out to enjoy themselves, despite reassurances to the contrary from both Sheila and Ralph.

It was over an hour and a half later that she heard Ralph's key in the front door, and she called out to him, 'is that you Ralph? I'm in the front room dear.'

Ralph sat down on the settee opposite his mother, who had been contentedly catching up on her knitting during his absence from the house.

'What do you think, mum; she's nice isn't she?'

'Yes dear, she appears to be very pleasant, and in all fairness my first impression is *very* favourable,' she emphasised the 'very'; but I'll bet she wouldn't take any prisoners.'

Evelyn smiled at Ralph, who sat there feeling pleased that Sheila had made a favourable impression on his mother.

Chapter 11

Ralph eased himself up from the bench, and started to saunter up the path towards the side door.

'Was all of that more than fifty years ago? I can't believe where all that time has gone, and so quickly, and yet the individual days seemed to have dragged,' he muttered as he walked.

Ralph entered the building through the side door, and was greeted by Everton who was walking towards him.

'Hello, Mr Ralph, you certainly seem to have made one young lady very happy. I am of course referring to Jessica, who rushed in about an hour or so ago, and poured out a bubble of words, which I eventually understood to mean that her and her mother had just been to look at the most beautiful house in the world, and they couldn't wait to move in; and that it was a dream come true. Then she went on to explain how she had booked her first driving lesson. From what I could make out, all of this had something to do with you.'

Everton put a big hand onto Ralph's shoulder, 'it's about time something nice happened to Jessica and her mum,' he smiled warmly; 'I have known them both for some considerable time, and their journey has not been an easy one. You may not realise it, but you are an answer to many people's prayers on their behalf.'

Everton had kept his hand on Ralph's shoulder whilst he had said this, but now removed it and added, 'the bar will be open again in approximately forty five minutes.'

Ralph felt a little embarrassed, and turned away to enter the lift. 'I only did what I thought would bring some pleasure to someone, because I realised that I could.'

Ralph had turned back to reply to Everton. 'I mean, I suddenly thought that there's not a lot of point selling the house, I don't need the extra money; I've more than enough to last my time out, and the house could be put to better use if I rented it out to someone who perhaps needed a house like that and that I know would appreciate it, and look after it as my mother used to do.'

He straightened his body and put his shoulders back smartly and said, 'right, I'm going to freshen up, and ready myself to visit the bar.'

He stepped into the lift and pressed the button.

As he entered his room Jessica, who was standing by his writing desk exclaimed, 'ooh, Mr Diggerby, you startled me.'

She was facing away from him and he couldn't at first glance see what she was doing, but as she turned to greet him, he saw the single orange rose in the stem vase and the framed photograph of Jessica and her mother, both of which items she had just placed there.

'The rose is from the front garden at seventeen Wellington Street, and if you are going to be my granddad, then you need a photograph of your granddaughter and daughter, where you can see us. Mum is just so excited; I don't think I've ever seen her so happy.'

She paused a moment before adding, 'I've never had a granddad.' She lowered her eyes and said quietly, 'I hope you don't mind, but I wanted to surprise you.'

'Well, you certainly did that,' laughed Ralph in a kindly way, 'and I suppose having the photograph is a small price to pay for becoming a granddad.'

'Haven't you ever been married? I – I mean it's not really my business and I don't want to pry, so don't answer the question if you'd prefer not to; it's just that there are no photographs in here; and if you're my Granddad now, then I do need to know something about you, don't I?'

'Yes I was married once, but we parted in tragic circumstances; circumstances that I do not like to think about, let alone talk about, my dear.'

'I'm sorry, I didn't mean to upset you. I won't mention it again.'

'No, don't apologise, my dearest Jessica; it's just that some things are too painful to discuss; but I suppose there are some memories that I could share with you; and I have to say that I think you are right; if I am going to be your granddad, then you do need to know a little about me. I'll have to give some thought to the matter.'

With that, Jessica skipped from the room, stopping in the doorway only long enough to say, 'tata.' She waved quickly and was gone.

Ralph stood a moment and looked at the orange rose, upright in the stem vase, and just to its left, the photograph of Jessica and her mother, obviously taken at the coast on a sunny day; and he smiled with happiness at the kind thought.

Within fifteen minutes, Ralph was seated on a stool in the bar, as Everton poured him a Cinzano with lemonade, a small piece of fresh lemon floating in the liquid; tiny bubbles rising up in the glass and popping at the surface. 'You sure that you don't want ice in that, Mr Ralph? It's a warm day.'

'No thank you, Everton. I do not take ice in my drinks, for several reasons; one, it makes my teeth on edge; two, you can never be sure just how fresh the ice is; three, it dilutes the flavour of the drink; and four, and this is the most important reason, it's not good value for money. I like my glass filled with the beverage, not frozen water. The landlord's profit is in the ice,' Ralph laughed, and took a small sip of his drink, feeling the bubbles tickling the end of his nose. He swallowed and continued, 'by the way, Everton, when you said you have known Jessica and her mother for some time; in what capacity?'

'Oh, Jessica and Margaret Darley are both members of my congregation at the Evangelical Church, of which I am the Pastor.'

Ralph was surprised at first by Everton's reply, but as he reflected, he could see that he had always felt there was something a bit different about Everton; he had a calmness; a serenity even; a gentle manner and yet he was strong of character.

'Everton, do you have a dream? I mean is there one thing, say in life that you would do if you could? If so, what would that dream be?'

Everton took up his classic pose of standing with his hands flat on the bar spread out, with fingers pointing outwards.

'My dream, Mr Ralph, is to have my own Gymnasium and coffee bar attached to my church, where people, particularly young men and women; boys and girls could work out and I could guide them to a healthier life, both spiritually and physically; with advice on diet, lifestyle, and keep fit regimes. A place where they could congregate in safety, and be able to seek help or a shoulder to cry on; or just hang out together, but in a safe environment. That's my dream and my prayer, Mr Ralph, but that ain't ever gonna come to fruition, without a lot of prayers, cos I'm gonna need more money than I will ever have just to get started; and where's a man like me gonna get that kinda money? Unless the Good Lord, Himself provides it.

My congregation is made up mainly of people in similar circumstances to Margaret Darley and Jessica, so there isn't a lot of money flowing in from giving. So, Mr Ralph, although it's my dream, it don't stop me sleepin' at night, 'cos it ain't gonna happen 'til the Good Lord wills it. No way, no how.'

The big man stood up straight taking his hands off the bar top and then, taking hold of his polishing cloth he wiped the glass that had been draining by the small sink. 'But the Good Lord is just that; The Good Lord. I trust Him that He knows when this is to come to pass, and when that time arrives, He will provide, somehow. That I do firmly believe.'

Bong! Bong! Bong! Bong! The six o'clock dinner gong sounded; Ralph eased himself off his stool and being careful not to spill his drink, for he had hardly touched it, walked into the dining room and took his seat at his table, nodding and muttering 'Good evening,' several times, as was his custom, when people on entering the dining room, acknowledged his presence.

After his evening meal Ralph was on his way back to his room when Jessica stopped him in the lobby as she was walking towards the front door saying, 'I'm off home now, to help mum start packing our things. She said it shouldn't take long as she has decided to take you up on your very generous offer of the use of the contents of the house. Apart from a few personal items and clothing and bedding and so on, we are not taking many of the contents of our present home. Mum says she just wants to move into the house as it is. She loves it so much.'

By this time Ralph had accompanied Jessica through the front door and realised that this was the first time in over a month that he had come this way. They stood in the evening sunlight, the sun, just reaching the tops of the trees to the right.

'We had a small steak and salad, with chips for dinner this evening. That's what my fiancé and I had at our engagement celebration in 1969, if I recall that correctly. Because neither my fiancé, Sheila nor I had any more extended family than just our respective mothers the four of us went to the Berni Inn, which was a real treat back then. As an accompaniment to the steak we shared a bottle of Mateus Rose; we were very daring that night; we shared a large bottle, just between the four of us; and then we took the empty bottle home to make it into a table lamp, which was something that everybody seemed to do at that time; it was just a fashion of the day. I wonder what happened to that old table lamp? I seem to remember getting a taxi home, and feeling very happy. Ah well....' his voice tailed off, but he suddenly said, 'you get yourself off home to your mum and give her a hand with the packing. Good night, Jessica. I look forward to seeing you tomorrow.'

'Goodnight, granddad.' Jessica kissed him lightly on the cheek, 'can we talk some more tomorrow?'

Ralph lingered a few moments watching Jessica as she appeared to be almost skipping down the road, stopping at the corner momentarily, to give a little wave.

He now turned and made his way back into the building and went to his room, where he sat in his easy chair, and pondered just what memories he felt he could share, and discarded the memories that he knew he couldn't.

There was one memory that he knew that he couldn't share, and that was his first involvement in "petting", as it was called in his day.

He and Sheila had been going out together for some three months when they had decided one Sunday afternoon to go for a walk, and they had hit on the idea that it would be nice to stroll, hand in hand through Bradbury Woods, which was not far from the canal. Crossing the canal by the footbridge and walking along the tow path for a quarter of a mile or so they reached the style that marked the beginning of the path through the woods.

It was mid-August, and really quite warm and neither of the young people were wearing much more than shorts and shirts, with pumps on their feet.

How funny that "pumps" were now referred to as trainers, he thought.

They had walked for a half hour or so and had come across a lovely grassy space in amongst the trees, where the dappled sunlight played tricks on the eyes, as the trees moved and the leaves rustled lightly in the slight summer breeze.

They had brought a bottle of fizzy and a KitKat each and finding a sun-warmed patch of grass they sat down. Having eaten the chocolate snack bar and washed it down with the drink, they both stretched out on the grass.

A large bumble bee buzzed very close to Ralph's face and he sat up abruptly, and swiped at it with his hand. He was just going to settle back down when looking at Sheila's face he noticed that she had a little piece of chocolate stuck to the edge of her top lip.

A smile spread across his face, 'can I have your last bit of chocolate, Sheila?' he had asked.

Sheila had opened one eye, and looked quizzically at him. 'If you can find a piece, you can have it' she had said, and then had closed her eye again.

The newly emboldened Ralph wasn't going to let this opportunity go by without taking full advantage, so he leaned gently across Sheila and moved his face above hers until his mouth was close enough to lick the small morsel of chocolate with the end of his tongue.

To his utter amazement as his tongue touched her lip she opened her mouth and her tongue met his. She curled her tongue around his and gently sucked; the next moment she slipped her tongue into his open mouth, and the sensation was unbelievable. His pulse was racing, he was finding it difficult to breathe, but the joyous feeling was......indescribable.

Ralph had been aware over the past month or so, as their kissing had become a little more passionate, that he was experiencing strange feelings in his groin area, indeed he was perplexed as to the effect that all this kissing seemed to be having on his, er, his thingy.

It embarrassed Ralph to think about this, but what embarrassed him more was that his thingy had become somewhat hard the last couple of times that Sheila and he had been kissing. He had felt acutely embarrassed by this and had tried to kiss Sheila with his back slightly rounded so that his groin wasn't in contact with hers.

This, to his horror last week, hadn't seemed to work because Sheila appeared to have deliberately gently thrust herself close to him until there was no way she could not have felt what was there bulging in his trousers. Sheila however, had never remarked on anything so Ralph had assumed that somehow she hadn't noticed the embarrassing lump.

They had been kissing each other goodnight as had become their usual custom, at Sheila's bus stop after a night out together. Funnily enough the stiffness seemed to have faded, by the time he had reached his own bus stop.

Now, however this was a different situation; there was that stiffness again, and it hurt it was so tight, and Sheila was actually pulling him tight to her body; there was no way she wouldn't be able to feel his hardness, especially through just two pairs of shorts; and there was no way he could readjust his body position. He would just have to keep still and hope she wouldn't be offended or something.

But she moved; only slightly, and her tongue was dancing round inside his mouth, and despite being somewhat embarrassing; it was also sensational; it was beautiful; whatever it was, that he was experiencing, it was heavenly. It was sunlight; it was icing sugar dusted onto the top of a fairy cake. That sweet sensation when you licked it off the top of the cake, and now Sheila was gently licking the tip of his tongue.

As quickly as it had started, it finished, as Sheila rolled onto her side.

Breathing deeply, she managed, 'aren't you a big boy?'

Ralph, of course, took this to mean that she thought he was now grown up enough to kiss in that fashion, which pleased him enormously, and brushing his hand across the stiffened groin area of his shorts thought that this was an apt choice of words.

Ralph knew he wanted to have that feeling again and the sooner the better, it had been delicious beyond description.

Ralph sat up and noticed that there was a small dark patch on the front of his red shorts. Aaagh! He had somehow wet himself. Now what was he going to do? Sheila looked so beautiful stretched out in the sunshine. She was gorgeous.

Twenty minutes or so passed as they both lay side by side, their hands gently touching. To Ralph's utter relief the wet patch on his red shorts had now dried, and before long they were walking back, retracing their steps along the woodland path until they reached the style, and the tow path stretched out before them, towards the footbridge.

No, thought Ralph, returning somewhat reluctantly to the present day, that's one memory I definitely can't share with young Jessica. But there are certainly a few memories of when I worked in the Bank, that I could share; although, come to think of it, she probably is wanting to know more about things surrounding my home life than what I did at work.

Ralph made himself a cup of tea, using the red kettle, for only the second time since he had moved into Downwood, three months previously. He couldn't explain to himself why, but he was aware of feeling more energised than he had done for several years.

When he sat with his cup of tea, and pondered a while, he did wonder if perhaps he had become a bit of a recluse, over the latter part of his life, and he quickly concluded that he had. Maybe shutting himself off from social interaction had not been as beneficial as he had intended it to be; maybe finding a "granddaughter" like Jessica, just someone to converse with and share some memories, would be a pleasurable experience; after all, not all his memories were sad and unhappy; in fact now he thought about it in perspective there were many happy memories too. Plus, he thought, how pleasant to have another human being to interact with; someone to care about and to be cared about in return.

He drained his cup, and rinsed it under the hot tap of his washbasin, and sat back down in the easy chair. Glancing at the time on his wrist watch, he reasoned with himself that ten past nine was too early to consider going to bed, so he resolved to try to recollect some of the happier times, that he could share with Jessica.

Of course; there was the one and *only* time that he had ever tried horse riding; and then there was the youth-hostelling, when they had stayed in a YHA hostel up above Grassington, in the winter; the rather scary occasion that he had heard ghosts in Sheila's house; and the first experience of flying, when they had travelled to Ostend, in Belgium, for the week.

Oh, yes these stories would do for starters, that is, if he could remember to tell them all. In fact Ralph started to feel quite cheerful when he recalled some of these adventures that Sheila and he had undertaken during their courtship, and also in the early years of their marriage.

Thinking back to those times, he readily conceded that he wouldn't have undertaken half of the things he had experienced, had it not been for Sheila, encouraging and daring him to stretch his, up until then, rather narrow boundaries.

As all these memories circulated in his mind, he found that he was widening his thoughts to take in Allan, and the moment when he had had to leave the Bank's employ. Ralph pondered for a moment, trying to get his thoughts into some semblance of order, and trying to remember all the details, but after fifty years or so it was difficult to recall everything in exact detail.

What he could recall was that he had gone to work, as normal on the Tuesday morning; it was definitely a Tuesday morning, because that was Securicor day, when they delivered all the cash, and took away the Banks excess coin or whatever. The Securicor guards had just finished their delivery and there were, as a result approximately twenty bags of mixed silver coin behind the counter, which would all require sorting and then storing in the racks in the strongroom downstairs.

There had been several customers in the Banking hall at the time, so the bags could not be dealt with straight away, and suddenly the Bank had been surrounded by policemen, probably twenty or so; they had rushed into the Bank and some, it was confirmed later had gone around the back of the building. It turned out that the Bank's alarm had been triggered as if there had been a raid in progress.

The procedure was that should a raid ever actually happen, there was an alarm bar at the foot of every till, and this was triggered by a cashier placing a foot under the bar and raising it; this would connect to the local police station silently, and the police would then attend the incident in some force.

However, on this occasion the bar had been triggered by a stray coin bag that had been pushed under the counter by a cashier's foot, and it had caught under the bar and triggered the alarm. Needless to say, neither the police nor the Bank Manager, Mr Lester were at all pleased, and disciplinary action had been threatened, although the actual culprit could not be identified as all the cashiers had been involved except Ralph, whose job had been to keep at his till serving the customers, whilst the cash exchange took place.

However, the real reason that Ralph remembered this particular day was that, after all this had been going on, Allan had been summoned to Mr Lester's room as there had been "an occurrence".

It turned out that a customer's account had had several unauthorised withdrawals of cash, going back over a short period of time. The said customer had complained to the bank that she had noticed that someone, at that time unknown, was withdrawing cash from her account. The culprit had been traced by the Bank's Inspectors to have been Allan; and the customer was reported as being a certain Mrs Sykes, who hitherto had been Allan's "friend".

It turned out that she had on one occasion asked him to withdraw some cash on her behalf from her personal account when she was unable to get to the Bank in person, but it had been an occasion when he was going to visit her the same evening. That had been alright, but, Allan had sadly realised how easy this had been to carry out, and knowing just how lax Mrs Sykes appeared to be in her vigilance regarding her financial affairs, and having one or two financial problems of his own, Allan had been tempted to solve some of his problems by helping himself to a portion of Mrs Sykes' funds.

Had he done this maybe just the once, she probably wouldn't have noticed, but he had become greedy and careless, and had repeated the trick several times more; so much so that even Mrs Sykes had noticed the drop in the level of her funds.

She had begun to tire of the relationship between herself and Allan in any case, and found this was an easy out for her. She had phoned the Bank, spoken with Mr Lester, leaving out the part about the relationship with Allan, and saying she had noticed cash being withdrawn from her account on a regular basis, and the rest, as they say, had been history.

Allan had been summoned in to see Mr Lester that Tuesday morning, had admitted the misdemeanours, and had been instantly dismissed from the Bank's service. He had not been prosecuted after the Bank and the customer had reached an agreement about keeping the publicity to an absolute minimum to minimise the adverse effect on both parties, namely Brackley's Bank and Mrs Sykes. Mrs Sykes had been handsomely reimbursed and the matter was considered to have been dealt with.

The reimbursement had not of course, been from either the goodness of the Bank's heart, nor from its own resources; but had come in fact from a new loan account opened in the name of a certain Mr Allan Briggs, the amount being loaned to him coinciding exactly with the amount reimbursed to Mrs Sykes. Allan had been required to sign an undertaking to repay the loan in full whenever he became able, through future employment or other means. The "incident" would be kept on record until such time as the loan would have been repaid in full.

This had all happened in the September, just nine months or so after Ralph had been married, and if Ralph had known at the time of his marriage what he had learned then, then Ralph would not have had Allan as his best man.

In fact Ralph had not seen Allan for some years after his dismissal from the Bank; he had just seemed to vanish off the face of the earth. That had never over concerned Ralph as he felt he would have been too embarrassed to have recommenced a normal social relationship with Allan, anyway.

Ralph opened his eyes and returning to the reality of the here and now again, he saw to his amazement that the time had moved on to ten twenty five, so he made himself ready for bed and lay down, with the light turned off some fifteen minutes later, and rather quickly drifted off into a sound sleep.

Chapter 12

For the second day running, Ralph was shaved, showered, dressed, breakfasted, and ready by nine o'clock, to commence the tasks he had set himself for the day; and he had just got back into his room when there was a knock at his door and on the call of 'come in', Jessica came bouncing in through the doorway, and Ralph looking up, felt his whole being lifted by her entering.

'Good morning,' she said. 'Did you sleep well? Have you thought up any stories you can tell me? Can I come and talk to you later please? Oh, and mum is going to ask Mr Greenwood, who's a joiner, if he would transport our few things as we are nearly ready to move. I know it was only yesterday, but she is so excited, and I am so excited; and Mr Greenwood has a van; and he has his lunch in Coopers Café nearly every day, and mum likes him because he is a kind man, and he has a van. Oh, I've already said that, haven't I?'

'Unless he's got more than one van,' laughed Ralph. He was enjoying watching the happiness pour out of Jessica. 'When is the move likely to happen, my dear?'

'Just as soon as possible. Mum's going to ask Mr Greenwood when he comes in for his lunch today and she's going to ask him to move us as soon as he is able. I'm so excited.'

She paused a moment for breath. 'I'm rambling a bit, aren't I?' she giggled. 'But I don't care, 'cos I'm so happy for my mum; and I'm so happy for me too. It's really *exciting*.' Jessica emphasised the last word.

Ralph just sat and allowed the excitement that Jessica was feeling, to affect him too. He found that he was enjoying this feeling immensely; so he laughed. He laughed at the warm feeling that was growing inside himself; at the realisation that a person like him could bring so much pleasure to another human being, simply by doing a kind act.

Ralph looked at the tin of spray polish that Jessica was carrying in one hand, whilst clutching a yellow duster in the other.

'Do you think there's going to be any chance of your using those two items at all, or are you going to be bouncing around like that Tigger thing in Winnie The Pooh, for the rest of the day?' Ralph laughed openly and enjoyed the sensation of fun, teasing this young lady.

Jessica laughed too, and bounced in the air. 'Boing,' she exclaimed loudly, and then she giggled.

'Just going to dust for the Misses Cotton,' she added. Quick as a flash, she kissed his cheek, turned around and was heading out through the doorway, in the direction of the Misses Cotton's room.

'Bye Granddad,' she shouted over her shoulder, and with that, she was gone.

Half an hour or so later, Ralph stood up and moved to the window and looking out at the gardens below, he saw Jessica carrying a coffee cup down the path, whilst supporting one of the frailer residents on her other arm. 'Bless you,' he said aloud and smiled.

Shortly after eleven o'clock, Ralph decided to "grab himself a corfee" as he had heard an American say recently on the television news, (this had impressed him, so he had been practicing to himself for over a week), descended in the lift and entered the lounge.

'Good morning Jessica,' he said. Then trying desperately to remember all he had rehearsed, he said in his best American accent, 'say ma'am, can I grab myself a coroffee?'

Jessica simply eyed him with a big smile on her face, then broke into another of her infectious giggles. 'Which part of Wales was that supposed to be from?'

They both laughed.

'Why don't you take your coffee down to the pergola area and I'll join you in a couple of minutes and you can tell me another memory story during my tea-break?'

Ralph did as was suggested and he took his coffee down to his favourite bench in the pergola area, and sat down, enjoying the mid-morning sunshine. Not many minutes later, Jessica came to sit with him on the bench; she was carrying her cup of tea and a plate with some digestive biscuits on. 'McVities'. She nodded her head in the direction of the plate, 'I love their digestives.'

'I love them even more, when they become *my* digestives,' laughed Ralph. 'Have I told you about my very first cooking experience?'

'No.'

'Well, Sheila and I; did I mention that my wife's name was Sheila?'

'Yesterday.'

'Oh, did I? Well, Sheila and I had been courting for about eighteen months I think, when one Saturday my mother decided that she was going out to the pictures with one of the ladies from where she worked, and as usual she had offered to prepare a meal for us both, but I recklessly, as it turned out, decided that it would be interesting to prepare and serve a special meal for the two of us. It was intended to be a romantic dinner for two.

I remember that I had obtained an empty wine bottle and softened the end of a candle and stuck it in the bottle neck and I had set it burning for two or three nights beforehand, just so it would have lots of candlewax running down the side of the bottle, for effect; just like in the restaurants. That was the first mistake, because the meal had only been underway for ten minutes or so when the candle guttered and went out; I'd used too much of it to create the effect. We had to turn the big light on at that moment which completely ruined the atmosphere.' Ralph laughed, and Jessica joined him.

'The next problem was that I had decided that I would do a Vesta chicken chow mein as the main course; you know, the one with the crispy noodles, but I had not realised that the contents of the box only contained enough for one person, and I'd only bought just the one box, so that left us feeling a bit peckish.

But I did win with my pudding; it was Arctic Roll. I'd bought one from the shop, and kept it in the fridge until I was ready to serve it, with the tin of custard. The only thing I hadn't realised was that the Arctic Roll had been frozen; the name was, I suppose the clue, so it was soft before I served it, and hot custard poured on top didn't help either; but, it tasted nice.

Then, right after we had finished the meal, I remembered the bottle of Mateus Rose in the fridge.'

How was the special meal? my mother had asked Sheila on her return home from the pictures.

It was different to anything I've ever eaten before, Sheila had answered, and then we had both collapsed laughing.

Mother had joined in with the laughter after we had described the meal to her.

Sheila did most of the cooking when we eventually got married, although my mother, with whom we lived in the early years, did like to keep her hand in as she used to say.'

'Better get on with my work,' Jessica said. She stood up from the bench and once again she kissed him lightly on the cheek, 'byee.'

She collected the cups, saucers and plate together and set off up the path towards the end door, turning at the top of the path to give him a quick wave.

By the time Ralph had arrived back in his room, Jessica was already in there; having made his bed, she was now on with the dusting and had the vacuum cleaner with the cable unwrapped and plugged in ready to go.

'Did you ever take part in any sort of sport?' she suddenly asked.

'Absolutely not.'

'No sport at all? Shooting? Snooker? Riding?'

'Oh, now you mention riding; there was the one and only time I tried horse riding, I suppose. Sheila had decided that she and Laura, her best friend; Laura's boyfriend and I should go to a local riding stable one Sunday morning and try horse riding. So she had booked an hour's riding lesson for all four of us.

Upon arrival at the local riding stable, we were each given an individual horse which the horsey lady said had each been matched to our personality, because it was a first time for each of us. Come to think of it, how she could possibly have known anything about our individual personalities, without having met us is anybody's guess.'

Ralph paused a moment, apparently considering this point, then he continued with his tale.

'Well, we set off along this country lane, there being about ten of us altogether, I think; my horse was a great lummox of a thing and just dragged along at the rear as if it didn't want to be there at all; so in that sense, the horsey lady was right, we were personality matched, as I'm certain that that horse didn't want to be there any more than I did.' Ralph laughed at the memory.

He continued, 'we had been given some basic instructions as to how to steer the horse and so forth; and I remember I was told to pull gently on the left rein to ease the horse into the side of the road if a car was trying to pass, for example.

Of course, as luck would have it, a car did come along, and I did do what I had been told to do, and gently pulled on the left rein, and of course we just *had* to be passing a very large private house with a huge main drive, which came down to the side of the road, and to crown it all the big double iron gates were open to the world, and my horse accepted the implied invitation and decided it wanted to investigate the garden.

The blooming great lummox simply started to walk up the drive. Nothing I could do would turn this stubborn old mare around and she proceeded to continue wandering up this drive and onto this man's immaculate lawn. We had got so far behind the others by this time that no one even noticed we were no longer behind them on the road.

Well, I looked up and there to my horror was the owner, at least I assumed him to be the owner, sitting astride his ride-on motor mower, thankfully heading away from us, and by now we were on his lawn. I cannot remember how I got that old mare back onto the road, but I did somehow, and spent a very tedious forty minutes or so, trying to urge this damned horse to catch up with its compatriots.'

Ralph broke off from his telling of the story, and looked at Jessica, who was giggling almost out of control by this time, 'it's alright for you to laugh young lady, but it wasn't you that was going through this purgatory.'

Ralph found that he was starting to share with Jessica in the laughter, for her giggle was most infectious, and for the first time in his life he started to see the funny side to this tale of woe.

Returning to his narration, he continued. 'However, when we reached a distance of about a mile from the stables, on our way back, this contrary horse suddenly decided that it wanted to be the first to arrive home, and set off galloping; and nothing I tried to do, would make it slow down; I repeatedly shouted "woah!" and I tried pulling sharply on the reins; all to no avail. From a standing start of some one hundred and fifty yards behind all the others we ended up returning to the stable yard, a clear winner by some one hundred yards.'

By now, Jessica was in hysterics, with happy tears running down her cheeks.

Ralph continued, 'I was terrified and ended up clattering into the stable yard lying flat across the horses neck and clinging on desperately to its mane and anything else that I could grab, to prevent me from falling to the ground whilst we had been travelling at some twenty five miles an hour or so.

By the time the horsey lady got to me in the yard, I was still clinging tightly to the horse, lying flat along it, with my arms firmly wrapped around its neck; the aforementioned horsey lady had to peel me out of the saddle.

I vowed then and there, that never again would I go within one hundred yards of one of those animals; and I never have. Horsey lady's only remark was, "well, Mr Diggerby, the theory goes that horse and rider should be as one, but not so attached that I have to prise the rider from his mount," and she had laughed, obviously deriving great amusement from my predicament.'

Jessica, who had returned to giggling after the hysterics, was now openly laughing, and Ralph found that he too was laughing out loud.

Once Jessica had settled back down she switched the vacuum cleaner on and ran it quickly over the carpet, then switched it off again curling the cord onto the back of the cleaner.

'Right, that's you done, granddad. Bed's made; room tidied and dusted and bathroom given the once over. See you soon. Byee.' With that she picked up the vacuum cleaner and was gone from the room.

Her departure left a silence in the room for a moment or two, but then a quick knock came at the door. Before he had time to say anything, the door opened and Jessica's face popped around the side, laughing she said, 'lunch is nearly ready; gee-up granddad.'

The door closed. Now Ralph laughed aloud to himself.

Ralph finished what for him was an unusually relaxed lunch, just taking his time to savour every morsel in front of him, adding some chutney to the plate of ham salad, which was a very unusual thing for him to do. Ralph normally liked his food plain, simple and unadulterated; but today he felt relaxed and relatively at peace with the world, and with his surroundings.

'You alright, Mr Ralph?' asked Everton, wandering across to his table, 'you seem to be eating in a more leisurely way than usual. Is today's ham salad *that* good?' Everton laughed in his deep booming way.

'I'm absolutely fine, thank you Everton. I'm absolutely fine. Oh,' he added as an afterthought, 'I'm going to my room to await a Mr Thomas Mercer, who's coming to visit me this afternoon, at an unspecified time. When he arrives would you mind directing him to my room, please Everton?'

'Yessir, Mr Ralph,' Everton said and saluted whilst showing his fabulous set of white teeth, in a broad smile. 'When this Mr Mercer arrives, would you like me to conjure up a couple of cups of something, and bring them up to your room? I can ask him on arrival if he prefers tea or coffee, and I know you like your coffee.'

'You are a very kind man Everton, that would be extremely helpful, thank you.'

Ralph had been making very little progress with his current reading material, Ken Follett's Whiteout; a book that he had started when he had first come to live in Downwood, but because of all that had been happening since his arrival, he had made little headway with the story, although he had tried unsuccessfully to read it the previous day. He resolved to rectify that situation straightaway, and sitting down in his easy chair, he opened the book where he had last left off reading and started from there. He'd only just managed the first two paragraphs of chapter 2 when there was a knock at his door.

'Come in,' he called, starting to stand up.

The door however, remained closed, so Ralph went to open it. In the corridor stood a very smartly dressed young man, carrying a beautiful expensive-looking red leather briefcase. The man was accompanied by an equally smartly dressed young woman.

The man spoke first. 'Mr Diggerby? I'm Thomas Mercer, and this is Sarah, my Legal Secretary. We're here by arrangement regarding an alteration, or more correctly, a re-writing of your will. May we come in?'

'Of course, of course,' said Ralph shaking the proffered hand and then backing into the room with a very slight bow and a sweep of his arm, indicating they should enter. 'I am afraid I only have the two chairs; I wasn't expecting two of you,' Ralph explained, now sweeping his arm again to indicate the dining chair and the easy chair.

There was a second knock at the door. Ralph opened it and there was Everton with one of the chairs from the dining room.

'Thought you folks might be needin' this,' he said walking into the room, with the chair grasped firmly in one of his large hands. 'I'll be back in a moment with three cups of coffee, although I thought I'd better bring this up first.'

'Thank you so much, Everton you are very thoughtful,' said Ralph, smiling at him.

Once they had all become seated, and after the coffee had arrived on a tray, together with some biscuits, Mr Mercer lay the papers from his briefcase onto the surface of the dining table.

'I have made out the new will to your exact instructions as discussed on the telephone yesterday, and Sarah has typed it up and prepared a copy for yourself, so we just require you to check through it to ensure it is drawn up as you requested. Once you've verified the contents are correct, we shall require you to sign the will in front of two witnesses, one of whom could be Sarah, here; so we just need one other.'

'I am right in thinking that a beneficiary cannot be a witness to the will signing, aren't I? Ralph asked.

'That is correct, Mr Diggerby,' nodded Mr Mercer. 'Maybe we could ask that extremely pleasant man, who just brought up the chair and coffees?'

'That wouldn't be appropriate, Mr Mercer,' said Ralph. 'After I've checked the contents of this document, I'll go downstairs and see if I can rustle someone up.'

Fifteen minutes later the documents had been duly signed by Ralph and then witnessed by the chef, who was happy to get away from the stuffy atmosphere of the kitchen for a while; and by Sarah. Mr Mercer folded the copy of the will he had brought with him and put it neatly into an envelope, which he handed to Ralph.

'The office will be in touch within the next few days to arrange settlement of our fees,' he said rising from his seat at the dining table. 'Do you have any questions at all?'

'What do I do with the copy of my old will; can I just destroy it now?'

'Yes, the new will is up and running and supersedes the one you have held the copy of. It has been very nice to have met you, Mr Diggerby. I'm afraid I do not recall your mother personally, who sadly had died long before I came to the firm, but I do know that your mother Evelyn, was very well liked and respected by my Grandfather, to whom she was Legal Secretary. Her name is still mentioned at our family gatherings. Thank you for entrusting your will to us, Mr Diggerby. I bid you a good day.'

With that, both Mr Mercer and his secretary Sarah, left the room.

Ralph sat back down, and enjoyed the momentary feeling of satisfaction and relief, that had resulted from the visit.

Everton knocked at the door and put his head round the opening. 'You alright, Mr Ralph? I just seen the two visitors leave; they said goodbye, so I thought I'd just come up and take the chair back downstairs to the dining room and the tray with the coffee things on, back to the kitchen.'

Everton smiled his big warm smile at Ralph, both with his mouth and with his eyes.

'Mr Ralph, I hope you don't mind me saying, but it's nice to see you so relaxed and happy.' Everton said this whilst collecting both the tray and the chair, and heading towards the door.

'I'll get the door for you, Everton; and many thanks again for your thoughtful kindness,' said Ralph holding the door open for Everton to pass through.

Ralph returned to the easy chair, and allowed himself to sink into its comfort, slowly. He sat a few moments, and then picked up his copy of Whiteout, opening it at Chapter 2 where the bookmark had continued to reside. Thinking to himself that there was little point in starting anywhere other than the first line again, as even though he'd already read the first two paragraphs earlier, it would help the flow, to start again. He had just re-read to the end of the second paragraph again when there was yet another knock at the door.

Laughing to himself, Ralph called, 'come in'.

'Hiya Granddad.' It was none other than Jessica, who despite the interruption, brightened his day. In fact, what was already quite bright was now shining.

'Mum's just popped in on her way home from work to tell me to tell you that Mr Greenwood, the Joiner, can move us tomorrow. If that's still alright with you?'

Without waiting for his reply, she continued with, 'it's soooo exciting! Mum says she won't sleep tonight. But she did say last night that it would be nice to invite you to come to tea one day, if you would like that? It wouldn't cause you any problems, or upset you, would it? To go back to what was your home for so long would it?' Jessica took a deep breath after such a long set of questions.

'No my dear, it wouldn't cause me any problems; and it would be very nice to have a meal in that dining room again, and to know and feel that the house is loved; and yes it is perfectly alright with me for you and your mum to move into your new home tomorrow.'

Jessica clapped her hands together several times in happiness, then kissed Ralph lightly on his mouth, and skipping to the door, giggled and said.

'Thank you Gramps. It's almost five thirty, by the way, and mum says to tell you there is a gin and tonic waiting with Everton at the bar for your pre-dinner drink this evening.'

She opened the door and her parting shot was, 'love you. Byee. See you tomorrow.'

Once back in his room after dinner, Ralph opened the top drawer to the writing desk and took out the folder, into which he put the copy of his new will, inside the same sleeve as the previous one had been, although he did leave the old one in there too, as company for the new one. He could never bear to part with any documents, "just in case".

He seated himself in the easy chair and reached down to the floor, to pick up the book; which he opened at the bookmarked page; but suddenly felt he couldn't be bothered to concentrate on reading, so shut the book again, replacing it back onto the floor, by his chair.

He sat instead, with his hands in his lap and let his eyes slowly close. Sitting like this, he had learned that he could switch on the video in his mind and send it running again.

He mused that by today's standards both he and Sheila had courted, and had been engaged for a long period of time. They had met, around 1966 and courted until 1969, when they had become engaged; then the wedding had taken place in January 1971.

The engagement celebration had been just himself and Sheila and their respective mothers; and the wedding had not been celebrated by many more than that in numbers. He remembered Sheila's friend Laura, had been her bridesmaid, and a couple of friends from Sheila's work, together with his best man, Allan. Mrs Sykes, Allan's 'friend' had been politely invited, but had declined the invitation, which in truth had been a relief to everyone concerned, including Allan.

1971 had been quite a year really, he thought; as it was both the year of his marriage, and it had also been the September of that same year when Allan had been dismissed from the Bank, leading to Ralph being trained to run the sub-branch on his own.

Chapter 13

'**G**ood morning Mr Melrose,' Ralph offered his customary morning greeting as he went to pass the First Cashier. Ralph seldom got a reply, dependant entirely on Mr Melrose's mood. But this morning Mr Melrose smiled at him and returned his greeting.

'And a very good morning to you Mr Diggerby; in the light of yesterday's events which saw your friend, Mr Briggs move on to pastures new, I need someone to replace him as an occasional stand in cashier for Ian Lambe at the sub-branch'

Brackleys Bank Thornston was responsible for the operating of a sub branch of the main Bank in the nearby village of Grillington. The sub branch was open and operated over similar hours to its mother branch, and was reached either by a fifteen minute bus journey, or a seven minute journey by car.

Ian Lambe who was the regular cashier, owned and ran a car; and he used this to transport both himself and the Bank Guard, a fifty year old retired Army sergeant-major, who went by the splendid name of Arthur Willow, a name, which for some reason caused much amusement to Ralph.

During Mr Lambe's annual leave or to cover for absence due to training courses or occasional bouts of illness, Allan, or Mr. Briggs, as Mr Melrose had always referred to him, had been the stand-in cover.

Now of course, things would have to change. So, this bright and cheery Wednesday morning, following the events of the previous day, Mr Melrose was going to need a favour from young Mr Diggerby; hence the unusually cheerful response to Ralph's greeting.

'I'm not sure that I would be actually able to cope with that job, at this time, Mr Melrose. I'm not sure that I have enough experience yet.'

'Nonsense, lad. You'll be fine. There's nothing to it. Just follow what you do here, and what could possibly go wrong? Starting today, you will accompany Mr Lambe to the Grillington branch and for today, Thursday and Friday he will teach you the ropes. There's nothing to it,' Mr Melrose repeated. 'There's little point in removing your overcoat, Mr Diggerby; Mr Lambe will be here in a moment or two to give you a lift over to Grillington. Of course in his absence you will be required to travel to the sub-branch by bus, for which you will be reimbursed by the Bank, at the beginning of the month in your salary, under the heading of expenses. Any questions?'

Before Ralph could think up any reply, Mr Melrose continued with, 'ah, he's here now is Mr Lambe. Good morning Mr Lambe. As discussed yesterday, I've got Mr Diggerby here ready, willing and able to accompany you to Grillington.'

Ralph accompanied Mr Lambe round the corner to the rear of the Bank where the latter had parked his car. Ralph went to get in the front passenger seat but on opening the door realised that the seat was occupied by a rather fierce looking man with a huge curling moustache.

'Oh, so sorry, I didn't realise that there was anyone there,' said Ralph, who was about to shut the car door again, when a noise came from under the moustache.

'Willow's the name,' he barked. 'Regimental Sar'nt Major Willow, retired; 14th/ 20th King's Hussars. Born and bred in Lancashire; destined from birth to serve Queen and Country in the finest Regiment in this fair Isle. You'll be Mr Diggerby? You'll be seated in the rear of the vehicle, if you please?'

Ralph pushed the front door closed and climbed into the rear seat, directly behind the moustache.

As Mr Lambe got into the driver's seat, the moustache uttered forth again.

'Mr Lambe will be our driver today, won't you Mr Lambe?' Turning in his seat to almost face Ralph, the moustache said, 'that's Lambe, with an "e", isn't it Mr Lambe? The "e" is most important, without that, Mr Lambe is just the Sunday roast.'

The moustache guffawed at his own joke. Ralph just sat still; but when he glanced up at the rear-view mirror he caught sight of Mr Lambe's raised eyebrows, with a pair of eyes to match.

To Ralph's relief, silence reigned in the car for the entire journey to Grillington, and Ralph was simply a bystander as the two other men went about the routine of unlocking all the doors; unsetting the alarm system; turning lights on; opening the strong room; wheeling out the till and installing it on the counter. Between them, they placed all the ledgers and papers on the counter, and on the clerk's desk to the back of the room.

There was just time to brew a cup of tea and drink it before the required opening time of nine thirty arrived, bringing with it the first customer of the day.

'Ooh; are you leaving us?'

'No, just showing Mr Diggerby the ropes.'

This question and answer sequence eventually advanced to reach the giddy heights of the old chestnut to Bank cashiers, namely "have you got any free samples?" In his relatively few years working as a bank cashier, Ralph had by now learned to totally ignore the latter remark.

He did find however, that it was somehow comforting to know that customers seemed saddened by the possibility of "their" bank cashier moving on to pastures new, and he thought with optimism that he would be alright when it came to the time when he would have to cover the sub-branch in Mr Lambe's absence, as the customers here in this large village seemed to be kind, thoughtful, and pleasant.

The first day passed without any untoward incidents and indeed Ralph found the time spent in his new surroundings to have been a pleasant change to the normal routine of the main branch.

Even Arthur Willow wasn't too difficult to get along with, once you got to know him, thought Ralph on the journey back to Thornston, in the car.

The bonus for Ralph, was that once he had returned to the main branch with all the day's entries, ready to be processed through the accounting machines by the operatives, Ralph's day's work was completed. He left the building some fifteen minutes before his usual time, and caught an earlier bus to go home.

As he turned in at the gate at number seventeen, he noticed that his mother wasn't in her customary place of fussing with the rose bush in the front garden. He put his key in the lock, opened the door, and called out to his mother.

'Hello, mum, I'm home.'

Evelyn came hurrying into the hall wiping her hands on her apron, a worried look on her face; 'are you alright, Ralph dear?'

'I'm fine thanks, mum. Why, don't I seem alright to you?'

'It's just that you're home early, dear, and I wondered if there was something the matter; some problem at work, or that you might not be feeling well and had been sent home early from work.'

'It's nothing like that, mum; it's just that I've been at Grillington sub-branch today and I was able to leave work a few minutes early, that's all. Not doing your usual spot of gardening this afternoon, mum?' Ralph added.

'No dear, I was finishing preparing the evening meal.'

'Will the rose bush be alright? I mean, will it survive the night without your tender care and attention?' Ralph smiled at his mother; love in his eyes, and understanding in his heart.

Evelyn simply smiled at her son, who she realised was growing up. She resolved that she would try to stop fussing with the rose bush whilst waiting for Ralph to appear into her sight, as he came from the bus.

She couldn't really help herself she thought, but knew that she must try, as she was concerned about her son's welfare and safety, but she thought, he is now old enough to get home without her worrying where he is. She had to untie his hands from the apron strings; it would be a struggle, but nevertheless, it was something she had to do both for him and for herself.

On the Thursday morning after the trio had entered the bank office in Grillington, Mr Lambe took it upon himself to explain the mysteries of the workings of the bank's alarm systems. He explained how the overnight building alarm was set; the correct codes to insert into the box, and the order of keys in the lock. Next he moved to the strongroom and explained the workings of that simple system. Finally came the unravelling of the "intruder on the premises" system, whereby the police station would be informed automatically if there were intruders on the premises during banking hours; in other words, if there was a raid in progress.

Ralph understood about the kick bar under the counter, as he had seen that operate at close quarters very recently, when the bar had been inadvertently raised by the bags of silver after the cash delivery the previous week. He was not however, familiar with the particular intricacies of the Bungo Alarm System, which was installed in the sub-branch.

'This system has been installed in this sub-branch for quite some years, and is somewhat antiquated,' Mr Lambe had explained, whilst showing Ralph the inside of an old cupboard in the rear of the bank office area behind the counter.

The interior of the cupboard appeared to only house an old record player on the top shelf, with a 78 rpm record sitting on the turntable, and a needle arm poised ready it appeared, to play the record at any moment. There were a number of wires and what looked like some altered form of telephone stand.

'This,' explained Mr Lambe, 'must be kept clear of any manner of foreign articles, at all times. When the alarm bar is raised under the counter, it automatically dials the number of the local police station, and then the record arm drops onto the record and it plays a pre-recorded message to the police, which will automatically advise the police that there are intruders on the premises, and also, of course notify them which branch of which bank is in trouble. They will then dispatch a squad of officers to the premises to render assistance, with immediate effect.'

Ralph took on board all of this information, finding it rather tedious but, he assumed, necessary; although, he conceded to himself that the need for assistance from the police should be a very rare occurrence indeed, particularly in such a small semi-rural area.

The second day at the sub-branch with his two colleagues, passed without any incidents of note; and the whole time was spent attending to the daily routine of serving the Bank's customers, and providing their needs as efficiently and courteously as possible.

Ralph did spend some period of time actually working on the counter, in order to familiarise himself with his new surroundings and potential new role. To his surprise, Ralph found that he enjoyed himself, and that as his confidence grew, he relaxed somewhat.

Fridays in Grillington sub-branch were a slightly different affair, as Friday was wage day for the local businesses; which meant that the wages clerks called at the branch with their company's cheques made out to "Wages" or "Cash" and an accompanying list of exactly how they wanted the cash amount broken down.

Of course, from the individual company's point of view they required exact amounts of notes and coin to enable them to make up the brown weekly wage packets.

To the Bank this was an essential service as it kept the customers happy.

But to the counter cashiers, this was purgatory as it took an age to serve each customer; and the queue grew longer, as the minutes passed.

Ralph could hear murmurings from near the back of the queue, which had by now stretched out beyond the entrance. It occurred to him that this was going to be the part that would cause him most stress when he had to do this on his own.

Mr Lambe seemed to have developed an indifferent attitude towards the situation, and kept his head down and just served each customer as they appeared at his till.

'Oh don't concern yourself about the muttering at the back of the queue,' he had said to Ralph, 'they all know the score, they all get served eventually.'

At one point, it became apparent to Ralph that he could assist Mr Lambe by taking in credits only, as this did not involve going into the till, which was strictly against Bank rules and regulations. He could take cheques being paid in with credit slips, and cash being paid in similarly, and stamp the paying in book and leave the pile of credits for Mr Lambe to enter into the ledger when a quieter moment appeared.

He suggested this to Mr Lambe, who shrugged and said that it would be alright if he felt the need.

'Is any one just paying in? Ralph asked shyly, 'I can take paying in only, if you wish.'

A few members of the queue moved towards where he was standing behind the counter, and this was working well until one of the customers he had dealt with, decided as an afterthought that he wanted some change for the shop.

'I'm afraid I'm not allowed to go into the till for change, Mr Butler, I did emphasise that I could deal with payments in only.'

'All you have to do is get two five pound bags of change from the bloody till lad, it's not like I'm asking for the world is it?'

'I'm afraid I am not allowed to go into my colleagues till,' Ralph repeated, feeling himself getting redder by the minute. 'I'm sorry, but I just can't do that.'

'Right stuff your bloody change then,' Mr Butler retorted, bad-temperedly. 'I'll go to the bloody Post Office.' Mr Butler turned away from the counter and made a great show of angrily stomping out of the Bank, heading off in the direction of the Post Office.

Ten minutes later he returned, somewhat shame-faced to the Bank queue, and attempted to walk in front of the people still queueing, to get to Ralph at the counter. However, a rather large, ruddy-faced man sporting a bloodied butchers apron, growled gruffly from the rear of the queue, 'Oi, Butler! Wait yer turn, like everyone else has to.'

'I've only come to get me ten pound note back that I gave to yon fella, for me change.'

'Aye, well, 'appen,' replied the butcher, 'be that as it may, but tha stomped off to t' Post Office, and in my book that counts as levin' t' Bank as tha'd bin served. So, get to t' back o' queue, thee.'

Supported by much muttering, the butcher seemed to have won the day, as Mr Butler shuffled out of the bank, and joined the back of the queue.

When it was the butcher's turn to be served, he stood in front of Mr Lambe, but he glanced across and he winked at Ralph, 'can't have the owner of t' sweet shop floutin' Bank rules, can we young 'un?' he said and laughed.

'For some reason, there's little love lost between Mr Butler, at the sweet shop and Mr Wells, the butcher,' Mr Lambe explained later in the day after activity at the counter had died down somewhat. 'Their shops are next door to each other, so there may be some history between them from the fact that they are neighbours. Sometimes it isn't wise to enquire.'

By the time he reached home that Friday evening, Ralph felt that he had actually learnt quite a lot from his three day secondment.

'I felt as if the butcher, Mr Wells, was very supportive of me in my slight altercation with Mr Butler, the sweetshop owner, and I found it wasn't as scary by the end of the three day's stint, as I had felt it was at the start,' he told both his mother and Sheila, as they all had sat down to their evening meal together.

By this time Ralph and Sheila had been married for just short of nine months, and Sheila had got used to going home with her mother, Sandra, after they had finished at the café on a Friday afternoon, in order that they could spend some quality time together; and then Sheila would return by bus into the centre of town; so she had got into the habit of standing outside the Bank on a Friday evening, from ten to five waiting for Ralph to finish work, so they could travel to seventeen Wellington Street together.

'How's your mother, Sheila?' Evelyn had asked.

'I think she's been looking a little tired of late, but generally she seems to be alright.' Sheila smiled at Evelyn.

She and Ralph's mother Evelyn had developed a rather pleasant easy-going relationship, where they shared the household chores and rather enjoyed each other's company. Sheila was pleased to take some of the household chores away from Evelyn as she too seemed to be a little more tired, by the time the evening came around, than she used to be.

Once the evening meal was finished and the pots had been cleared away and washed up, Sheila rushed upstairs and came back down almost immediately clutching her wedding photo album.

'Please can we just look through the photos again?' she asked placing the album, opened at the first page, on the table surface.

They had done this as a group several times since the wedding which had been over eight months previously, in January 1971.

In one of the photographs there could be seen a slight dusting of snow which had blown into a corner of the square paved area, outside the Registry Office; one of the penalties of a January wedding.

Because of the paucity of family members on both sides, the wedding had been a very small affair, and consequently only a sparse collection of photographs had been preserved in the album, but it gave Sheila a great deal of pleasure to go over the photographs and the memories of all the details of the day.

Allan Briggs had been the best man, basically in the absence of anyone more suitable; both mothers; a very distant Aunt on Sheila's side; a couple of friends from the café, and Laura as bridesmaid; and Laura's current boyfriend made up the entirety of the assembly. They had decided between them to have the ceremony in the Town Registry Office; the reception, at the café, where Sandra, Sheila's mother had done all of the catering, ably helped by Evelyn.

Both mothers had insisted that Sheila should not be involved in the catering for her own wedding, so both Sheila and Ralph had been shooed away from the café the evening before, so they had gone to the pictures to see, appropriately so they thought, *Diamonds are Forever.*

Evelyn had poured each of them a glass of sherry, as they slowly turned the pages, discussing in great detail the memories that each photograph provoked. There, was the one where Sheila arrived at the Registry Office in a large saloon, a white Ford Zodiac. Here, everyone had agreed that Sheila had looked really lovely in her white wedding dress.

The two mothers, Sandra and Evelyn; and Laura and Sheila had gone to get Sheila "kitted out", as they had described the expedition.

The four had set off early one Saturday morning, and they had made a day of it. They had travelled together into Leeds by train into City Square Station and had walked from the station up Park Row, and turning right onto the Headrow they had progressed to wander around the whole of Eastgate, and beyond.

They had finally ended up in C&A's large store on Boar Lane; where the dress had been purchased, eventually.

Before this, there had been much toing and froing, between all the different dress shops; including Pro Nuptia, and other outfitters dotted around the centre of Leeds. Once the dress had been literally "in the bag", they had undertaken a grand tour of some great number of other shops, including shoe shops, like Dolcis and Stead & Simpsons; accessory shops, selling handbags and gloves and all the paraphernalia they thought necessary to complete Sheila's big day; not forgetting of course, the lingerie shop.

They had managed to pause at one point of the proceedings; that was once the dress had been decided upon, and had enjoyed a slap-up lunch in Whitelock's Ale House in the wonderfully named, Turk's Head Yard; but had then continued with the shopping for another couple of hours or so afterwards; before setting off to travel back home on the train, heavily laden with parcels and bags. They had, however all agreed that a wonderful time had been had by all, and they all arrived back in Thornston tired but very content.

By contrast, Ralph and Allan had popped into Thornston town centre, to O S Wains where each had been measured for a new suit. Whilst there they had both purchased a plain white shirt each, together with a new tie to round off the outfit. The tailor's assistant had promised faithfully that both the suits would be ready in ample time before the wedding day, which at that time had still been some three months away.

On the second page of Sheila's album was the photograph that faithfully recorded the result of the men's trip, being the one of the groom and best man both resplendent in their new suits, standing stiffly to attention on the pavement outside the Registry Office; and if you looked carefully at the photograph you could just make out the front of a passer-by's shoe in the bottom edge of the frame.

There was of course the obligatory group photograph which only had nine people on it, but as "happiness doesn't depend on numbers," as Sandra had said, the day was still fondly remembered, around the dining table at seventeen Wellington Street.

Once Ralph had returned to the here and now again, he did allow himself to feel just a little saddened by the fact that he had not kept any of those photographs; the wedding album having long ago been destroyed.

So now, he only had his memory to rely on, although he was able to control the images in a selective sort of a way.

As Ralph continued to sit awhile in his easy chair, he looked back on his day, and he felt quite satisfied by all that he had achieved, and pleased by what he had allowed himself to recall, and he went to bed a more contented man than he had felt for some many years.

Chapter 14

Ralph had risen early again and had been prepared for the coming day, just as he had been on the two previous days. The only difference this morning being that there had been no sign of Jessica.

Time had passed slowly until the clock showed nearly time for lunch, when there was suddenly a knock at his door, and Jessica bounced inside, almost before he had time to call, 'come in.'

'Hi Granddad,' Jessica sang, 'we're in. Mr Greenwood came at seven o'clock this morning and the three of us loaded his van and then we drove to Wellington Street. I've chosen the bedroom at the back. It's lovely. The carpet in there is so squishy; it's so soft and thick.'

'That was my mother's room,' said Ralph. 'Originally, she used to sleep in the front bedroom but she moved into the back bedroom after Sheila and I were married and we had gone to live with her. It was intended that we would only live there whilst we were saving up to buy a house of our own, but subsequent events changed all those plans. She had insisted that we take the front bedroom, although both Sheila and I would have been more than content to have used the back bedroom, which as you have seen is a very nice room; and it gets the sun first thing in the morning as I recall.

The room is pretty much as she left it, and the carpet was her special treat to herself; she loved that carpet. She even used to take her slippers off outside the room door, so she could feel the wool on her bare feet. Although it has been many years since that carpet was originally laid, the room has been hardly used.'

'But the carpet feels almost new,' Jessica said. She looked down shyly, 'in fact that's just what I did, I took my shoes off and loved the feel of the wool on my bare feet. That's what I'll do from now on, I'll always have bare feet in there, just like grandma did. Oh, she'd have been my great grandma, wouldn't she, if you're my granddad. What a lovely thought.'

Ralph was very deeply touched by these last few words, which were made with such obvious sincerity and feeling. He looked at Jessica's eager young face, and felt a tenderness and a warmth towards her that he had not felt towards any human being for over forty years or so.

'The back bedroom was left untouched, after my mother sadly died. We had only lived with her, Sheila and I, for just over one year, when she had gone to work one Wednesday morning, as right as ninepence, as we used to say. Around three in the afternoon Mr Mercer; he was mum's employer, had phoned the Bank to speak to me and inform me that mum had collapsed whilst at work, and the ambulance had been called, and they had rushed her to the hospital, where they discovered that she had had a heart attack. We managed to get to see her within an hour of the phone call, but she died later that night. Wednesday February 9th 1972. Nine forty seven pm.' Silence.

'Poor mum; I still miss her.'

Despite her young years, Jessica sensed that now was a time to allow a silence.

A moment or two passed before Ralph motioned her to the chair and said, 'why not sit a while, if you've got time, please my dear.'

Jessica pulled the dining chair from its place tight up under the table and turned it to face Ralph, and having sat down she leaned forward and lightly placed her hand on his. 'Go on, granddad,' she encouraged softly, 'please tell me more.'

Ralph smiled at Jessica, and encouraged by her genuine eagerness he continued.

'Well, it seemed to change everything when that happened. It was so sudden and without warning. I cannot recall much about that time; the funeral for instance, I cannot remember at all. I think I was allowed some time away from work, but I can't say for sure. I seem to remember people being very understanding and supportive to me; in fact to both Sheila and I at the time; although I remember it seemed to make a difference between Sheila and I at first, but I suppose that was inevitable.

I think we came to terms with the situation only slowly, and of course it changed our need to save up for a house of our own as I was able to take over the tenancy of the property with the Council. This meant, of course that we then had our own home, and so life started to settle down again slowly after that.'

Jessica sat quietly listening and after a few moments of silence, after Ralph seemed to have finished saying all he wanted to say, she looked at him and asked him a question.

'Do you believe in ghosts?'

'Why ever would you ask a question like that?' Ralph responded, a quizzical look on his face.

'Well, it's just that your mum's bedroom seems to have a peaceful feeling about it, as if there's something or someone looking after the house, and it seems to be centred in that room.'

Ralph smiled an acknowledgement at Jessica and said, 'well, ordinarily speaking I would say that I do not believe in such things as ghosts, but you have reminded me of something that happened during my courtship with Sheila.'

He shifted in his chair.

'We had been out for the day and had gone back to her house and we had had our meal there. Her mother, Sandra had gone out for the evening and so we were left in the house on our own. Anyway we were sitting watching telly about seven thirty when I heard some children crying. You have to remember that Sheila had no relatives, so I knew we weren't babysitting for anyone in the family. Sandra's mother lived in a ramshackle old farm house; although the farm itself and most of the outbuildings had long since been disposed of, and houses had then been built all around it; but nevertheless the house itself was detached and some distance from its nearest neighbour. Well, as I said, I heard these children crying, and it seemed to be coming from upstairs.

I mentioned to Sheila, that she hadn't told me that we were babysitting for a friend or a neighbour, to which she had replied that we were not.

So who are the children I can hear crying upstairs? I had persisted.

"Strange isn't it?" Sheila had said, "mum and I sometimes hear those two children, not often, but nevertheless, we definitely hear them.

The crying seems to always come from the small bedroom at the end of the landing, and rumours are that there were once two children, many years previously that had died here from whooping cough."'

Looking up at Jessica, Ralph continued, 'I never heard them again, but I certainly did hear them that night; so do I believe in ghosts? Maybe, maybe not. I know what I heard, and there was no one else in the house other than Sheila and I; so your guess is as good as mine.'

'Oo-err,' said Jessica and shivered, 'I've got goose-bumps.' She sat thinking for a moment, and then continued with; 'so granddad, were you in fact born in what is now our house, in Wellington Street, and did you always live there?'

'Oh yes, I was born there; brought up there; and lived all my married life there,' here there was a pause before Ralph concluded the sentence with, 'and the remainder of what could best be described as my single life there too. I left it for the very first time to move in here, just over three months ago. No regrets though; it's been good to me, has that house.'

'It doesn't look like you used the dining room all that often,' said Jessica.

'No, not since....' Ralph stopped, and then continued with, 'no, I hadn't used the dining room for some considerable time.'

Jessica stood up from the chair and turned and replaced it under the table, tight up as it was always kept.

'I suppose that I'd better get a move on with my chores,' she said. 'I may as well start in here.' Jessica looked at Ralph's bed and laughed. 'What is that?' she laughed, pointing at the bed that was a tucked in mess.

'Well I thought that by the time it had got to eleven forty five you'd not be coming to make it,' said Ralph, defensively; but couldn't prevent a short bark of a laugh escaping.

'Honestly, what are you like?' Jessica said whilst stripping the top covers off, and straightening the bottom sheet. Laughing, she added, 'left like that it'd be like trying to sleep on a corrugated garage roof.'

She gave him a very old fashioned look, the laugh turning into a giggle, as she wagged a slim finger at him.

Ralph looked suitably chastened, and was rewarded with a swift kiss on the top of his head, as Jessica went out of the room into the corridor and immediately returned with the vacuum cleaner saying, 'you've missed your coffee, this morning haven't you, do you want me to make you one from here?'

'That's very kind of you my dearest Jessica,' Ralph replied, 'I think that I'll wait until lunch time, which isn't far away, but thank you.'

The sound of the vacuum cleaner seemed to invade the whole of Ralph's being, and the relief he felt when Jessica had finished and it was switched off, was almost a physical sensation. She disappeared out of sight into the bathroom and the sound of cleaning could be heard.

Eventually, she popped out of the bathroom, and stood in front of him saying, 'there, that's you finished. Mum has taken a day off work so she can settle herself into the house; unpack the boxes; and familiarise herself with the house and its surroundings. Actually, I've taken a day off work too, but I thought that I'd just come in to sort your room out.'

She took the dining chair from its place under the table, turned it around and sat down opposite him again, in the same position that she had been in a while ago.

'You can tell me another story now. We've got a few minutes before your lunch.'

Ralph sat for a moment trying to take in what Jessica had just said to him about although having a day off, she had come into work just to look after him and make sure that he was alright. He had a sudden realisation that after being alone for more years than he cared to remember, it seemed as if someone actually cared about him. Even loved him. Ralph looked at Jessica as only a doting grandfather could, and then he put his finger to his chin, and was silent for a moment.

Then, 'did I tell you about the weekend that Sheila and I went Youth Hostelling over Grassington tops? She had this brilliant idea of trying youth hostelling, so she had booked us in overnight at the YHA at Linton, near Grassington. We had caught the West Yorkshire Road Car red bus to Skipton, and the local bus from there to Linton. It must have been after four in the afternoon when we had eventually arrived there.

Did I mention that this was in February? No? Well it was in February, so it was very cold and almost dark, by then.

Once we had booked in to the hostel, we had to help with the catering and tidying up and then we sat around in a lounge sort of place and chatted, before we were told it was bed-time. Men and women slept in separate dormitories of course, so we split up and went our separate ways to bed. I say bed, actually it was a bunk, and it was so uncomfortable, and I was in a room with several other chaps, all of whom seemed to snore.'

Ralph paused a moment thinking, before he asked Jessica rhetorically, 'how come if there are five people in a room and one of them is snoring, the only one that isn't kept awake by the noise, is the one that's making it?'

He laughed in Jessica's direction and said, 'there's no need to even think about an answer to that, because I don't believe there is an answer.'

Before continuing on with the tale, Ralph paused a moment to recollect where he'd got to.

'Now, where was I? Ah yes. Well, I hardly slept a wink all that night and it was so cold; there was no heating and it was the middle of winter, so it was almost a pleasure to get up in the morning, and get washed and dressed. Shall we just say that the facilities, bearing in mind that this was the late nineteen sixties, were very basic?

We breakfasted, and got all the tidying up done, and everything, and I mean *everything* had to be cleaned, dried, and put back exactly where it had come from; and then we got togged up in these outdoor walking things that we had bought for the occasion and then we set off.

As we were walking across the tops above Grassington, and down into the village, or town or whatever it is; it started to snow. It was very cold, and we didn't really know where we were or what we should be doing. About an hour into the walk we were coming downhill across a very large field, which had some sheep in the top corner. Glancing at them we could see that they were all huddled together to keep warm in the snow, which by now had started to fall quite thickly; when Sheila said I should whistle the sheep, just to see what would happen.'

Ralph stopped speaking and looked at Jessica, who was giggling behind one hand held to her face.

'This was not funny, I'll have you know, young lady,' he said, but he caught the infection of her giggle and laughed too, 'actually, I suppose it is funny looking back, but it certainly was not at the time.

Anyway, like a fool, I whistled; and suddenly there were sheep coming towards us from all directions; at first they were just walking, but we turned to run towards a nearby wall, and as we ran, so did they. Within a few moments we were surrounded and being buffeted by a hundred sheep or so; it was quite scary; at least I found it scary, but Sheila just wouldn't stop laughing. They kept butting me in the backside with their heads and nudging my thighs.

Afterwards, Sheila thought that they must have assumed we were there to feed them in the snow. Somehow though, we managed to get to the wall and clamber over it, and we sat down in its lee to catch our breath. Obviously the sheep could still smell us through the dry stone wall, and kept bleating, the bleating getting louder and louder. After a few minutes respite we made a run for it. Needless to say we didn't try youth hostelling again. I think Sheila might have just tried again, but there was no way that I wanted to.'

'You didn't seem to like outdoor activities, did you?' laughed Jessica, 'or is it that they didn't like you? Ooh look, it's nearly ten minutes to one, you're going to miss your lunch if you don't go now.'

Jessica stood up and returned the dining chair to its usual place, tight up against the table; then she leaned forward slightly towards Ralph and taking hold of his hand she half-pulled him up out of his chair.

Jessica then accompanied Ralph downstairs in the lift and they parted company outside the dining room; Jessica skipping off towards the front door and Ralph ambling into the dining room, to his table.

'Good afternoon Mr Ralph,' Everton greeted him in his golden brown voice, 'where you been hidin' this mornin'?'

'Hello Everton, I've been in my room. At first I was just sitting enjoying the peace, and then that delightful storm swept in, even though she had taken a day off; so we have just sat and chatted about memories.'

'Hope you don't mind me saying, Mr Ralph, but you two's good for each other.'

'I don't mind you saying that at all, Everton. In fact I believe that you are correct. I have not realised over the years how pleasant it can be to reminisce. Pleasant memories of course.'

Everton glanced at Ralph, and paused, before saying quietly, looking him in the eye, 'sometimes it helps to recall the not so pleasant ones too, Mr Ralph. It clears the mind, cleans the soul.'

'I'm not too sure whether I've actually got a soul,' replied Ralph.

'That's one thing you can be assured of, Mr Ralph; you gotta soul.' After a slight pause, he added, 'you also got a Maker, and one day you and Him gonna be havin' a chat. I just hope and pray that you have readied yourself for that chat.'

'Hmm, is there any mayonnaise?' asked Ralph.

Ralph started to eat his lunch slowly, even before Everton brought the mayonnaise.

'Thank you, Everton,' he said.

For just a split-second Ralph was unsure what he was actually thanking Everton for; the mayonnaise or…. the seed of a thought that had started to germinate in his mind, which he attempted to push to the back of his mind's seed tray.

After lunch was finished, Ralph took himself down to the pergola area, and sat a while quietly thinking. He allowed his eyes to close with the warm sunshine playing on his face.

Several minutes had passed before he was brought back to the here and now again by a bright and cheerful, 'hi granddad.'

Ralph opened his eyes, and shielded the sun from them with his hand.

'Hello, my young granddaughter,' he said and smiled. 'I thought you were supposed to be having a day off, helping your no doubt long suffering mother to unpack?'

'I'll have you know, I've done my bit, and anyway, mum asked me to call to see you, just to let you know, she says, that there is a lot of police blue and white tape all around the rear of number nine Wellington Street, and a couple of police forensic vans, and people in white plastic suits wandering in and out. I wonder what happened there?'

'I wonder,' said Ralph seemingly absent-mindedly. 'I wonder.'

'Who lives at number nine, Granddad?' asked Jessica.

'I'm afraid I don't know who lives there now, as the house was sold before I came in here, and it has changed hands.'

'Well, do you know who used to live there?' Jessica persisted.

'Oh, yes.'

'Granddaaaad?' pleaded Jessica.

There was quite a long silence whilst Ralph seemed to be weighing up something in his mind. Jessica had enough sense to allow that silence.

'A man called Allan Briggs,' eventually came the answer.

Jessica was herself then silent too for a few moments.

'Isn't he the man that you got that letter from The Weighbridge about?'

'Yes, the very same.' Ralph looked away towards the stream at the bottom of the valley garden, and didn't comment further.

'Sorry, Mr Diggerby. I didn't mean to ask questions that would cause you upset.' Jessica sat down on the bench next to Ralph, and put her hand on his.

'I much prefer it when you refer to me as granddad, 'he said, unable to make eye contact. But after a moment or two, Ralph turned his head, and saw the loving, concerned expression on her upturned face, and he managed a kindly smile in her direction. Then Ralph grasped the small gentle hand that was placed on top of his, and couldn't help but notice the comparison between the two; her small soft smooth-skinned pale hand and his; elderly, liver-spotted and with wrinkly skin.

'Everton said something at lunch today that is causing me to think. He said that sometimes it helps clear the mind and clean the soul to remember and maybe share the not so good memories, and that one day, probably sooner rather than later,' he laughed, 'I will have to have a chat with my Maker. Can I ask, what do you think about that, as a young person?'

'Well, Granddad, I know that there is a God, and I do know that we will all have to give an account of ourselves one day to Him; and I feel that a trouble shared is a trouble halved, from just a human point of view. Mum says that. She also says that we all need someone to talk to.'

Jessica sat a for moment quietly, then added, 'I could be that person for you if you'd let me. I can keep a secret, if I'm needed to. Plus, you've helped me and mum and I'd like to try and help you if I could. I can't give you anything, as I've nothing to give; but I can listen, and we can be friends. I can try my very hardest to love you, just like I'm your real granddaughter.' She quietly added, 'I already love you as a nice person.'

There was a prolonged silence between them, and Jessica continued to cling tightly to Ralph's hand, her thumb gently massaging the wrinkled skin over his knuckles.

Ralph took a deep breath and drew himself up straight; taking both Jessica's small hands in his he looked into her face, and started to speak.

'I was once held up at gun-point,' he breathed out. 'I was doing my first session as a stand in for Mr Lambe, a cashier, who ran the sub-branch in Grillington. It was the Tuesday. Everything seems to have happened on a Tuesday, except mum's death, which had been on a Wednesday. Anyway, on the Tuesday in question I had opened the branch and let the first customer in at nine-thirty, and just finished serving her, when a young man wearing a scarf over his face and a crash helmet on his head, suddenly ran into the bank and pointed, what I am sure was a gun at me, and screamed at me to give him the money from the drawer. Looking back, he was obviously young and foolish, because he should have done this later in the afternoon, when there would have undoubtedly been more money in the till; but instead he chose the early morning when there was only the cash float in there. It was terrifying. It all happened so fast.'

'Oh, Granddad,' exclaimed Jessica, 'what did you do? Were you hurt? Did he fire the gun?'

Ralph continued with, 'I don't know how, but actually I managed to follow the correct procedure. I kicked the alarm bar to activate the automatic alarm to the police station; gave him the notes from the till, and as he was running off I ran round from behind the counter and shut and bolted the Bank door. And then we waited.

Both Arthur Willow, the bank guard and I were quite badly shaken up. After a few moments Arthur asked how long I thought it would take the police to arrive, and I answered that I didn't know. Then he suggested that I should contact the main office in Thornston, so I picked up the phone and dialled the number. In the meantime, there was a loud thumping and banging on the bank door, and we both cowered down behind the bank counter, as we thought he had come back for more.

As it turned out, it was just Mr. "Wishing" Wells the butcher who was trying to pay in his takings and didn't realise of course, what had happened. But then, why would he?'

'Mr. Wishing Wells? Was that his name? Wishing?' asked a wide eyed Jessica.

'No,' laughed Ralph, 'we called him "wishing" because he was for ever wishing something would happen; I wish it would rain, when it was dry; and I wish it was spring, in the winter; I wish it was warmer, when it was cool; and I wish it was cooler, when it was hot, and so on, and so on.

Well he shouted through the door at us, that he wished we would just open the door and let him in, and Arthur shouted back to tell him we had been raided and that we were waiting for the police to arrive. Then he shouted back that he wished the police would just hurry up so he could pay his money in. Meanwhile I was talking to the Chief Clerk, Mr Mawson, at Thornston, who told me he was on his way.'

'What did the police say when they got there?' asked Jessica, who was sitting listening open mouthed and wide eyed.

'Well,' continued Ralph, 'you see, that was the thing; they didn't turn up, well not until a long while after. Mr Mawson had arrived, and the first thing he said was that the bank doors should have remained open, something to do with the Bills

Of Exchange Act, and shutting Bank doors was preventing the exchange of bills, or some such rubbish. At least it sounded like rubbish to Arthur Willow and myself at the time; we couldn't have cared less about Bills being able to be Exchanged. Eventually the police did attend the incident, but it was about forty five minutes later.'

'Why did it take so long? I mean, it was a serious thing to have happened, wasn't it?' asked a wide eyed Jessica.

'Well it turned out that the Bank's wonderful Bungo Alarm system, which had been installed some years earlier, had been responsible for the delay.

When I had kicked the bar, an automatic telephone call should have been triggered to the nearest police station. Which, in fact it had been but, as soon as they answered the call, the record arm dropped down onto the record and this played, in theory a pre-recorded message which was supposed to say something like, "This is a Bungo alarm message. There are bandits on the premises at Brackleys Bank Grillington. Please attend urgently."'

'So why didn't they?' asked Jessica.

'The powers that be, after an investigation had taken place both by the police and the Bank's Inspectors, discovered that the record arm had dropped onto the record after the police station had answered the call; exactly as it should have done but, there had been it seemed a large gathering of dust and fluff on the surface of the record and the needle had stuck. All the police got was a message that said, "This is a Bungo..... this is a Bungo..... this is a Bungo." So they were aware a raid was taking place, but didn't know which branch of which Bank. It had taken them some considerable time to find out which Bank branch it was, simply by a process of elimination. Then they had attended as soon as they had known where it was that they were actually meant to be going.'

'Oh poor Granddad, I'll bet you were scared.'

'Yes, my dearest Jessica, I have to admit, that I was scared. Also, it really upset both my mother and Sheila when I arrived home early from work that day, and explained to them both, what had happened.

Of course, I had had to be interviewed by the police and by the Bank's Inspectors, but was allowed home and given the rest of the week off work to allow me much needed time to recover.

Looking back, it might have upset my mother more than any of us realised, as it was the following February, that she had had the heart attack and died. I mean, it might not have had anything to do with her illness, but we'll never know will we?'

'Did they catch the man?' asked Jessica.

'Yes, I believe that they did do. Unlike with Allan, whom they didn't prosecute, they did prosecute the armed raider.'

'Allan?' asked Jessica, 'is that the same Allan as we mentioned earlier? The one who used to live in the house at number nine?'

'The very same.' Ralph repeated the exact same answer as he had done a few minutes previously, but instead of turning away and looking down the valley at the stream, this time Ralph looked into Jessica's face, as he said the words.

'Do you want to tell me about Allan?' she asked quietly.

'Actually, I rather would,' breathed Ralph. 'But not right now, not at this moment.' He patted the back of her hand gently. 'Let's go and have a cup of tea, shall we? Its thirsty work is all this sharing of memories, although I must admit I am finding that it is quite liberating.'

Before they set off for the lounge Jessica suddenly asked, 'is Mr Lambe, in the story about the bank raid, the reason why you are so averse to lamb, as you put it?'

'No, my dear young lady, I am averse to lamb for a completely different and unrelated reason. Now, let's go and get that cup of tea.'

After they had shared the pleasure of each other's company over a cup of tea in the lounge, Ralph suggested that it might be a good idea, if Jessica went back home to make sure

Mrs Darley was managing alright, 'to show togetherness,' he had said.

'I'll come back this evening after dinner, if that's alright with you?' Jessica asked as she went to the front door accompanied by Ralph, and she left him there as she half skipped her way down the road, turning to wave as she reached the corner.

Ralph decided to make his way up to his room, either perhaps to read or, as he thought more truthfully to himself, that he was going to have a short nap.

Chapter 15

No sooner had Ralph's eyes shut than there was a knock at his door.

'Come in'

Everton opened the door and stood in the gap.

'I'm sorry to disturb you Mr Ralph, but there's a gentleman to see you, says his name is Carter and he's from Maunday's Solicitors. He says that he has to hand you something in person.'

Everton stepped to one side and a tall slender gentleman in a dark navy suit and highly polished shoes, stepped into Ralph's room. Everton closed the door and went back downstairs. During the time this interaction had taken place Ralph had stood up, and he shook the hand that was offered.

'Good afternoon; Mr Ralph Ernest Diggerby?' the man queried. My name, as you have just heard is Mr Carter, I represent the firm of Maunday's Solicitors. We have been instructed to hand you this envelope which hitherto has been kept securely by the firm for a few years now; to be hand delivered I am sorry to say, on the death of a certain Mr Allan Francis Briggs. Mr Allan Francis Briggs, I have to inform you, sadly passed away at the Weighbridge Nursing and Care Home in the early hours of this morning; so here I am.'

With that Mr Carter put his hand into his inside jacket pocket and withdrew a plain white envelope, which he handed to Ralph. The envelope simply had, *Ralph Diggerby,* written in black ink on the envelope. Ralph instantly recognised the distinctive style of Allan's handwriting, which was neat and flowing, with a slight forward lean. How often had he seen that neat script when they had worked together all those years ago? It had always struck Ralph as odd that a man whose father was a builder with big rough gnarled hands should write with such neatness and precision.

Ralph took the envelope from Mr Carter's hand saying, 'thank you Mr Carter.'

'I'll need you to sign a receipt for this item, if you please, Mr Diggerby.' Mr Carter, reached into his other inside jacket pocket and produced a typewritten form, pointing to the blank dotted line on the paper; he also handed Ralph a pen, 'if you'd be so kind, Sir. Thank you.'

The task duly completed, Mr Carter picked up the signed receipt form, folded it neatly and returned it into his inside pocket, and again stretched out his hand towards Ralph.

'Nice to have met you, Mr Diggerby. It could perhaps have been under happier circumstances, but there we are, that's life, I suppose.'

'Or death,' Ralph replied quietly.

'Quite, quite. Well, I bid you good afternoon, Mr Diggerby.'

Mr Carter turned and let himself out through the doorway, leaving Ralph standing in the centre of his room holding the white envelope in his hand. Not being quite sure what he wanted to do with the envelope he stood for a few moments, then he lay it down gently on his dining table top.

The letter continued to lie unopened on the dining table, until eventually, a very indecisive Ralph chose to leave it where it was, still unopened. What he did decide however, was that it was time to proceed downstairs for his pre-dinner drink, so he left the room and went down to the bar.

As usual there was only Everton in the small bar, and no one else had yet entered the dining room, so the two men shared a few words of general chit-chat before Everton said, 'I hope the envelope wasn't bad news, Mr Ralph. I'm not tryin' to pry or nothin' but I hope it was not bad news.'

'I simply can't answer that,' said Ralph, staring at the bubbles rising in his glass of Cinzano and lemonade (with no ice); 'as I haven't opened it yet.'

'You've not opened it yet?' exclaimed Everton. 'What if its good news?'

'Then it'll just have to wait the same as if its bad news,' answered Ralph with a thin smile.

Just at that moment, a man whom Everton recognised walked into the dining room and looked around as if seeking someone. Seeing Everton through the open doorway of the bar he waved a blue envelope towards him.

'Hi Everton, I've brought sad news for your Mr Diggerby, about his friend Allan Briggs. Allan sadly passed away in the early hours of the morning and I've just...' Ralph had slid off his bar stool and come into the man's view, 'oh, he continued, now looking directly at Ralph. 'I'm sorry to have to say, Mr Diggerby that Allan passed away in the early hours of this morning. It was peaceful. Sorry you didn't have chance to say your goodbyes.'

'Thank you kindly, my friend. I did say my goodbyes to Allan, but that was some time ago when he was still Allan,' said Ralph quietly. The shell that was left was not Allan. But I do thank you for your kind thoughtfulness.'

'Well, I must be off. Nice to have met you Mr Diggerby, don't let me delay your evening meal.' The residents had started to file into the dining room, in readiness, and anticipation.

Bong! Bong! Bong! Bong! The six o'clock dinner gong sounded on the dot, but most of the diners were already in situ.

In contrast to the lunchtime when he had felt relaxed and had enjoyed his meal, Ralph felt somewhat tense and out of sorts, and ended up just toying with his meal, as he seemed for some reason to have lost his appetite.

Having decided not to bother with his sweet, he excused himself from the table and went to his room. Once inside, he opened the blue envelope which contained a simple note, advising him that Mr. Allan Briggs had passed away at four twenty that morning, peacefully. Details of the funeral to be advised in due time.

Ralph went to the window and stood on tiptoes and stared into the distance towards where the Weighbridge Nursing and Care Home was. He saw the old arched entrance, with the setting sun glowing amber on the stonework, and then relaxed his feet and turned away from the window.

He lifted the dining chair to its position in front of the writing desk and unlocked the desk top drawer and having taken out the orangey-brown folder; he opened it and pulled out the newspaper clipping from three days previously. He looked at the photograph of the police activity and striped tape draped across the rear of the house in the story, and re-read the article, not smiling inwardly as he had done at the first reading three days ago. Was that just three days ago? So much seemed to have been crammed into those three days. He felt like he had nearly re-lived his life in that short time; in fact he had re-lived it after a fashion, but not, he conceded, all of it.

There was a gentle tapping on his door.

'Come in,' he called.

The door opened and in bounced Jessica, who, he acknowledged to himself had become the light of his life. His whole being once again seemed to be lifted, as it was whenever this delightful young lady came into his presence.

'Hi Granddad,' she beamed, shutting the door behind her. She walked across to the writing desk and removed from the vase, the single orange rose that she had put there from the front garden of number seventeen, and replaced it with another identical one.

'There we are,' she said turning on her toes and standing in front of him. 'Oh, that's number nine Wellington street,' she said, looking down at the newspaper clipping that Ralph was still absent-mindedly holding in his fingers.

Ralph was caught in the headlights as it were, for just a moment, but Jessica didn't seem as if she was particularly attracted to the article, neither did she seem to especially notice the orangey-brown folder; instead she sat down in Ralph's easy chair with a sigh.

'Ooh, this is comfy Granddad; I love it.' she giggled her infectious giggle. 'By the way, mum was talking to the lady next door this afternoon, and she told mum that you used to own all those four houses on that block and two houses across the road at numbers sixteen and eighteen and that you bought them from the Council, and that the occupiers then used to pay you the rent. Wow, you must be very rich.' she laughed

'I'd say comfortable,' Ralph answered, raising one eyebrow, and laughing at her cheekiness. 'I'll tell you just how that came about, shall I?'

'Yes please,' she said drawing her legs up under herself, and wrapping her arms over them. 'I'd say, I'm comfortable too, in this chair,' and she giggled again.

'Do you remember that I told you when my mum died, Sheila and I had lived with her for just over a year?'

'Yes,' said Jessica, and screwed her eyes up tight as if trying to remember something, 'Wednesday February 9th 1972. Nine forty seven pm.' she said, 'poor great grandma.'

'That's mightily impressive,' exclaimed Ralph, feeling genuinely surprised that she had remembered the time and date exactly.

'Granddad, I've never had any relatives. My mum's mum died when I was little; I never knew who my proper granddad was, as he left grandma before I was born, and I don't remember my dad because he left mum when I was really quite small. My dad had been brought up in an orphanage, so we didn't know who his parents were or what happened to them. You are the nearest I've ever had to a granddad.'

She stopped suddenly and tears filled her lovely grey eyes, 'please don't be cross,' she said, 'but I love you just like you are my real granddad. Do you think it's alright to do that? Do you think it's ok to say that? Please say it is.' A huge tear rolled down her right cheek, and Ralph watched it splash onto the easy chair.

'Do I think it's alright to think and say that? I most certainly do. Furthermore, I'd like to say that I find that I love you like a real Granddaughter.' He smiled warmly at her, 'so dry your eyes young lady and don't drop any more water onto your proper Granddad's favourite chair.'

Jessica lowered her head for a moment and then smiling to herself she raised her face, and their eyes met in a warm smile of understanding. It was an unspoken moment of affection between a young mind and an elderly one, and the moment left them both with a feeling of inner satisfaction and warmth.

'Now, where was I? Oh yes, Sheila and I had lived with my mother for just over the year, before she died. Mum had very little money, and in fact had it not been for her small policy that she had with the Man From The Pru we would have struggled with the cost of her funeral, but as it turned out there was enough for that and a few pounds to spare.

After that we had just Sheila's wage and my Bank salary, and although we lived carefully there was never that much money to spare. We had been very fortunate in that we had lived with mum, as taking over the tenancy agreement was a relatively simple affair; so we always had somewhere to live, and so we got by.

It was ten months after my mum's death, that Sandra, Sheila's mum was taken ill, complaining of shortness of breath, dizziness and weight loss, all of a sudden. It all seemed to happen in just a few weeks. She had seemed to go from a healthy woman, vigorous, and running a busy business...'

'Did she have something to do with the café?' Jessica interrupted.

'Sandra, Sheila's mum had been left the café business and the building and the rambling old farm house by her husband, Sheila's father, after he had died, and so she ran the café and Sheila worked there, that's how we met.' Ralph sat a moment quietly.

'As I was saying, she seemed to be a healthy and vigorous woman one minute and being treated for cancer the next, and it was actually, as I said, about ten months after *my* mother had died that Sandra was diagnosed with cancer, and mercifully it was all over within another three months. It really shook Sheila up a lot and it took her a long time to recover from that, and I'm not sure she ever did, really.

For the three months that Sandra was ill, the responsibility for keeping the café running as a going concern, fell to Sheila. Sheila was a very hard worker, but she did not possess a business head. Consequently she found the management of the business a terrible strain, and what with coping with the emotional side of watching her mother die as it were, before her eyes, it turned out to be a very difficult period in Sheila's life. I did my very best to support her both emotionally and practically, but I'm sure that I fell well short of the required mark.'

Ralph sighed loudly, and paused before continuing, 'Sheila had been Sandra's only child and so she was left everything, but she didn't want to try to cope with taking over the running of the business, so she sold it to someone who already had a café but wanted to expand.

She sold the farmhouse too, which the purchaser, a local builder eventually demolished, and then he erected half a dozen new houses on the resulting land. In total we inherited around £30,000, which was an awful lot of money in those days.'

'Didn't Sheila want to go and live in what had been her house? After all she did own it, then.'

Ralph smiled at Jessica, 'oh no, she didn't like the old farm house, as it was very cold and damp and too large for what we wanted, besides she always said that she would feel funny about living in a house where her mother had died.'

Ralph paused for recollection. Then he continued again.

'Obviously Sheila was now in possession of a considerable amount of money, and she had made the decision to give up working in the café, partly because she no longer needed to work for the money, and partly because she felt she would be unable to work there for the new owner, however nice he might have been. I fully supported her in this decision, and she had a period of two or three months when she was just at home as a housewife. To be honest, I thought it was a wonderful time, as Sheila was just at home, and to be fair, she did seem as if she enjoyed that relaxed lifestyle, which I'm convinced she did for a while.'

Jessica was sitting listening intently to all that Ralph had been saying, but as he paused for a moment, she asked if he would like a cup of tea. When he said yes, she jumped up off the easy chair and proceeded to make them both one. It was only then that she realised there was only the one cup and saucer, so she dashed from the room heading in the direction of the kitchens downstairs, to get herself a beaker.

Ralph took this opportunity to replace the items back into the folder and return it to its home in the writing desk drawer.

He had just patted the key through the material of his trousers, as was his habit, when Jessica dashed back into the room, breathing heavily, and clutching a beaker in her hand.

She poured tea into both the cup and the beaker, adding the milk and sugar, passed his cup and saucer to Ralph, and re-took her seat in the easy chair, curling her legs up beneath her as she had done before. She took a sip from the beaker, sighed contentedly and urged Ralph to continue from where he had left off.

Ralph smiled at her and refreshed his dry mouth, by taking a sip from his cup.

'Life occasionally has a habit of providing chances and coincidences, and roundabout this time was one of those episodes.' Ralph steepled his fingers and looked at Jessica from over the top of the apex.

'We had had several discussions about what we should do with this money she had inherited, and we were both aware that this was a potential life-changing opportunity, for us both, and that we needed to proceed with some thought and careful consideration.

Well, one Saturday morning around about this time we had a letter from Thornston Council, informing us that they were looking to restructure their housing stock, and as a result of this they were intending to sell off to the private sector, all such houses as ours; that was to say they had accumulated over the years a motley collection of ad-hoc houses to go along with their purpose built Council housing stock.

At the time, this seemed too good a chance to miss; here we were being offered the chance to buy our house, and we just happened to have the cash. We subsequently visited the Council Offices and arranged the purchase of our house and whilst doing that one of the older members of staff happened to remark that they used to have a Mr Diggerby who had worked in that department, but had died some years previously. He had asked whether there was a connection?'

'What was your dad's name?' Jessica interrupted the flow.

'Eric, Eric Diggerby.'

'Sorry to interrupt, but I need to know.'

Ralph continued, 'that was another of life's coincidences; the man I spoke to and who dealt with the transaction for us had worked with my father, remembered him and had liked him. He needed to know about our means of purchase of the property; that was, were we going to take out a mortgage? Or did we, and he said this with a smile, did we have the cash? We surprised him by explaining we actually had the full amount for the house in cash; and we also explained of course how we had come by this money. He then suggested that as an investment we might want to think about purchasing, maybe one of the neighbouring houses and then that would enable us to obtain an income from the rent.

This triggered an idea in our minds and after much discussion we revisited the Council and put in a bid to buy the other three houses in our block of four, and two houses across the road that the Council also owned. To our surprise this offer was accepted, and within a few weeks we became the landlords of the five houses; well, the five houses and the one we now owned and lived in. There was a lot of complicated legal work that was all sorted out by the firm my mum had worked for. So, there we were in our mid to late twenties, property owners.'

'Did you stop working at the Bank, Granddad?' Jessica had finished her tea and was now looking at Ralph's face, whilst supporting her head on her two hands, one up each cheek, cupped together under her chin.

'I did consider giving up my job, but I quite enjoyed my work, and it brought in the extra money we needed; but it did mean that Sheila did not have to work, and so she took on the task of rent collecting and dealing with any repairs that needed doing to the houses. I do remember that we did enjoy one luxury, we decided to fly to Ostend in Belgium for a week's holiday.'

'Ostend? Not Spain? Or not Greece?' Jessica questioned.

'Well, the great Spanish and particularly Greek holiday boom hadn't really taken off by then, and Sheila fancied Ostend, for some reason. Actually we had a really good break and we were pleasantly surprised by how nice Ostend was.

There was one funny thing that happened, now that I remember, and that was that we had one day of rain that week, so we looked around for something to do indoors. Round the corner from the hotel was an old cinema, and for some reason they were showing a film called The Longest Day, which had first been shown in England some ten, maybe more years before. It was a film about the second world war, and it was a film that I had never seen, and remembered that I had wanted to. The thing about this film is that it was sort of in two parts and looked at what the Allies were doing, and then what the Germans were doing, separately. It was made to be realistic and authentic so the German parts of the film were all spoken in German and then the translation was dubbed onto the screen. That would have been fine except we were in Belgium, so the English script we naturally could follow, but the German speech was dubbed into French and Walloon, so despite sitting all the way through what was a very long film, I never got to find out what the Germans were actually saying.' Ralph paused and laughed.

Jessica laughed too.

'You mean, you had all that money, only spent a small amount on a week in a Belgian port, and the only thing you remember about the whole week is sitting through some film where you didn't understand half of what was being said?'

By now tears of a different sort were rolling down Jessica's face.

'Granddad, what are you like?'

A little cloud of seriousness passed over Jessica's face.

'I love it when you tell me about you when you were young. I've never had anybody to tell me stories of when they were young, apart from mum; but I know most of her stories, as I was there a lot of the time.'

She thought for a moment. 'Will you still tell me about Allan? You did say that you wanted to, but I don't want you to feel pressured; and if it's something that's not nice, I can keep a secret; and I think that I am old enough to understand most things.'

'Well, it's gone eight forty five, and I think it's time you were on your way home to keep your mum company,' Ralph reasoned, 'and I've got an unopened letter to read, before I tell you Allan's story. Thanks to you, I feel as if I am now able to tell the story but we'll have a go at that tomorrow, if you've got the time.'

Jessica nodded, and uncurled herself out of the easy chair, kissed Ralph on the cheek, squeezed his hands, skipped to the door, called 'night, night Granddad,' over her shoulder and closed the door behind her.

Ralph picked up the envelope from where it still lay, on the dining table top, and started to slit it open using his finger. He read the contents of the envelope three times before returning the two sheets of paper to the envelope. He got ready for bed, and finally lay down to attempt to sleep at just gone ten thirty five.

Chapter 16

Ralph awoke early from what had been a fitful sleep; his
night had been full of jumbled memories and thoughts
and concerns; and people from his past had kept visiting him
throughout the night, in the guise of dreams. Only his mother,
of whom he seldom dreamt, had smiled at him and seemed
pleased to greet him.

As a result of all the night's disturbance his muscles ached
and his joints were stiff; so he stretched and lay still under the
duvet, in an attempt to relax and unwind his body.

Nevertheless within thirty minutes of waking, he had
shaved, showered and dressed ready to face the day; and when
he had glanced at the time displayed on his mobile phone as he
unplugged it from its charging point; it was showing seven
fifty. He slipped the phone into his pocket, and now he felt
that he was fully ready to descend to the dining room to have
his breakfast.

There was a light knock at his door, a knock that he had
come to recognise in the past few days. His face lit up and his
mood grew instantly brighter as he recognised that it was
Jessica's knock.

'Come in,' he called, happily.

The door opened more slowly than usual before one of
Jessica's entrances, but open it did and there was Jessica with a
big tray loaded with breakfast things. Ralph moved quickly to
hold the door open to allow her to enter, and in doing so he
looked at the tray as it moved towards, and then past him, and
ended up being placed carefully on the dining table.

Then Jessica turned around and smiled lovingly at Ralph.

'Good morning lovely Granddad. Here is your breakfast. I was up extra early this morning as both me and mum had a wonderful night in our new home. I love my room. I love the squishy carpet. I love the bed. I love it all. So I got up and came into work early so I could bring you your breakfast upstairs on a tray.'

'That is extremely thoughtful and kind, my dearest Jessica,' enthused Ralph.

'Well, it's partly because it's my way of saying thank you to you, but also it gives you the opportunity and the time so that you can tell me about Allan whilst you are having your meal,' said Jessica, whilst starting to unload the contents of the tray onto the surface of the dining table.

There was a cooked breakfast of bacon; egg; sausage; fresh tomatoes, which were fried until black and caramelised; Ralph's favourite, scrambled eggs; a spoonful of beans; and something that always reminded Ralph of the hatch gratings on board old wooden sailing ships, a hash brown. Jessica had also brought up a bottle of his favourite (in fact the *only* sauce that Ralph would use) HP sauce; a tea pot full, of what Ralph considered to be "proper" tea; that is loose leaf tea, **not** tea bags; toast, butter, and some Frank Cooper's Oxford thin cut marmalade, which was another of Ralph's all-time favourites. A single orange rose in a stem vase put the finishing touch to the lay out.

'There we are.' Jessica said, as she stepped back from the table to assess her handiwork. 'That's everything I think.'

Ralph just smiled at this enthusiastic, lovely young lady, who had become his friend, his granddaughter, and someone of whom he had become extremely fond, in such a short space of time.

The elderly man took his seat at the table and dropped two sugar lumps into the cup of freshly poured tea.

'Thank you so much, my dear. Go on then, sit yourself down in the easy chair.'

Ralph gestured to the chair with his right arm and then he picked up his knife and fork and cut a bite-sized piece of bacon and pushed some scrambled egg onto it, and lifting it to his mouth, savoured the delicious smell before popping it into his mouth.

Meanwhile Jessica had curled her legs under herself into her signature position, and sat watching but waiting in anticipation to hear about Allan, for that was the primary purpose of the delivery of Ralph's breakfast tray, as they both knew.

Ralph first took the edge off his appetite, and slaked his thirst with the cup of tea, and then in between mouthfuls started to talk.

'I can't say that Allan was a friend, not in the true sense of the meaning of the word; in fact he wasn't somebody who I ever felt totally comfortable with, to tell the truth. What we did have in common, was that we had started at Brackleys Bank on the same morning, so we tended to go away on the same training courses together; and the same night-school classes together; although I did notice that Allan did tend to be not as conscientious as I was.

We went for a drink after work on a couple of occasions, but not that often as I liked to get home to my mother as she was alone apart from me, and I did tend to worry about her somewhat. Of course Allan had other fish to fry on some evenings too.'

'Did he work part-time in a chip shop on a night, then?' laughed Jessica.

'No, he did not,' smiled Ralph. Ralph had come to love Jessica's cheeky wit, and despite the fact that she had interrupted his serious flow he couldn't help but laugh, particularly after he looked up and saw the expression on her face.

'Allan was having a liaison with one of the Bank's customers, a rather attractive financially independent woman, whom he would visit, up to twice per week when her husband was at the golf club, where he spent a good deal of his time. To be fair, Mrs Sykes was a pleasant enough lady and was a prime example of the expression "a golfing widow", whose husband sadly neglected her in favour of the 19th hole.

I do think that she and Allan were genuinely fond of each other, but Mrs Sykes was not in a position to take the relationship any further as, although she was financially independent, the source of the finances was her husband, if you see what I mean.'

Ralph paused whilst he cut a piece of pork sausage and dipped it into the HP sauce, before raising the fork to his mouth; he savoured the flavour of the pork sausage, mixed with the sauce, before resuming his story.

'Allan's parents were quite well off; his father had his own business, he was a builder; and his mother was a very nice lady, who worked part-time in a fancy, ladies dress shop. I had at first thought that Allan had been an only child as I think, he had had a younger sister, but she had died at a young age. That sibling was not a subject that was spoken about in the family context, but I had learned through a remark about men being from Mars and women being from Venus, that in fact Allan had had three sisters.'

Ralph paused again whilst he poured himself a second cup of tea, and buttered a slice of toast, ladling a thick layer of marmalade on top. He pushed his breakfast plate away from him and said, 'thank you for that, it was delicious; and for this toast which, with this particular marmalade, is my favourite.'

Jessica just nodded and smiled before taking a mouthful of liquid from her screw top coke bottle, which she had suddenly produced.

'Originally Arthur, that was Allan's father, had wanted Allan to follow him into the family building business, but Allan was not cut out to be a builder, as I will explain later, much to his detriment. So the next best thing in Arthur's eyes, was arranged. He pulled a few strings at the Mason's Lodge and Allan was offered a position with the Bank. I don't think that Allan was ever that keen, but it was a living.'

'Wasn't he your best man at your wedding?' asked Jessica.

'Yes, he was. There was really no one else I knew well enough to ask at the time. He did the best man's speech and all that, but we weren't really that close to be honest.

A few months after our wedding, Allan fell afoul of the Bank when he committed a rather silly act. Mrs Sykes, who was quite disorganised when it came to her finances, had at one time asked him if there was any way he could draw some cash from her account, and take it to her, as she was unable to get to the Bank in person on that particular day. He had drawn the cash from her account and found that no one at the Bank had queried the transaction; and as he had one or two financial problems, from occasional visits to the big casino in the centre of Leeds, he decided to try the same trick again, but not at her request.'

Ralph stretched to see whether he could squeeze a third cup of tea from the pot, which he found he could – almost.

'So, of course he found that he had got away with taking the money once without being found out, so like all fools having got away with it once he tried again, and then again. Of course even Mrs Sykes eventually noticed these regular, for they had become regular, withdrawals from her account, and unfortunately for Allan, Mrs Sykes had been tiring of the relationship, which to be fair had been going on for some four or maybe five years; so she had made a complaint to the Manager. The matter was investigated by the Bank's Inspectors and it was found he had secreted a considerable amount of money from Mrs Sykes' account without her consent and knowledge; so was sacked on the spot.'

'What did he do? Where did he go?' Jessica asked, wide eyed.

'To be honest, I have no idea. I did not see him again after that day nor did I hear from him for a few years until he suddenly turned up at number seventeen Wellington Street one evening, and announced that he had bought number nine, which had been on the market for some weeks previously.

He explained that he had been working away as a salesman, and he had spent his time travelling the country. It was something to do with stationery, I think. However, his father had recently died and Allan had been left a small house in Grange-Over-Sands, but as he explained, he felt he needed to move back to Thornston to be based nearer to his mother in case of her needing him.

He had, he explained, sold his own house and had been living in the house left to him in Grange-Over-Sands. He had decided to keep the house in Grange as a sort of holiday home; in fact he did let it out privately from time to time.

In the meantime he had married this lady named Maureen, who he had brought with him that same evening as he had come to call. She had seemed a nice enough person but not, from what I could tell, was she Allan's type at all. However, that was not our business.'

'So, was that when he moved into the house that's got all the police tape all around it?'

'Yes,' said Ralph, 'he moved in there around about 1974; to be honest, I can't remember exactly when. He was away a lot of the time travelling, as I said, as that was his job. Sheila and Maureen got along alright-ish and Sheila used to keep Maureen company on occasions, but they were never really that close.

Things between the two of them, Allan and Maureen I mean, didn't seem to be that good within a short space of time of them moving into number nine, both from what Maureen told Sheila and from what we just observed, in fact they would argue frequently in front of us, much to our embarrassment.

Well, one Wednesday evening Allan asked me if I would like to go with him to see Thornston United, in a big league match playing at home to Blackburn Rovers, which Thornston won by two goals to nil. This was the first time I had ever been to a football match, and of course I was hooked from that moment; I loved it. I started going on my own to home matches and really enjoyed the atmosphere and being surrounded by people shouting and swearing out loud. It was something I had never experienced before in my life, and I loved it.'

'Do you still go?' asked Jessica.

'No my dear, it's been quite a few years since I have bothered, although I still look out for their results on a Saturday, or whatever day they are playing these days. It used to be just a Saturday afternoon; and midweek matches were always on a Wednesday; but now what with the TV they all play any time of the week, and at any time of the day and night it seems. All to satisfy the money men on the telly.'

Ralph paused for a moment, and wiped his lips using the serviette provided by Jessica.

'Anyway, there came a time when Allan decided that he wanted to prove his father had been wrong in his assessment of Allan's building skills. The fact that his father had died a couple of years before, didn't seem to matter to Allan, who set about building an extension to his property at number nine. It seemed to have taken weeks before he had got the footings in and was ready for the concrete to be poured as the base to the construction.

He was working away a lot at the time so he had arranged for a friend of his father's to tip the concrete early one morning whilst Allan was away somewhere; so that by the time Allan returned home from his travels the base would be ready to erect the extension on.

As I say, Maureen and he had been having a particularly bad time of it at that period and she had, if I remember correctly, accused him of having an affair, which of course Allan had vehemently denied.'

Jessica was just sitting listening intently as Ralph imparted this story; she was absorbed in the narrative as it unfolded from Ralph's lips.

'Well, Allan had, as I say got the footings dug out and the preliminary work completed to the building up to the damp proof course, and the next step was to be the concrete, but all of a sudden Maureen upped and left.

She had written him a note, on blue paper, as I remember it and he showed me the letter saying that she had decided to leave him and never come back as she was very unhappy and that she was convinced that he was having an affair. It was definitely her hand writing, as she had a very peculiar way of forming a capital 'A'. She seemed to be there one minute and completely gone; vanished off the face of the earth, the next. We never heard from her again.' Ralph took a mouthful of what was now cold tea.

'Did you ever find out if Allan had been having an affair; and if he had, who he'd been having the affair with?' asked a wide eyed Jessica. 'Had Maureen been right?'

Ralph sat a minute and picked up the white envelope that still lay on the table from the previous evening. He slipped his fingers in between the jagged torn top of the envelope and slowly extracted the folded note paper from within.

'Up to the point I have reached in the story, I had no idea who he might have been having an affair with, although it didn't come as any surprise at all to think that he was actually having an affair.

At that time, as far as I was concerned things between Sheila and I were fine and dandy; we hardly ever argued or disagreed. Let's face it, I was in love with her, always had been since the day when I had first met her in the café, all those years before. I loved her deeply then, and I suppose, the truth is, I still do now.'

There was a silence in the room for a few moments during which neither moved nor spoke; until this was broken by Ralph as he handed the note papers from the envelope to Jessica.

'Can you imagine how I felt when I found out for real, about the contents of this letter, from Sheila one day. That is to say she informed me of the part that she had played in there,' he indicated with his head, towards the letter, 'but not of course the part about Maureen. You will realise when you read that, just why the police are there now with the blue and white tape.'

Jessica took the letter from Ralph's shaking hand and opened it. There were two sheets of white paper, with a neat script covering just one side of each of the two sheets. Unfolding the pages she started to read.

At first the tight, neat script seemed to play with her eyes and she found difficulty with concentrating on the words, but as she read on the letters formed more clearly in her mind.

February 1981

Dear Ralph,

Well, old man, now that you are reading this, it means that I have recently died. I am no more. I'll either be standing in front of a God, who I've never acknowledged or I'm nowhere, which is what I believe will be happening. All will be blackness.

Today as I write, it is a very typical miserable February day, cold and wet. I feel cold and miserable too and so I am setting out to do something that I feel I need to do to put the record straight between us, or as we used to say in the Bank, to balance the day's work, at least as best as I can.

You probably are wondering why? Well I always did consider you to be the best sort of bloke I had ever met and I have felt somewhat guilty, so now I can write this letter safe in the knowledge that its contents will never come to light whilst I am still alive.

Firstly, I want to say how very sorry I am that things didn't work out for you and Sheila, and that it was mainly my fault.

We had been having a relationship for a short while, prior to her leaving you.. To be fair to Sheila, it was me that did most of the encouraging, so I take most of the blame, although it does take two to tango, as they say.

You had been going to the football on a Wednesday evening and Sheila had called round to see Maureen, one time, (more about Maureen later) but Maureen had gone to Bingo. How I hate Bingo!

Well, as time passed and we chatted, one thing led to another and we ended up sleeping together, except there was very little sleeping if you get my meaning?

I have to say this became a regular occurrence for a while and we decided to go away together. I had a place in Grange Over Sands, that my father had left me in his will, and we planned that she should live there, and I would visit regularly, until at least I had completed the building of that damned extension. (more of that later, too)

At this point Jessica stopped reading and looked up at Ralph, with tears in her eyes. 'Oh poor Granddad. Is this the first time you knew?'

'No, Jessica. Sheila had left me a note saying she was leaving me and I found it when I came home from work on that particular day. In the note, she did tell me that she was going away with Allan, and mentioned the house in Grange-Over-Sands, but of course she didn't mention exactly where it was.'

'Didn't you ever try to find her, Granddad?' Jessica asked.

'No my dear, I didn't see any point. If she no longer loved me, then there was little point chasing after her. So I just closed the book on that particular chapter of my life.'

Jessica looked back down at the white pages before her, and recommenced reading.

There was also of course the problem of Maureen, who quite frankly was not my type, and why we ever got married, I have absolutely no idea.

Anyway, as it turned out Sheila and I had arranged for Sheila to join me in Grange Over Sands, but she never turned up on the agreed day. You might recall my phone call about the concrete on the footings of the extension; well that was actually just an excuse, as I didn't expect you to be there when I phoned to see where she was, as it was in the afternoon and you should have been at work. Anyway, as I say, Sheila never turned up and I don't know why, or what happened to her. She never made contact, and I never saw her again. You did say that she had written you a note to say she was leaving, which was what she told me that she was going to do, but as to where she went as she didn't join me, I never knew, and you never said.

Now, the explanation regarding Maureen. This is where this gets difficult.

We, as you will have been aware at the time had not been getting along at all well, for the weeks before she left me. We were just not suited, and furthermore she had suspected about Sheila and we had had a row about that, just another row of many that we were having at that time.

We had sort of made it up and I had convinced her that she was imagining about me and Sheila, and we had got a bit drunk one evening and she had suggested, just as a drunken daft idea that we should each write a letter to the other explaining why we would leave that person. I have no recollection as to the actual point of us doing this, apart from the fact we had drunk too much wine. Well we did this just for a laugh, but it occurred to me as I went to throw them away that it might just be worth hanging onto the letters, because it had given me a grain of an idea.

I had decided to prove my dad wrong in his assessment of my building skills, even though he had died a couple of years previously and I had set about building an extension to number nine, if you recall, and I had got as far as the footings, when Maureen had another go about her suspicions about me and Sheila, only this time she was adamant, and I finally confessed to her, and she threatened to tell you.

It was then that I hit on the brilliant idea that I could put a pillow over her face in the evening, and bury her in the newly dug footings, and cover her over with some cement, and then when the concrete was poured for the base, that would be that. I had the letter in her own handwriting explaining why she was leaving me, so I let it be known she had found out about an affair I was having and consequently that she had left.

Except she hadn't left. She was under the floor of the extension, and you unwittingly helped put her there.

'Oh, Granddad, said Jessica, 'how was it that you helped, unwittingly?'

'Well Allan had phoned from Grange-Over-Sands and asked me if I could just make sure that all the damp proof course was safely and securely in place for when the man came to tip and lay the concrete base on the morning after Allan's phone call. So of course I did go round and made sure it was all safe and sound, except unbeknown to me poor Maureen was lying under a thin layer of cement that was already there. I actually got up very early the following morning to ensure that everything was in order, ready for the concrete to go straight in, and I even helped shovel it.'

Jessica looked back down at the letter and finished reading the contents.

I subsequently returned from Grange Over Sands and completed the building of the extension, which I have to admit now, proved my father right in his assessment of my building skills. It was a disaster. It should in all honesty, have been demolished and rebuilt properly, but I couldn't could I?

But I'm safe from all that now. My fate is now known to me, I fully expect that I am in never ending blackness, as I've said before; in my opinion there is nothing after this life.

If you've died before I have, then the contents of this letter will never become known, because I have left careful instructions to deliver this to you on the day of my death or as soon as possible thereafter, or for this letter to be destroyed in the event of you predeceasing me.

Cheerio, old chum

Allan

'But this means Allan is, or was, a murderer.'

Jessica looked at Ralph as the truth of this was slowly sinking in. 'But that's awful. So the police are there now because of Maureen, Allan's wife? Ooh, how terrible.'

She slowly handed the letter back to Ralph, who took it from her, refolded it and replaced it into the envelope.

'Yes, my dear Jessica, that's exactly what it does mean. Allan was a murderer.'

'And he was best man at your wedding, too.' Jessica said indignantly.

'Yes but that wasn't too bad a crime, was it?' Ralph laughed and the sombre mood lightened.

Jessica suddenly uncurled herself from the easy chair, stood up straight, stretched herself and announced to Ralph.

'I'm just going to have to start work, it's coming up to nine o'clock.' She took hold of Ralph's hands and squeezed gently, 'try not to be too upset about the letter granddad. I'll try and pop back later.'

Jessica collected up all the breakfast things and put them back onto the tray, and then as she went to open the door, she turned to Ralph.

'Oh, mum says would you come for your evening meal this evening? We'd both love it if you can come, but I'd understand if you felt that you couldn't.'

'Please thank your mum very much Jessica for me, would you and tell her I'd love to come.'

'Oooh goody.' And with a characteristic, 'Tara, Granddad,' she left the room.

Having sat still, thinking for a while, Ralph got up from the table, and shuffled towards the writing desk, and he went through the procedure of opening the top drawer and letting down the top. Taking the orangey-brown folder from its place he opened it on the desk top, and took out the newspaper cutting from four mornings ago, and re-read the whole of it.

There was a knock at the door.

'Come in'

The door opened and there was Everton, carrying two beakers of coffee. He came into the room and closed the door behind him.

'Thought you might need one of these, Mr Ralph,' he said placing the beaker in front of him on his desk top.

'Thank you, you are most kind, Everton. Jessica's gone about her duties,' said Ralph nodding at the second beaker in Everton's hand.

'Oh, this one's for me, Mr Ralph. That is if you don't mind me sittin' a while and talking with you whilst I drink it?'

'I don't mind at all. In fact I welcome your company, Everton,' said Ralph. 'Why not sit in my easy chair, or more correctly, as it's becoming known, Jessica's easy chair?'

As Everton sat down with a long and gentle sigh, Ralph turned his dining chair away from the desk to face him. They sat silently, sipping their coffees for a few moments.

Chapter 17

━━━━━━━━━━━━━━━━━━◯◯◯◯◯━━━━━━━━━━━━━━━━━━

Everton placed both his hands around the beaker; his hands were so large that they seemed to engulf the whole of it. He stared into the brown liquid for a few moments more, took a draught of coffee, and looked up at Ralph.

'Jessica tells me that you have received a distressing letter,' he said. 'Was it the one that was delivered yesterday by the sombre gentleman in the suit? Do you want to talk about its contents, Mr Ralph? Would it help you to talk about it?' A pause. 'Or to talk about anythin' else?'

'I don't think there's very much to discuss about the contents of the letter, in one sense, Everton; it was all a long time ago.'

'Except that things that happened a long time ago and have never been put to rest properly, as you might say, can often clutter up the soul and the mind and stop us from thinkin' straight about the present and just as importantly maybe, about the future. Perhaps we can start by you lettin' me have a read at that letter for myself, Mr Ralph? If you don't mind, that is?'

'I don't mind one tiny bit, Everton, but I don't want to keep you from your work and I certainly don't want to be a burden on you.'

Everton sat up straight and smiled at Ralph, his big eyes opening wide, 'you ain't heavy Mr Ralph; you's my brother, and as far as the work issue goes, I regard this as being the Lord's work, so you're only keepin' me from my work, by us not talkin' to one another.'

'Thank you Everton, I really appreciate your concern but there's nothing I can really say to you about the issue, other than what I've related to Jessica.'

Everton took another draught from his beaker and looked at Ralph. There was a pause as if he seemed to be working out what to say. 'So, let me be havin' a read at the letter first, cos I've got a couple of questions of my own for you, unless the contents of this here letter answer those questions first.'

Ralph passed the two sheets of white paper to Everton, who took some spectacles from his top pocket, and placed them on his face.

'Age. It catches up with us all Mr Ralph,' he said and smiled.

There followed several minutes of silence whilst Everton read Allan's letter through twice, pausing momentarily several times as if absorbing the meaning of certain passages. Eventually he folded the letter and removed his glasses from his face, wiping his mouth with the back of his hand.

'This letter should be handed to the police, straight away, Mr Ralph. This is evidence which will help to identify one of the two ladies in there.'

Ralph looked up suddenly, with just a moment of panic across his face. 'Does this mean I'll have to talk to the police?' he asked.

'It would certainly help them in their efforts to identify both the young women who they have found.'

'How do you know they have found two bodies?' asked Ralph.

'Because, Mr Ralph, I read the same newspaper as you do, and I saw the article you cut out of your copy, in mine; and it clearly said the police had found two bodies. Now at the moment they are treating this as a sort of a serial killing. But of course, as you and I know very well, the perpetrator of the one crime, confessed to here in this letter has died. The question is, of course, if we have what is basically a confession as to how one victim got there, who is the other, and when and how did she get there, Mr Ralph? The second question being; is, or was this Allan a serial killer, and more importantly, if he's not, then who else should they be looking for? And furthermore if they can identify the second woman, then she can be laid properly to rest after all this time, couldn't she Mr Ralph?'

There was quite a long silence as Ralph fidgeted and Everton sat looking at him. Eventually, Ralph looked into the file that was still open on his desk, and pulled out a piece of paper from one of the plastic files, held it a moment and then passed it to Everton.

'This was left for me on the day that Sheila disappeared. It was on the mantlepiece in the dining room at seventeen Wellington Street, waiting for me when I got home.'

Everton took the piece of paper, and read it.

Ralph,
I find this letter difficult to write, so I'll keep it brief and to the point.
Things have not been good between us for some time, and I no longer love you. I have to tell you that Allan and I have been seeing each other for some time. So I am leaving you, and by the time you read this letter we will be in Grange Over Sands. I know that you love me but I am sorry to say it hasn't worked for me.
Do not try to get me to come back as I don't want to see you again.

Sheila.

Everton read the letter carefully, and said to Ralph, 'so, what you are saying is that you saw Sheila before you left for work that morning? You came home from work and found this letter on the mantlepiece, and Sheila wasn't in the house, and you've never seen her again since that morning? You know what this looks like don't you?'

'What?' asked Ralph, now staring blankly at Everton.

'It looks like Allan got cold feet about running away with your wife, or for some reason he changed his mind or maybe she changed her mind, so he killed her too, and buried her next to his wife under the extension. The only other plausible answer is that the second body was put there by someone else, an opportunist, shall we say; and Allan's confession in the letter is true and full, and he was not in fact responsible for the second body. Will we ever know, I wonder?'

Ralph sighed and said, 'Everton, it says in that letter from Sheila that things hadn't been good between us for some time, but I was not aware of that. I truly thought that we were happy; at least I was happy. Sheila had never mentioned anything to indicate she was not happy, so this letter, or note came as a complete shock to me that day when I got in from work. I remember Allan phoning up and asking me about the water-proofing, or damp-proofing or whatever it's called, on the base of the extension he was in the process of building, and I did make sure that it was in place properly as he requested. There was only a cemented area to one side where he had brought some pipes into the site, but that was all.'

Ralph paused and took a sip from his nearly cold coffee, and then continued.

'You're probably right in what you say about the letter being evidence, I hadn't considered it from that point of view. I suppose I'm going to have make a visit to the police station, sometime in the near future.'

'I could do that for you if you like,' answered Everton with a kindly smile.

'Thank you, Everton, but I think that this is a task that I should undertake personally; after all the letter was addressed to me and they are bound to want to ask me lots of questions about Allan, for starters. Then they are going to want some background information and then there's going to be questions about Sheila and the identity of the other body. Oh dear, that's going to be quite a difficult visit, one that I'm not looking forward to at all.'

'I'd be happy to go with you, in fact I'd like to help by driving you there, and perhaps waiting with you,' offered Everton. 'I could even sit in on an interview with you as moral support, if that would help?'

'Actually, that would be very helpful, thank you.,' Ralph replied.

'By the way, I understand you've been invited for your evening meal at your old house, this evening? said Everton, suddenly, changing the subject, 'I've been invited too. Shall I call and give you a lift in my car, and then I can see you safely back home again afterwards?'

'Thank you most kindly, Everton; I would appreciate that very much. I also look forward to your company in a purely social setting, as it were. Perhaps we can discuss going to the police station at this evening's meal and maybe you could take me there tomorrow?'

'That seems like a plan to me, Mr Ralph,' said Everton. 'I can collect you from here about five thirty, I've just got to pop down to my church when I get off duty from here at four thirty, but I'll come back for you; unless you'd like to visit my church with me, and then we can go on to Wellington Street from there?'

'Actually, that would be rather nice, thank you Everton. I think I'd really rather like to see your church. I'll be ready and waiting for four thirty then.'

In anticipation of what he thought might be a big meal in the evening, Ralph had only had a very light lunch, so by the time four thirty came around he found that had developed quite an appetite.

He had a second shower of the day early in the afternoon in readiness for the evening; and he had dressed very smartly in his best suit and shirt and tie, and donned his very best shiny brown shoes. If he had allowed himself to think about it closely, he would have admitted to feeling a tad nervous, however he quickly dismissed this thought from his mind; although as the appointed time of four thirty approached, Ralph did experience a slight dryness of the mouth.

'Come in,' he called, in answer to the knock at his door.

Everton stepped inside the room; he was wearing a very smart black suit with a black shirt and a clerical collar. Against Everton's skin tone, and the shirt and suit, Ralph noticed the clerical collar shone out like a beacon. He had never seen Everton dressed in this manner before, and he thought the man looked mightily impressive.

'Goodness me,' Ralph exclaimed, 'I think you look amazing, dressed like that.'

'Which can only mean that you don't think I look amazing when I'm not dressed like this,' Everton laughed. 'Thank you kindly, though. Are we ready to go, Mr Ralph?'

They went down in the lift together, and walked across to the car park. Everton's car, a five year old Nissan was parked nearest to the exit, and the lights flashed and there was a beeping sound from the vehicle as they got to it, as Everton pressed the button on the fob to unlock it.

They travelled in near silence as they drove along together; Ralph felt slightly uncomfortable for some reason, and the drive to the Evangelical Church seemed to last a lifetime, despite the fact that the journey actually took only a few minutes.

Having locked the car behind them, Everton went to the Church main doors, unlocking one side and letting them inside the building.

As soon as Ralph walked inside he could feel the peace of the interior. He looked around at all the wonderful coloured stained glass windows, with the afternoon sun streaming through them on the south side, but throwing reflections of the colours at an angle, onto the pale blue carpet. Ralph looked at the wooden chairs all set out neatly in slightly curved rows, making them appear to him as if they were a series of very large long bows and he now saw reflected onto the backs of the chairs all the colours from the windows. Dust motes danced in the multicoloured sunlight, but the thing that gripped Ralph most of all was, the silence.

Ralph felt the need to whisper. 'I don't think that I've been inside a church building in all my adult life.'

Everton put his hand on Ralph's shoulder and gently squeezed. 'That's a great shame, Mr Ralph,' he said. 'Why not just sit awhile and enjoy The Father's peace, the peace that passes all understanding. I'm just going into the office for a few moments, but I'll be back shortly.'

Ralph sat still, absorbing the silence.

He had no idea how much time had elapsed before Everton quietly came and sat beside him, placing a hand on Ralph's knee. 'It's good to feel completely at peace, isn't it?' he said gently.

'To be absolutely honest I don't know what it's like to feel completely at peace.' Ralph emphasised the word 'completely'. How do you get to feel at peace, completely?' he asked.

'By asking God the Father, to forgive all your wrongdoings; by confessing those wrongdoings to Him.'

'But,' said Ralph, staring ahead, not feeling able to look Everton in the eye, for some reason he couldn't quite fathom, 'but, surely an all seeing, all knowing God would know what I've done? Why would I need to confess to him?'

Everton breathed in slowly, 'that's such a good question, Mr Ralph. Confession is really our acknowledgment to God, that we know, what He already knows.'

'It would be too late for me, though wouldn't it? I mean, I've reached the age of seventy four and I can't have that much time left to put right the things that I've done wrong. It would take one hundred years for God to forgive me for the things that I've done.'

'Mr Ralph, it don't work that way, Jesus isn't like that,' said Everton who now placed his hand on Ralph's shoulder again, and continued, 'if you will only confess your wrongs, we call them sins, and then ask for His forgiveness, if you are sincere, and you repent, and ask Jesus to join you in your life, and guide you from here on in, then that is all it takes.'

'Surely not?' Ralph's mind was whirring.

'It is surely so, Mr Ralph.'

'So, would I have to come to church on a Sunday to do this?' Ralph was now intrigued.

'No sir, Mr Ralph; we can do that right here, right now. That's if you want to. You've got to _want_ to. Behold, I stand at the door and knock, says Jesus; if any man hears that knock and opens the door, I will come in. You notice that He does the knocking, but you control the door. It's up to you, you have the power to say no, and to keep the door closed.'

Ralph sat very still and very quiet for some few moments; his mind racing, and his eyes began to mist over, and tears formed at the rims.

'I wonder if my mother is in Heaven? I'd like to see her again.'

Ralph was silent again.

'Can I use the loo, please? he asked.

'Surely,' said Everton pointing, 'it's just through that door.'

Ralph returned a few moments later and sat back down. He drew in a deep breath and let it out with a long sigh.

'Ever since Sheila went from my life I have been a somewhat bitter and lonely man; living life almost as a recluse. I suppose, if I was asked, I would have to describe myself as a diffident individual. I did not allow anyone into my life; I have no family, that I'm aware of, and no friends. I have never shared anything of my life until I came to Downwood, and you and Jessica showed me such kindness, that I felt the need almost, to share something of my past, particularly with young Jessica. I find that I can feel genuine affection for her, as if she was indeed my actual granddaughter.'

Everton just smiled his recognition, and replied, 'Jessica, and her mum, Margaret, are very dear to me. I managed to obtain the job at the home for Jessica. She is such a hard worker; a good girl, very kind, and genuine and loving.'

Ralph nodded his recognition of these attributes. He breathed in deeply again and continued.

'Once Sheila had departed, I felt there was no need or desire to continue working at the Bank; I had sufficient income from the rents; indeed, I had more than I really needed in income terms, so I resigned. I spent my time travelling a little, and reading a great deal. My only port of call away from the house was the library. Oh, I used to go for long walks, just to get fresh air into my lungs but, I can't say that I ever actually enjoyed walking. There was a certain amount of time and energy taken up with managing the houses; the repairs and so forth, but apart from that, I did very little.'

'Right,' nodded Everton, 'that's taken care of what happened after Sheila and you parted, but what about before?'

'Well, as I said to you earlier today, as far as I was concerned, everything between Sheila and I was fine and dandy. Ok, we did of course have our moments, but all couples do that don't they? We had a quite comfortable life financially; we ate well and didn't really want for anything, materially anyway.' Ralph hesitated a moment before continuing, eyes firmly focused on the blue of the carpet.

'The er, physical side of our marriage wasn't exactly desperately exciting, but that didn't seem to bother Sheila too much, and after life's first blooming of the passion buds had withered, it didn't seem much of a problem to me either. Obviously looking back at the letter, and the affair with Allan, I had misjudged that issue.'

'What about Sheila's behaviour before she left, was it noticeably different in any way,' asked Everton.

'Not that I can recall.'

'So, how did you react when you got home from work that evening and found that Sheila was gone?' asked Everton, flicking a piece of white cotton from his immaculate trousers.

'Do you think that God is listening to this conversation; right now, right here?' Ralph suddenly asked as he put his hands together and trapped them between his knees.

'Oh, yessir, Mr Ralph. He is surely listening right now, as indeed am I.'

Ralph drew in breath and as he did so he glanced up at a poster on the wall slightly to his right; he was taken with the depiction of Jesus that it had on it; standing with his arms open as if in welcome, and underneath was written, "I am the Way, The Truth, and The Life" John 14:6.

'Well, here we go,' Ralph said, switching his gaze from the poster towards Everton, 'The Way, The Truth and The Life. Hmm.' Ralph glanced down at his hands, still together between his knees, and then returned his gaze to concentrating on the carpet.

'I was meant to be working at the Bank on the following Saturday, and Sunday morning as we were having the interior decorated and they had asked for volunteers to be in the building as, tradesmen were not allowed in the Bank unsupervised, whilst it was closed. The manager Mr Lester, had suggested that I could either be paid overtime or have time off in lieu; so I had opted for the time off.

Because of that I had come home early in the afternoon, letting myself into the house, and went into the kitchen, carrying a frozen leg of lamb. I had decided that I would buy a leg of lamb, which was still a bit of a treat to be having mid-week, and cook it and prepare the evening meal on the following day, which I had off. I didn't often cook, but I had thought it would make a pleasant change for both me and Sheila.

I heard her moving about upstairs, so I went to the bottom of the staircase and called up to let her know I was home.'

Ralph glanced at Everton to assess his reaction so far, but Everton was just sitting looking at Ralph with a compassionate look on his face.

After returning his gaze once again towards the carpet, Ralph continued speaking, but in a slightly lower tone.

'Now I've always been a tad on the absent minded side, and I was wandering around the house carrying the frozen leg of lamb, why I don't know, but there we are. For some reason I went into the lounge and there I saw an envelope on the mantlepiece, addressed to me. I opened it and the letter I showed you earlier today was in that envelope. I had just read the letter, which as you can probably imagine shocked me greatly, when Sheila came running down the stairs and ran into the lounge.

"Oh," she had said, "what are you doing home so early? You're not supposed to be home until five thirty, and its only two forty-five, and you're here now. You're not supposed to have seen that letter until after I had gone. Why have you come home early?"

She was obviously very upset, as I seemed to have unknowingly spoiled her plans. I honestly had no idea that she was unhappy, let alone unhappy enough to be leaving me; and leaving me for Allan at that.'

Everton placed his big hand on top of Ralph's, and gently squeezed it.

'You're with a friend Mr Ralph, you can tell me whatever it is, that's on your mind after all these years.'

'Thank you,' Ralph said. There was a tear starting to gather at the rim of each eye.

'I asked her why she felt that she had to leave, and couldn't we talk about it, and why hadn't she mentioned something before now, so that maybe we could have tackled the problem and rectified the situation. But she had just said that it had all gone too far to be rectified and besides I was just boring. I asked her why Allan, but she just laughed.

I remember mentioning something about having the following day off work and that I was intending to cook this leg of lamb, which I had at that very moment realised that I was still holding in my hand; when she laughed in a mocking way, and suddenly I became very angry and very upset.

I was never a bad tempered person normally and I hated, still do, trouble of any kind but I felt the frustration rise in me and the anger got worse, and when she mocked me again and called me a soft wimp, with no back bone, and I freely admit that I lost it momentarily. I lashed out with my hand, the one with the frozen leg of lamb in it, and just at that split second she threw her head back and laughed again, and .... I, ..er, it caught her right on the back of her head, just where it meets the spine. I must just have snapped her spinal cord just at the base of the skull. It was sickening.'

Although he tried hard to constrain his emotions, Ralph couldn't hold back the tears and once the floodgates opened it took him some while to regain his self-control. Everton just sat with his hand on Ralph's; saying nothing and just waiting patiently for this to happen.

Eventually Ralph had regained his composure and he continued.

'It was awful. She just went very still, very quickly; and her eyes sort of rolled and she went blue and purple like she was suffocating, and then she slumped in the chair. There was no blood, in fact there was hardly a wound to speak of.'

Ralph turned to look into Everton's face and spoke as if pleading.

'Everton, I loved her, and in fact I still do; but I had killed her. She was just dead; just like that. I stood and stared for a moment and then I jumped towards her and tried to revive her, but she was just – dead. I am so, so sorry for what I did, but it was a sort of accident. One minute she was laughing at me and the next minute I had killed her. I didn't know what to do. I just went numb. I don't know how long it was that I just stood there looking at her; my lovely, lovely Sheila.'

Ralph just sat for a moment, staring straight ahead, before continuing the story.

'Suddenly the telephone had rung, and without thinking I answered it, and guess who it was? Yes, it was that bast... sorry, Allan.

Looking back, he must have been surprised to find it was me answering the phone as he would obviously have thought that I would still have been at work. To cover himself he asked some stupid question about the damp proof course material on the extension, and could I make sure that it was in place ready for the following day, when the concrete was to be tipped and laid. I remember saying I would see to it, and put the phone down.

It was then that an idea had come into my head. I know it was wrong, so wrong, but I was panicking. I hit on the idea of wrapping Sheila up in some damp proof sheeting and burying her in the extension at Allan's. So, when it was getting twilight I went down to his house and borrowed the wheelbarrow and took a roll of the plastic sheeting, and went back to number seventeen. I wrapped poor Sheila up in the sheeting and put her into the wheelbarrow and took her down to number nine. I scraped a shallow grave and put her into it, and then carefully replaced the plastic sheeting.'

Ralph paused, 'do you think I could have a drink of water, please?'

Everton leaped up saying, 'of course, of course, sorry,' and he ran towards a door; coming back a few seconds later carrying a white coffee mug, which he handed to Ralph. Ralph took a couple of mouthfuls and set the cup on the floor beneath his chair. Everton had only just regained his seat when Ralph continued again.

'I got up really early on the following morning; I say I got up, I hadn't really had any sleep; but I was down at number nine well before seven in the morning, when the concrete was due to arrive.'

Tears now started to flow freely from Ralph again, and in between the sobs he managed to explain further.

'I even helped lay the concrete. I was sort of numb. It was most peculiar; I didn't seem to have any *feelings.*' He leaned on the word feelings, and let out a quick hard sigh.

Several moments of silence ensued, which Everton felt he shouldn't interrupt, so he continued sitting with his head bowed, waiting for the next utterance.

'Once I'd done all that, I felt that I couldn't undo it in any way. I had been trapped by my own actions. Of course, I didn't realise that poor Maureen was lying next to Sheila.

But I do know in my inner being that it was not a deliberate attempt to kill Sheila; I just wouldn't; it was just a momentary madness. But having then buried her, it dawned on me that it had turned it into what appeared to be a deliberate act. But it wasn't, it wasn't; I loved her. I would have let her go wherever she wanted to, if only she had just asked; but she laughed. Why did she laugh? Sheila, Sheila, why did you laugh at me?'

Everton just sat still, his big arm around Ralph's slender shoulder; which allowed him to realise just how frail Ralph actually was.

'Shall we pray together?' he asked gently, after a while.

'Yes please,' answered Ralph.

'Desperately, at this moment I want to be right with God; to acknowledge Him; to seek His Forgiveness; just to know His Peace and to be rid of this terrible feeling of guilt, after all these years. Can that happen, Everton?'

'It surely can, Mr Ralph. Just as a thought, what happened to the leg of lamb?'

'I cooked it and I ate it. I have never been able to face lamb since; I hate the sight, the smell, and the taste of lamb.'

'Oh, now I understand where the aversion to lamb originates from. Seems to me that you inadvertently had discovered the perfect murder weapon, Mr Ralph. Come on, let's pray.'

As they prayed, and Ralph asked for forgiveness, and for Jesus to change his life, one of those strange quirks of life happened. The sun, which had been moving round slowly, suddenly reflected very strongly into Ralph's eyes from the highly polished brass cross on the alter table, temporarily blinding him.

The light was unseen by Everton, sitting alongside; however, had he noticed it, he would have been reminded of Saul's conversion on the road to Damascus.

After a few moments of silent contemplation, Ralph looked at the man sitting next to him.

'I suppose I need to go to the police as a matter of some urgency, Everton. Do you think you could accompany me, please?'

'Could I make a suggestion? Why don't we keep our pre-arranged dinner date with Margaret and Jessica first, then get a good night's sleep, and I will take you to the police station tomorrow morning? I mean, it's not like you're going to run away overnight, is it?'

Ralph nodded his agreement saying, 'it'll be a bit like the Last Supper, then,' and laughed.

They both laughed, as the tension had dispersed, and then instinctively they hugged.

'I'm gonna have to call you Brother Ralph, from now on,' laughed Everton, 'welcome to the Church, Brother Ralph, may God guide you and bless you.'

'Amen.'

Chapter 18

The front door to number seventeen was opened by Jessica, who had a large smile on her face and she gave both men a warm embrace.

'Come in, come in,' she said stepping back from the threshold, 'we thought you must have got lost on your way here.'

'We had some serious business to attend to first, down at the church, also known as the office,' laughed Everton and winked at Jessica. 'We can praise God that your new Granddad, is also your newest Brother too.'

Jessica's mother Margaret, popped her head around the open kitchen door saying, 'welcome Pastor, welcome Mr Diggerby; dinner's almost ready. Jessica, why don't you take the gentlemen into either the dining room or the lounge and then we can have a drink before dinner, although it won't be that long before it's served.'

She wagged a finger, laughing towards Everton, 'you did say five o'clock, Pastor...'

'And now it's almost five thirty Margaret, I know. But we had some business to attend to before we could come, didn't we Brother Ralph?'

Ralph nodded shyly.

'Shall we go and sit around the table, and have a drink and a chat before mum brings in the starters?' Jessica suggested. Once all three of them were comfortably seated around the table, she continued, 'Pastor James, when mum comes in from the kitchen please would you say grace for us in our new home at our new dining table?'

'Yes, Jessica, I surely would be delighted to do just that. My, my; what a lovely room,' Everton turned from side to side on his chair and looked around the room, admiringly.

The dining room door opened and in came Margaret with a small tray on which she had placed three glasses of sherry and a small tumbler of water.

'Oh, how that takes me back,' said Ralph, 'my mother used to do exactly that when we had a special occasion; she would bring in some sherry in small glasses on a tray, before we ate the meal.'

'Well Ralph,' Margaret said, 'I hope you recognise the glasses; I found these yesterday, they were at the back of the kitchen cupboard.'

'Oh yes, my mother's sherry glasses. I had totally forgotten about them. How wonderful.'

Everton waited for a short break in the conversation, and then said grace.

'Amen,' resounded around the table.

Margaret immediately excused herself from the table and disappeared into the kitchen, returning a few moments later with a larger tray than the first one she had brought in. This one was supporting four fruit dishes, with a half grapefruit in each, slightly browned on top, where the spoonful of granulated sugar had caramelised, after having spent a few moments under the grill; and there, right in the centre of each one was a bright red glacier cherry.

'I know this is a very simple starter, and somewhat dated, but I wondered if perhaps it might have been the sort of dish your mother might have served when someone came to dinner,' Margaret offered as an explanation; 'I do hope so. I hope it reminds you of her, here in your home.'

Jessica looked at her mum, and then across at Ralph, and saw they were both smiling warmly at one another, 'Mum, that was a lovely idea.'

Then turning towards Ralph she said, 'Mum has not told me what we're having for dinner tonight. She told me it's all going to be a surprise; to remind you of when you lived here with your mum. Mum thought that would be a nice treat.'

Looking at Margaret across the table, Ralph just said, 'it's so very thoughtful of you. May I call you Margaret?'

'Yes, of course, dear,' she replied, 'please do.'

'My mother always called me dear,' said Ralph.

Jessica was the first to start, making a bee-line immediately for the glace cherry, and savouring the sticky syrupy coating and the unique flavour.

'Hmm,' was all she said, but it was sufficient comment.

They all proceeded to finish their grapefruit; the eating of which was made easier by the painstaking incisions between each segment. Margaret had gone to a lot of trouble, obviously.

There was a slight pause in the proceedings as Jessica and her mum cleared the table and then Jessica came back into the dining room and returned to her seat.

The three of them made small talk at the table whilst Margaret was dishing up the main course in the kitchen. The sound of potatoes being mashed, and vegetables being strained over the sink drifted in from the kitchen, before Margaret brought two tureens into the room on a tray and offloaded them onto the table. She quickly turned about and disappeared back into the kitchen only to return with a gravy boat, and another tureen. She spent a couple of minutes arranging these on the table, placing a serving spoon into each tureen, and making a space for the next serving dish, which was still to be brought in. After a few more moments in the kitchen, Margaret arrived in the doorway with a look of some pride and pleasure on her face as she placed onto the table, the meat carving plate, containing a leg of roast lamb.

'Oh no, mum,' Jessica was first to react, 'oh why didn't I think to tell you about Granddad not eating lamb?'

Immediately Ralph reached out his arm and placed his hand on Jessica's, 'don't upset yourself, my dear; after this afternoon's long discussion in Church with Everton, there is no longer a problem with the lamb. All that has been satisfactorily resolved. The situation with the lamb has been resolved by the Lamb; the Lamb of God. Isn't that correct, Pastor?'

Ralph looked at Everton for confirmation of his words, and Everton simply nodded his agreement, saying, 'the Lamb of God who taketh away the sins of the World.'

Ralph turned his head back in Jessica's direction and said, 'it's alright, my dear Jessica, lamb as the main ingredient, is all of a sudden quite acceptable. I intend going to the police station tomorrow, as I believe I possess certain information that will assist in the identification of the two bodies discovered down at number nine. Either Everton or I will maybe explain soon enough about that, but in the meantime I would prefer it if we could just enjoy this wonderful meal, and this wonderful company.'

'Are you going to be alright Granddad?' Jessica looked at Ralph with big doe eyes, tears not far from spilling over the rims.

Ralph in return, placed his hand onto the back of Jessica's hand which was resting on the table and said, 'my dear, I haven't felt so much at peace in some forty-odd years. Now, do you think,' he said smiling warmly at her, 'that we could just serve the lamb. Lamb was always my favourite meat, until something came between me and it; but now I feel liberated, and I would like very much to savour the taste of lamb once again, after all these years.'

Ralph glanced sideways at Everton and said, 'you could say Everton, that having savoured the Taste of The Lamb, it has left me free to savour the taste of the lamb, couldn't you?'

'Amen to that,' said Everton.

The lamb was duly carved and served onto the four plates; each person helping themselves to the vegetables, and gravy.

Ralph looked up at Margaret and said, 'I'm so sorry, Margaret, I should have brought a bottle of something. It's the polite and correct thing to do on an occasion like this, but it completely escaped my mind.'

'Oh,' exclaimed Margaret, jumping up from the table. 'I did buy a bottle of red wine, Merlot I think; I'm not very good at wines, so I trust it'll go alright with the lamb. I had forgotten that too until you reminded me. How silly of me.'

She excused herself from the table and dashed off into the kitchen again and there followed the sound of cupboard doors opening and closing; the chink of wine glasses; and the grating sound of the metal bottle cap being unscrewed, before Margaret scurried back into the dining room and placed the three glasses on the table and the opened bottle of wine in front of Ralph.

Turning to Everton she said, 'I'm sorry Pastor, what can I get you to drink?'

'I would be fine with just a glass of plain water, thank you Margaret,' Everton smiled at her.

Jessica looked at Everton for a moment and then asked, 'Pastor, don't you like wine? Is that why you don't drink it?'

'No my dear Jessica, I'm afraid the opposite is true; I like wine too much; and beer; and vodka; and cider...'

'Then why don't you drink some?' Jessica interrupted, not understanding the poignancy of the remark being made.

'Jessica,' cautioned her mother.

Perplexed, Jessica flushed, but looked at Ralph. 'What?' was all she said, shrugging her slender shoulders.

Before Margaret could say anything more to her daughter, Everton smiled at Jessica and explained, 'I am what they call a recovering alcoholic. I was rescued literally from the gutter by a very kind angel of a man a few years ago. I did not know him, but he took me into his home and cleaned me up, fed me and gave me a change of clean clothes, and a bed for the night. What he did give me, the thing that meant the most, was a signpost.'

'A signpost?' asked Jessica

By now all the food was served onto the plates; the wine was poured, and they had all commenced eating. Between mouthfuls, Everton continued. 'Yes, a signpost. He pointed me in the direction of Jesus, and from the time I met Him, my life was turned about. So much so that I eventually became a Pastor, and I do not touch alcohol, because I know where that would lead me back to; and that's some place that I do not want to go.'

Ralph savoured the morsel of lamb in his mouth and swallowed.

'All my life I have thought that it was only the good people who went to church, and I knew that certainly did not include me,' he said.

'No, really the opposite is true, or certainly should be,' answered Everton. 'It's for the people who are in recognition of their wrongdoings; and who know their need for a Saviour; those of us who know we can't do this on our own; so we come together to praise, to worship, and to support one another, through love and understanding; and not by judging; and not by pointing fingers.'

'Amen,' said Margaret, who had been sitting quietly eating, listening to Everton. 'People like me don't know the half of it,' she said. 'I was respectably brought up; we never had much money; but I was loved. I've never had much in the way of money and possessions since, but I've never been to such places in life as the deep despair that comes from deprivation and poverty, and drugs and drink and so forth, thanks be to God.'

By now the main course had been finished and all of their plates had been cleared of every morsel, apart from a few smears of gravy.

Ralph placed his knife and fork together on his plate, as he had been taught to do many years before in this very room. 'Thank you so much, Margaret, that was beautiful.'

'There is some more lamb if you'd like some,' Margaret replied, with a warm smile.

'Thank you no,' said Ralph, returning her smile, 'I am, as they say, replete.'

'You can say that again,' laughed Jessica. Looking at Ralph, she asked, 'did you get that, Granddad?'

'Jessica, what are you on about?' asked Margaret.

'Say that again; replete?' Jessica looked at her mum's face, and giggled. 'Oh mum, I do love you.'

Slightly embarrassed, Margaret turned to Ralph and said, 'There's a special treat for pudding, if anyone would like some?'

'Ooh, a special treat for pudding, I am intrigued to find out what that could be,' answered Ralph, 'so I'll say yes please.'

After a slight nod from her mother, Jessica stood up and the two of them started to clear the table of dinner plates, tureens and serving dishes. They both disappeared into the kitchen, returning a couple of minutes later with a covered bowl, and four smaller, matching pudding bowls. Jessica handed out the smaller bowls, and Margaret placed the large covered bowl in the middle of the table. All eyes became fixed on the large bowl; Margaret raised the covering with a flourish, and there it was.

'A perfect arctic roll,' she announced, looking directly at Ralph and laughing.

They all caught the humour of the moment and laughed.

'Shouldn't the perfect arctic roll be covered in custard?' Ralph joked.

'Maybe, or maybe not,' Margaret replied, 'but one thing is for sure, it should never ever, be preceded by a single box of Vesta Chicken Chow Mein.'

They all laughed, although Everton didn't know what the joke was, but Ralph, looking at Jessica, and still laughing said, 'you grassed me up.'

He then turned to Everton and said, 'the joke is about my first attempt at home cooking. I was telling Jessica that the first time I attempted to cook a meal for Sheila and I, was when I did a Vesta Chicken Chow Mein, but only bought one box as I thought there was enough for two in each box, and then I served arctic roll and custard but I'd kept the arctic roll in the fridge instead of the freezer, and it became very soft, particularly after I had poured a tin of hot custard over it.

I told Jessica that story in the strictest confidence,' he added, looking sternly at Jessica and laughing.

Ralph, whose face had now turned serious, looked across the table at Margaret and said, 'thank you so very much for the meal. Thank you for the thought that has gone into it. I feel as if I have come full circle in this house, and you all have helped me to lay several ghosts from my life. I feel as if I can face the future with a peace that I have never known.'

Suddenly, Ralph put his hand to his temple, 'ooh! I've got such a pain, here in my head. Goodness me that's really painful.'

'Jessica, take your granddad into the lounge and let him sit a while 'til the pain passes. It's probably all the laughter; plus by all accounts he has had a full-on day.'

Jessica did as she was asked by her mother and helped Ralph into the front room, which was so familiar to him. He sat carefully on the end of the settee, and she propped him up with a couple of cushions.

He smiled at her, 'thank you my dearest girl,' he said. 'Because of you, I feel fully restored to the human race, and so very content. Because of you, I have learned to love again, and to experience the feeling of being loved.'

Jessica smiled lovingly at him. She too felt grateful, that because of him she had experienced something that she had thought could never have happened, to experience the feeling of having a loving Granddad. Jessica left the room to get Ralph a drink of water from the kitchen.

Ralph closed his eyes.

Chapter 19

'I've brought you a glass of water, Granddad,' said Jessica, smiling at Ralph as he sat on the settee with his eyes closed.

Thinking he had fallen asleep, she tip-toed from the lounge into the kitchen. 'He's having a quick nap,' she said, to nobody in particular.

A couple of minutes later, Everton decided it would be a good idea to just check up on Ralph, and leaving the kitchen he walked through into the lounge.

'You ok Mr Ralph?' he asked gently.

He moved closer to Ralph and realised that the elderly man's chest was not moving up and down; he took hold of his wrist and it was limp and heavy; he lifted one of Ralph's eyelids gently and tenderly; the eye stared back not seeing.

Everton sat on the settee next to Ralph and uttered a whispered prayer, that Ralph could now be at peace and could be with the Lord for ever.

Then Everton took his phone from his pocket and dialled 999.

'Emergency, which service please?'

'I think we need an ambulance, but the person is already dead,' said Everton. 'We might even require the police, but there are no obviously apparent suspicious circumstances.'

'I'm putting you through to the ambulance service. Please hold, caller,' the operator's professionally calming voice said.

Once connected to the operator at the ambulance service, Everton explained the circumstances and provided all the required details; after which he sat back on the settee, sighed deeply and pressed the phone's off button.

He stood up to go into the kitchen but as he glanced at the doorway he became aware that both Jessica and her mother were standing just outside, in the hallway, with the door wide open. At that moment Jessica turned to her mum and flung her arms around her and started to emit a keening sound.

'Granddad; Granddad,' she sobbed. 'Why? Why now, just when he had become so happy?'

Everton gently shepherded the two women into the dining room and sat them down at the table; then he returned and quietly closed the lounge door. Proceeding next into the kitchen, he found some clean glasses in a cupboard and filled each of them with fresh cool water from the cold tap, and returning to the dining room, he proceeded to sit and attempt to comfort Jessica and her mum. His first thought was one of gratitude; thankfulness that he had been invited to the meal; mainly from the point of view that, had he not been there he realised, the two ladies would have had to deal with this dilemma themselves.

As he sat quietly at the dining table, Everton was filled with a deep sense of satisfaction; he pondered over the happenings of that whole afternoon, and he felt that he had been used directly to help another soul to find his home with God; and now sitting here, he was able to give practical assistance and comfort to the living.

'I'll go and unlock the front door,' said Margaret, and stood up from the table.

'I'll do that, Margaret. Where are the keys?' Everton asked, standing up from the table.

Margaret sat down again and Jessica put her arms around her mother's shoulders, burying her face into her neck, and starting to sob again.

'Thank you, Everton,' Margaret said, 'the keys should be in the front door.'

'You stay here, Margaret' said Everton indicating with his head in Jessica's direction, 'someone needs comforting.'

He left the room and walked the short distance to the front door and turned the key that was, as Margaret had indicated, already in the lock.

As he pivoted to go back into the dining room the reflection of a blue flashing light appeared through the frosted glass of the front door; Everton waited for a few seconds as a pair of paramedics let themselves in, following a quick cursory knock on the door.

'Good evening,' said Everton, 'I'm Pastor Everton James, I was the one that made the 999 phone call. The patient is in here.'

He turned and led them to the lounge door, opened it and indicated that they should enter in front of him. 'Do you need me to stay here with you, or is it better that I leave you two to do what you have to do?'

'We'll manage ok, thank you,' said the first paramedic, who had the name Richard, embroidered onto the badge on his jerkin front.

Everton returned once again to the dining room, and sat down once more in the seat he had occupied earlier.

'I'd be very happy to stay with you two ladies for tonight, if you'd like. I can sleep on the settee or on the floor, I'm not bothered, either way. I'd rather not leave you two alone in the house tonight. It might help you sleep more soundly if I'm here.'

'Oh yes please,' said Jessica immediately, and after a short pause, 'thank you, Pastor. I know that I'd feel better if you were here for tonight.'

'Well, you'll not be sleeping in the lounge; neither on the settee nor most certainly not on the floor; we've got a bed in the spare room, which I will make up,' said Margaret sternly, but the words were accompanied by a warm smile.

'I can assure you Margaret, that in my time, I have slept in very much worse places, and in much worse conditions than those that are to be found on your lounge floor,' nodded Everton.

There was a light tapping at the door, and Richard the paramedic put his head around the gap, and beckoned to Everton, who immediately got up from the table and walked briskly into the hallway.

'I'm afraid the elderly gentleman is deceased,' he informed Everton. 'It appears that he has had a severe bleed to the brain. I'm sorry to have to inform you of this, although all of this will have to be confirmed by post mortem but it should be a formality. The police will have to be informed as he had not been attended by any medic before actual death; this is just to formalise matters.'

'Thank you er, Richard,' said Everton, confirming the man's name with a glance at his name badge. 'I shall have to be making an appointment to see the police, or maybe just to call in anyway tomorrow, as there is an unfinished matter that requires their attention.'

'We'll just need to remove the body to the mortuary, so we'll be a few more minutes making the necessary preparations.' Richard turned back into the lounge as he spoke these last few words, and Everton returned once again to the dining room.

'Poor Granddad,' sniffed Jessica, who seemed to have calmed down a lot in the last few minutes. 'How awful, after all those years when he didn't know what happened to Sheila, and not being able to eat lamb and now he could, but he can't anymore because he's dea...' She couldn't bring herself to complete the word, and started to cry again, but a much more controlled burst of tears than the deep sobbing of before.

Everton looked at Jessica's face and smiled with compassion at the red-rimmed eyes; the tear-stained face, and the little drip on the end of her nose, which she removed at that moment deftly with the back of her hand. Realising instantly what she had done, she smiled through the tears, at Everton, 'sorry,' she said.

'You have to remember Jessica, that until Ralph met you, he had been a deeply troubled man for most of his adult life, and had become somewhat of a loner, with little or no belief in his Maker, and no hope. But because of you, he found himself, and more importantly, he found his God; and peace, and forgiveness, and he found love from you, which I know he cherished and valued. Furthermore, I believe that you were used by God to bring about his redemption, and you cannot do anything but rejoice in that. What greater memory could you possibly have than that; that God used you as his vessel to give Ralph His Eternal Peace.'

Jessica sat still and silent for a moment or two. 'Did I do that?'

'Oh yes, believe me, you did just that,' affirmed Everton.

There was a banging and clattering from the hallway as the covered stretcher was removed down the front steps and placed inside the ambulance. A few moments later, Richard stood in the dining room doorway and said, 'I'm so sorry for your loss, but we'll be on our way now.'

A silence descended upon them all which was only broken by the sound of the front door closing and then they faintly heard the ambulance engine starting up, and the diminishing sound of it driving away.

Everton suggested that they say a prayer for Ralph and for themselves too, and afterwards, at Margaret's suggestion, they drifted into the kitchen and set to with some of the washing up. However, they hadn't done much of the washing up when Margaret sighed and said, 'let's leave the rest of this until tomorrow. The washing up is not that important. I'll go and make up a bed for you Pastor, in the spare room. Meanwhile, let's go and sit in the lounge for a while.'

Jessica went into the lounge accompanied by Everton, and they both sat down on the settee, whilst Margaret busied herself upstairs, making up the spare bed. After a few moments, Margaret re-joined the other two in the lounge, and they indulged in quiet conversation.

It was not until the early hours that they all felt as if they wanted to retire to bed, but once there they all three slept surprisingly well despite, or maybe because of the traumas of the day.

Early, the following morning, Everton woke up to the sound of Margaret stacking cleaned plates onto the draining board, and the sound of cutlery being dropped into its various sections in the kitchen drawer. He stretched and yawned and made his way downstairs to the kitchen and found that the previous evening's dishes were mostly washed, dried and put away. They exchanged morning greetings.

'Can I get you some breakfast, Pastor? There's already a cup of tea in the pot, if you want one.'

'A cup of tea would be most welcome Margaret, thank you. I'll not trouble you further, as I know I'm going to have a busy day today. I'll have to call into Downwood and inform them that Ralph is not going back; and that I shall need to be away from the home today; and that Jessica will not be in today either. I could call at Cooper's Café and inform them that you can't make it today either, if that would help you; and then – then I'll make my way to the police station.'

Whilst he had been listing his day's tasks Margaret had poured a cup of tea for him, and he had gulped down some of it already in between naming the day's listed items.

'You know my telephone number, if you need to talk or perhaps if Jessica needs to talk. Don't either of you be afraid to phone. It's what I'm here for.'

Brushing his creased trousers with the palm of his hand he picked up his jacket, and felt for his car keys in the pocket. Margaret stretched up and put her arms around his neck, 'thank you, you lovely, lovely man.' She kissed him.

Everton just smiled into her face, more with his eyes than with his lips.

'I'll call by, later,' he called over his shoulder as he made his way to the front door, which he opened without having to turn the key. 'Well fancy that, we all went to bed last night without locking the front door. Thanks for the tea.'

Having first driven home and showered, Everton dressed in his second black suit; and put on one of quite a few black shirts that he possessed together with his clerical collar; and then having breakfasted on porridge with honey stirred in, Everton got back into his car and drove first in the direction of Coopers Café.

He parked as near to the café as he was able and walked the remainder of the way. The café was still closed and the door was locked, so he banged on the window until someone came to open the door. He explained the situation regarding Margaret to the chef, and then walked back to the car and set off once again, in the direction of Downwood.

After his arrival at Downwood, he spent some considerable time explaining the situation regarding Ralph, to the Manager of the Home; he also requested some time off to be able to deal with Ralph's affairs with the police, although he declined to go into any details about that; and he also mentioned that Jessica probably wouldn't be coming into work that day, describing how upset she had been, and indeed still was, and how she needed time to come to terms with Ralph's death.

Everton then proceeded up to Ralph's room and let himself in with his pass key. He closed the door behind himself and walked slowly across to the easy chair and sat down in it, with a deep sigh.

He was not sure how long he had just sat there, in the easy chair, and thought about the elderly man who had become his friend, and for the briefest amount of time a member of his congregation. He had come to really like Ralph, and it warmed his heart when he thought of the wonderful effect that Ralph had had on Jessica and her mother, Margaret.

Eventually he became aware that he was really just putting off the moment when he would have to visit the police station, so he raised himself out of the chair, glanced around the room, and went towards the door. But, before he had reached it, the door opened and in walked Jessica.

'I had to come to clean his room and tidy it, not that it needs much tidying; I suppose it's just an excuse to sit in here for a few moments and remember,' she said.

Everton smiled warmly at her, 'I just beat you to it,' he said. 'But now, I'm going to the police station to settle Mr Ralph's account with them, as best I can. I can't say I'm looking forward to this part of the day, but it's something that's just got to be faced and done.'

'Can I come with you, please?' asked Jessica imploringly. 'Please?'

'Well, first I'll have to check with your mum to make sure that would be alright, and second, I must inform you that there will be things that I will be telling the police about Mr Ralph that might make very uncomfortable listening for you.'

'I don't think there's anything I could hear about Granddad that would stop me loving him,' Jessica said defiantly.

'Well, it's alright with me,' Everton answered, 'but let's just call at seventeen Wellington Street first, and check it out with your mum on our way, shall we?'

So, off they set, calling to see Margaret on the way. She was somewhat reluctant to agree at first, but after some persuasive, plaintive, begging by Jessica on her own behalf, Margaret relented and gave them her blessing. 'You must come and share lunch with us, after you have finished at the police station Pastor,' she said.

Standing at the desk in the Police station reception area, they waited a moment or two until a large Sergeant appeared and asked how could he help?

Everton asked to see the detective in charge of the investigation at number nine Wellington Street, the one that had featured recently in the newspaper. 'That'll be Detective Inspector Radcliffe, who's in a meeting at the moment.'

'Well, could you tell him that I have information that will identify both the victims in the case, and the way in which each of them met their end.' Everton stood as tall as the sergeant and looked him straight in the eyes.

'Just take a seat Reverend, please. I'll see if someone can have a word,' the sergeant seemed to have changed his attitude, all of a sudden.

A few moments passed, and Jessica and Everton found themselves glancing around the walls at all the posters, and speaking in whispers; somehow, neither thought it was a place in which they felt they could talk in a normal voice.

'Good morning, I'm Detective Inspector John Radcliffe, I'm in charge of the investigation at number nine Wellington Street, and the desk sergeant tells me that you might have some information that would assist me in that task.'

Everton nodded. 'Your name is?' asked the Detective Inspector.

'I'm Rev. Everton James, Pastor of the Evangelical Church, and this is Miss Jessica Darley, who works with me at the Downwood Retirement Home; she's also one of my congregation.'

Inspector Radcliffe shook both their hands, and then he showed them through to an interview room, which was situated at the rear of the building. They had to wait a few moments as the Inspector used a code to open the door to the side of the front desk.

Once in the room, and after her eyes had adjusted to the light level, Jessica gazed around wide eyed; the room was bare, painted a dull green; a single light fitting hung from the ceiling; the table was fixed to the floor; and there was a strange stale smell, that she couldn't quite identify. There was what looked like a recording machine placed at the end of the desk, but attached to the wall, and a camera fixed at an angle half way up the same wall.

They were motioned to be seated at the opposite side of the desk to the Detective Inspector, and he placed a buff coloured file on the desk to his right-hand side.

DI Radcliffe took some blank paper from the buff file and a pen from his pocket.

'Right. Firstly thank you for coming in and sparing me your time; secondly, it would help me a great deal if you would allow me to record what you say, it'll help with the flow of the discussion and it'll save me making frantic notes as we go along.' Everton nodded his consent, and DI Radcliffe spoke again.

'Right, let's see what you've got for me.'

Everton started by explaining how he knew Ralph from the job that he had at Downwood; he explained Jessica's role in the Home and how she had especially befriended Ralph, and how he had "adopted" her as a granddaughter; and through that relationship how he had gradually opened up and told them both, but mainly Jessica, things from his past.

Everton related the tale of the letters, both from Sheila to Ralph and from Allan, and how that letter had arrived from a solicitor's office after Allan's death.

'Would you happen to have brought those letters with you?' asked DI Radcliffe.

'No,' said Everton, 'but I know where Ralph er, that's Mr Diggerby kept them. He always kept the key to the drawer in his trouser pocket, so we need to get that back from the mortuary, along with his other effects.'

All of this information so far, Jessica had been aware of, as Ralph had shared it with her too, but Everton braced himself on her behalf, as he started to relate the contents of the previous afternoon's conversation in the Church.

'You must realise, Detective Inspector, that what I have told you thus far, I can corroborate with the written evidence in Mr Diggerby's folder, but what I am about to relate, I have no proof of, other than as a Church Pastor I have heard Mr Diggerby's confession, and I can relay that on to you. I cannot prove anything of what I am about to tell you, but I have absolutely no doubt that this is nothing but the truth. He had no reason to tell me anything but the absolute truth.'

Everton became aware that he was telling of the previous days happenings as much for Jessica's information as for the policeman's.

'Ralph, that's Mr Diggerby, told me how he had thought that he and his wife Sheila had been happy, but that he had come home from work unexpectedly early one day as she was about to leave him. She had left him a note to say that she was going away with Allan Briggs who lived at number nine Wellington Street. She had expected to have been long gone by the time he had arrived home from his work, but in one of life's many quirks, he had come home early on that particular day. He had explained how she had laughed at him and that he had been holding a leg of frozen lamb in his hand.

He had purchased the leg of lamb, on his way home, in order to cook a meal for them both on his day off the following day. She had laughed at him several times and finally he had had a sudden rush of temper; which I have to say, I had never seen any evidence of temper, Inspector; he was always a very mild mannered man. Anyway, he had had this sudden rush of temper, and lashed out at her and caught her on the back of the head, and by all accounts she had died instantly.'

Opening his folder and shuffling through a few sheets of paper, DI Radcliffe said, 'as far as the autopsy, or the post mortem examination shows us, the mode of death to one of the victims appeared to be as a result of a single blow to the head, severing the spinal column, so that appears to tie in with what you have just said. Also, according to the pathologist, death would have been pretty much instantaneous.'

Everton went on to explain how Ralph had, well not panicked exactly, but how he had been in a confused state, and how he had buried Sheila under the concrete, but that he had no knowledge of Maureen, lying near her.

Everton explained about Ralph's many years of sadness and withdrawal from society, and how he had become, in his own words, a near recluse. Everton commented on how there were no family photographs in his room, and no memorabilia and that the whole of his past life could seem to be contained in the orangey-brown folder that he had kept in his writing desk top drawer.

Jessica had just sat quite still throughout all of this discussion, staring ahead at the green wall. 'Poor Granddad,' she whispered aloud to herself, and both the Detective Inspector and Everton smiled in her direction.

When the interview was over they all stood, and DI Radcliffe offered his hand to both of them.

'Thank you so much for coming in to see us today. This information will save us many hours of police work, and after making a few further enquiries, it will help us in probably closing this case. I'm going to have to get this typed up into a formal statement, which you will be required to sign, but I can phone you about that, Reverend James. In the meantime, I thank you again.'

Duty done, the pair set off back to seventeen Wellington Street, where they were welcomed back by Margaret with a bowl of home-made soup and some crusty bread.

'I made soup and bread as I didn't know how long you would be, and soup can be ready to serve at any time,' she said.

Several days had passed, and as Ralph had no known next of kin, Everton decided that he wanted to handle Ralph's funeral himself, so he had liaised with the police and Ralph's solicitors, Page Mercer and Foreshaw, in order to be allowed to conduct the funeral service.

The police allowed Ralph's funeral to take place three weeks after Ralph's death, after the Coroner had released the body; and so it was held at the Evangelical Church and was attended by Everton, who presided; Margaret Darley; Jessica, and two members of the staff from Downwood; Mrs Thompson who lived at number fifteen, and had been Ralph's neighbour for over forty years; and Thomas Mercer from the Solicitors' office.

It turned out to be a very simple affair but no less meaningful despite the paucity of mourners in attendance.

They all went from the church to the Thornston Crematorium for the committal, and ended up at seventeen Wellington Street for an intimate gathering and buffet tea afterwards. Margaret had insisted on being the one to provide and prepare the buffet tea, 'as the least that she could do, after all he had done for her and Jessica.'

During the course of the tea, not very much was said about Ralph as, in truth none of those attending really knew that much about him, but Mr Mercer from the solicitor's office at one point did say to Everton that he could do with a private word with both him and Jessica Darley, who he presumed was the young lady of the gathering.

With Margaret's permission both Everton and Jessica went into the lounge with Mr Mercer and after all three were seated, Mr Mercer introduced himself to Jessica, as he already knew Everton from his previous visit to see Ralph at Downwood.

Mr Mercer had some papers in his suit jacket pocket and he produced these and then looked at the two people seated in front of him.

'Mr Ralph Diggerby has left a will instructing our firm to act on his behalf in all matters pertaining to his estate. There will, you understand be a delay in settling the will, as Letters of Probate are required and then the retrieval of all the assets prior to distribution in accordance with Mr Diggerby's wishes. As well as numerous bequests to, in the main, local charities, there are two main beneficiaries in his will, namely Miss Jessica Darley,' and then he looked from Jessica to Everton, 'and Mr Everton James. Looking at your attire Mr James that should I suppose, technically read, Reverend Everton James.'

Mr Mercer turned to look at Jessica again, who was sitting upright with her hands clasped together between her knees.

'To you Miss Darley, he has bequeathed his house at number seventeen Wellington Street, the house we are in fact in, right now. There is a proviso in the will that although the house is to be yours, you are to allow your mother to live in this property for as long as she wishes, and for the rent to be nil. You are both to maintain the rose in the front garden to the best of your ability for as long as it remains as a living plant. There is also a sum of £50,000, to enable you to attend either university or college, as you so desire; although this sum of money may be disposed of in any other way that you might see fit.'

Jessica was now sitting with her hands over her face, trying to take all of this in, but was otherwise silent.

Turning now to Everton, Mr Mercer said, 'to you Reverend James, Mr Ralph Diggerby bequeaths, the sum of £300,000 to be used as you see fit, but he hopes it will enable you to see your dream of a gymnasium and coffee bar to be incorporated into the church for the use of local young people; to come to fruition.'

Everton sat, looking stunned.

'Can we tell mum?' Jessica asked suddenly, jumping up and going to the door, where she hesitated for a moment, awaiting confirmation.

'By all means, said Mr Mercer.

Jessica came rushing back into the lounge with Margaret in tow, looking a little flustered.

'Please Mr Mercer, will you tell mum what Granddad has said in his will about her?'

Mr Mercer, who had in the meantime stood up from his chair, sat down again, and re-opened the will document. He looked at Margaret and repeated what he had said earlier.

'Basically Mrs Darley, Mr Diggerby has left this house in his will to your daughter Jessica, with the proviso that you are to be allowed to live in it, rent free for the rest of your life, or for as long as you choose. Oh, with the proviso that you tend the rose in the front garden, to the best of your ability.'

Margaret's eyes filled with tears, and she flicked one away with the back of her hand before it had chance to run down her cheek, her reaction not going unnoticed by Mr Mercer, who smiled in her direction.

'And, Granddad has left me £50,000; so now I can go to college and do my A-levels and then on to university, so I can do nursing; or I can do whatever I want with it.' Jessica clapped her hands. 'But it really means that I can become a nurse. Oh Granddad, I love you. Thank you.'

Jessica then looked from Everton to her mother and said, 'Granddad also left Reverend James, a lot of money; enough for him to build the gym and coffee bar that he wants for the church.

Margaret glanced across at Everton, and said, 'the Lord's Face certainly shined down upon us the day Ralph came into our lives, didn't it, Pastor?'

'Amen'

Chapter 20

R alph opened his eyes and looked about him. He appeared to be sitting; except that sitting was not quite how he would have described his situation; he was aware of his existence; he could see and feel and he was conscious, but not in the way he had been used to.

He was aware of being in what he imagined was a small room, but there was no door, in fact there didn't even appear to be a front to this room. He was reposing on what was seemingly a stone bench; and everything appeared to be white; the walls were white; the stone bench was white; the ceiling was white.

The atmosphere that surrounded him was not cold, but neither was it warm; the light was not gloomy, but nor was it bright. There were no specific noises that he could recognise, but on the other hand there was not silence. He appeared to be floating and yet was grounded; he imagined he felt like he was weightless, and yet somehow of substance.

He felt peaceful and relaxed, and when he looked down at where he remembered his best suit had been, what to him seemed to have been only recently and yet, somehow, to have been so long ago, his legs were now dressed in a robe, his feet were in sandals; soft comfy sandals. He looked again and realised that the robe covered his entire body; it appeared to be made from some rough, course material, and yet it did not irritate his skin, nor did it even feel in the slightest bit uncomfortable.

'Hello Ralph,' said a voice that appeared to float towards him. 'Welcome to Eternity. Please, just relax; we'll be taking you to your Life's Reflection Time, shortly. You won't be needing anything; all your requirements have already been dealt with. I'll be back with you in a while. In the meantime, please be at Peace.'

Ralph tried standing, but he seemed to glide into position with no effort from his muscles. He became upright and he felt secure on the standing surface, but did not feel as if his feet were actually in contact with the ground.

That pain in his head had gone, he realised; in fact he felt really well and rested, and yet – and yet he couldn't really say that he *felt* anything. Yes, he realised that he was aware, rather than had feelings; he was aware of having emotions but strangely, only peaceful ones. He remained still for an indeterminate length of time, listening. He didn't know whether he actually expected to be hearing something or someone, perhaps; but he heard nothing.

'Hello,' he called, and his voice echoed around in a gentle, soft way. 'Is there anybody else here?'

His spoken words hung in the air, but there was no immediate reply.

He tried walking forwards, but he seemed to move with a floating sensation; he came to a halt at the edge of the room he was in and turned around to inspect it. It resembled a stone cell, a little like how he imagined what a monk would sleep in, except it was white. Everything appeared white.

The stillness was broken by a voice that floated across to him from somewhere nearby.

'Are you waiting too?' it called.

The voice appeared to have come from somewhere behind him, and when he looked he became aware that there was another cell similar to the one he was in, some distance from his; this cell wasn't connected to his; it just *was*. Somewhere over there. Although it could be seen, somehow Ralph knew it couldn't be reached.

'Waiting?' answered Ralph, 'waiting for what? Where are we? Where are you? *Who* are you?'

'We're waiting for our Life's Reflection Time,' answered the voice.

'Life's Reflection Time? What is that?' Ralph looked around but couldn't see anyone, nor could he locate precisely where the voice was coming from.

'That sounds like Ralph,' said the voice. 'Is that you Ralph?'

'Yes, my names Ralph, but I'm sorry to say, I don't recognise your voice, although I can hear it clearly. I can't see you either. Where are you and who are you?'

'It's Allan. I've been here for a couple of weeks already. I say a couple of weeks, but the truth is time just seems to be at a standstill, and yet I am aware of its passing. I can't explain what I mean, you'll simply find out for yourself. I do keep asking how long it's going to be before my Life's Reflection, but they keep telling me that they are just waiting for some others to arrive, before they can process me. I hope that you are one of the others.'

'Allan?" Oh yes, Allan. Of course, I read your letter; it was to be delivered to me on your death, so naturally you would be here. Yes, of course.'

'Ah, the letter,' replied Allan's voice. 'I'd appreciate it if you wouldn't mention that whilst we are here, if you could possibly avoid it, old man.'

'I don't think it's any of my concern, actually,' replied Ralph. 'In fact, all that's behind me now.'

As if a door had suddenly opened, a bright light filled the space, and Ralph saw a person coming towards him. He was similarly dressed to Ralph, in a robe and sandals, and he came towards Ralph with outstretched arms. 'Welcome Ralph; it's time for your Life's Reflection Meeting; come this way, please.'

'What about me?' called Allan from across the invisible divide. 'When do I get my Meeting?'

'It won't be long now,' answered the robed man. We're still awaiting the return of the other two persons, and then you can be processed.'

The robed man took Ralph firmly, but gently by the hand and then they went through the doorway that had previously appeared, as if from nowhere. Ralph looked back as the door was silently closed behind them.

The light on this side of the doorway was very much brighter, even so it did not affect Ralph's eyes; he did not need to screw up his eyes against the bright light, nor did it effect his vision.

He was led by the hand into an area, that could not be described as a room as such, for it was not enclosed, or so it appeared to Ralph, and yet it gave the impression of being self-contained.

There were a couple of the white stone benches which were set adjacent to one another, not too close, but then not too far apart either. The space that surrounded the white stone bench that was set in the corner was shaded, and appeared to have green backlighting.

Ralph was guided to the second bench, more in the open and more in the light.

'Do please be seated and make yourself feel at Peace, comfortable, and at ease. He will be with you very shortly.'

The robed man moved away and was soon swallowed up in the brightness.

Ralph looked about him; it was very pleasant here. He had been sat waiting for a few moments before the brightness appeared to part and a second man in a similar robe to the one worn by the first man, and also similar to the one that Ralph was wearing, approached and seated himself in the part shaded green area.

The man appeared to be glowing from within, and it was as if His eyes saw right through Ralph.

'Peace to you Ralph,' the man said. Ralph instinctively knew that he was not to speak at this juncture, and so he remained silent.

'What would you like to reflect on at this, your given opportunity?' asked the Man.

Ralph waited a short moment, collecting his thoughts before replying.

'I suppose there are very many things that I can reflect on from my earthly life; but the one action that stands out is the terrible thing that I did to Sheila, and then the continuance of that by hiding her body, and then the lifetime of hiding away from the truth; and I realise now, the lifetime spent in my denial of God.'

'And what do you feel about all of that now?' asked the Man. It seemed to Ralph as if the Man smiled gently at him, and Ralph could feel His warmth.

'I am desperately sorry about all of those actions, and I wish that I had never done them, or at least, I wish desperately that I had owned up; and I am particularly sorry that I never acknowledged God, the Father, or God the Son, or God the Holy Spirit or at least acknowledged Him a lot earlier in my life, instead of leaving it to the last minute.'

'The important thing is that you did acknowledge Us at the time appointed for you to do so, which means that all of that is behind you now.'

'Oh, so there's an appointed time for that, is there?' responded Ralph.

'Well there may be several, depending on your life circumstances,' answered the Man.

'Am I allowed to ask questions?' asked Ralph.

'Of course you are; what do you wish to know?'

Ralph looked at the Man, his face half obscured by the shade. 'Who are you?'

'I AM who I AM,' He said simply. 'I am the Alpha and the Omega. I am The Beginning and The End'

Ralph realised that he had full understanding, at that moment.

'May I ask another question, please?'

'As I said, you may ask what you will.'

'Well, couldn't you have sent me an angel to assist me when it was my time, and then I might have responded how you wished?'

The Man looked at Ralph, with eyes that knew all. He simply answered Ralph's question with, 'I did send you an angel when it was your time and you did respond.'

'Did you send an angel? Did I respond? I don't recall either.'

'Did I not send you Jessica?' was the simple reply.

'Oh, I didn't realise,' said Ralph, startled. 'But it all makes sense now.' After a short pause, Ralph added, 'and I did respond, didn't I?'

'You see now, don't you? And there was also her assistant Everton? Neither are, or were, specifically aware of their roles, but they both make themselves available to me, to work My Purpose out.'

Ralph quietly asked the next question, hardly daring to look the man in the face.

'Is my mother here? Do I get to meet her again?'

'Your mother is indeed here, and you will get to meet her soon.'

'But what about Allan, and Sheila and Maureen? What will happen to them?'

'It should not cause you any concern what will happen to them, Allan is somewhat unrepentant about killing Maureen and is unrepentant of his affair with Sheila; and Sheila is unrepentant of not returning your love even though she vowed to love you, and unrepentant of her adultery; and Maureen is unrepentant of hating Sheila for having the affair with Allan; so they will spend eternity together, locked in a situation of their own making. Joined together, but separated from the Father, and His Peace, which passes all understanding. They will be Together Through Eternity.

'Ooh, that sounds like a type of Hell to me,' said Ralph.

'Yes, you see Ralph, Hell is not a big fiery furnace full of devils with pitchforks prodding at everyone all the time; Hell is eternal separation from the Father's Love. I experienced Hell, the separation from the Father's love on the Cross, and whilst I was in the tomb; but on what you call Easter Morning I triumphed over Death and Evil and the Father caused Me to rise from the dead, and I sit now with Him, at His right hand. By the way, I have interceded with Him on your behalf, because when the summons came, you responded and acknowledged me and were sorry for all you had done. You did reach out to me, and I did respond; as indeed I do to everyone who reaches out.'

Ralph felt he shouldn't have asked what would happen to the other three, and apologised.

The Man acknowledged the apology and explained that that was a normal human reaction, which was fully understandable.

The Man looked kindly at Ralph and the Man then smiled.

'There is a story that my friend John wrote down in his gospel in the Bible in John chapter 20. It happened during the time between the Crucifixion and the Ascension. My friends had been out fishing and they had caught nothing during the night. When they came ashore at dawn, I was waiting on the beach for them; I had a fire going, with some fish cooking on it, and some warm bread, in my hands. I knew they had caught nothing, so I shouted to them to let the net down on the right side of the boat, which they did; and behold, they brought up the nets unbroken, with 153 fish caught up inside.

I beckoned them to come, and I know they did not recognise me at first, partly because of the distance and partly because I was shortly to return to the Father.

However, after we had broken the night's fast, I asked my good friend Simon Peter, whether he loved me; in fact I asked him three times on purpose, to teach him the lesson about denying me three times, and then the two of us went along the beach a short way for a walk, and Peter had then looked over his shoulder.'

The Man paused and laughed, 'what's going to happen to him he had asked me, pointing towards John, and I had said the same to him as I say to you now. Do not concern yourself with what will happen to him, concern yourself with what will happen to you. What is that to you? *You* must follow me,

I had said. With that I had put my hands on his shoulders, and explained to him what would happen to him at the end of his long life. I love Simon Peter for his impulsiveness, and his strength; he is as solid as a rock.'

As he said this, Ralph's gaze was instinctively drawn to the Man's hands, and he saw the nail holes, and from there his gaze went to the Man's feet, and there too he saw the holes.

'My Lord, and my God,' Ralph gasped.

~~~~~~~~~~~~~~~~~~~~

About the Author

Born and raised in Bradford, Ian Robinson was educated at Thornton Grammar School, a place he was eager to leave and jump into the world of work.

He eventually found his niche as a financial advisor, a career he maintained for 30 years. Taking early retirement from the financial world enabled Ian to fulfil a life-long dream of working at his beloved Bradford City Football Club. Leaving there, he went on to work as a doctor's receptionist but this occupation was sadly cut short due to a heart attack.

Ian became a Christian at the age of 62 and is a member of the church family at St. Luke's Church, Holbeck Leeds. He is happiest at home with his wife Christine, especially when they are together in their garden, catching up with friends and strumming away on one of his several guitars.

Lightning Source UK Ltd.
Milton Keynes UK
UKHW041228230322
400398UK00002BA/37/J